time and the
mystic's
MOKSHA
METER

C. Pic Michel

HeartStudio *Books*   Cincinnati, Ohio, USA

More from HeartStudio *Books*

Gold Lamé *(that's le-mayy)*
first in the Gold Lamé series
C. Pic Michel

Enlightenmeant Cartoons: Now What?
written and illustrated by C. Pic Michel

My Five Careers:
Increasing Brain Power and Longevity
Through Strenuous Exercise of the Mind
written by Joseph Taylor
illustrated by Pic Michel

visit heartstudiobooks.com

HeartStudio Books is a registered trade name of The HeartStudio LLC, email: TheHeartStudio@fuse.net

ISBN: 978-0-9825934-1-7

PRINTED IN THE UNITED STATES OF AMERICA

Guide to Font Usage

"Text in quotes"
Spoken aloud

Text in Italics
Spoken in thought
also spoken by Narrator in Webinars

"Text in *italics* in quotes"
Emphasized aloud

Pause, pause, pause...
Narrator changing channels

Double line space
Slight change, same-scene

Pronunciation Guide with Loose Definitions

Tetta...tĕt-ah, etheric lady guru
Hrim...hrēm, an etheric guide
Moksha...mŏk-shuh, liberation
Rishi..rē-shē, wise sage
Jiva..gē-vuh, similar to one's soul
Nirvana...nir-vah-nuh, heavenly freedom
Bodhisattva.....bō-dĕ-sŏt-vah, postpones personal nirvana to help others
Namaste...nah-muh-stā, greetings!

Dedication

I have had parts of this story kicking around in my mind for a long time. One such plotline involves a young girl who mysteriously disappears under suspicious circumstances. While the story is purely fictitious, I wrote it at a time when our community was processing the loss of two teenage girls to violence. One of them had attended my after school art classes. One was loved by other artists I know. Aware of the ongoing heartache associated with such loss, I feel compelled to share that there is no violence in this novel, there is hope, the hope that endures and inspires humanity to live better even under the most difficult circumstances – the hope of openness, kindness, and mirth. My stories tend to feature challenged youth as heros and teachers. May we always feel so inspired as when we witness the wonder and wisdom of a child.

With particular appreciation
for the bodhisattva in my life
and special thanks to June, Melissa,
Rob, Daniel, Connie, Vince and Dan.

Contents

1. Time 101, Moksha 0   1
2. Which Way Did She Go   29
3. Clang! Clang! Clang!   55
4. Who's Been Sleeping in My Dreams?   77
5. Hijacked, Hysteria, and Princess Peeking   105
6. Reunions and Defections   133
7. Déjà vu   163
8. Smack! Thwack! Splash!   183
9. Bing! Bang! Boons!   203

Time 101, Moksha 0

The fluorescent lights inside the city bus made it seem like a giant glow worm lumbering over the dark, cobblestone streets of Cincinnati's Over-the-Rhine neighborhood. If riding a bus could be considered a spectator sport, fifteen-year-old Ardin True was a dedicated fan. Through her window, she could easily view the ever-changing scenery of various bus routes or change her focus to monitor a diverse range of fellow passengers, from suit-shrouded professionals to the tattered, homeless poor. After years of enduring the enforced company and well-meaning inquisitions of caseworkers, guardians and foster parents about how she felt, Ardin came to see the buses as a sign of emancipation. People's probing questions made her feel like maybe she had cancer or something. If she was suffering from anything, Ardin decided, it was nothing more than just being a kid. Somehow the adults failed to appreciate her position on that issue. They called it "at-risk", said she had a "behavioral disorder" and tried to medicate and relocate the symptoms away. Nevertheless, Ardin remained an enigma who at once taxed their patience and challenged them to stifle their amusement over her silly tricks and pranks.

Ardin had been in the custody of the county since she was found as an infant on the steps of a half-way house. No one knew anything about who her mother or father might have been. Nor had anyone ever proven able to become her mother or father. Every placement Ardin's case managers tried had failed. The prospective parents didn't appreciate her sense of humor or her tendency to disappear. Sometimes Ardin would go missing for days.

At first the police would search for her and the foster parent or potential adoptive candidate was questioned. They never found her, Ardin always came home on her own, and when asked where she had gone, she claimed she was visiting with invisible friends in another world. The way Ardin described it, she could dream instantly and transport herself to other dimensions. The way the county social service agency interpreted it, she suffered from psychosis.

Ardin couldn't understand why the adults had such a problem understanding that she could leave the dreary world of physical existence and hang out with celestial nymphs and wise sages who helped her deal with everyday life. The caseworkers just didn't see it as being all that helpful and told her they were concerned for her welfare. Ardin wondered what there was to be worried about. Even when she met with demons, she found them to be quite likeable.

Ardin shifted her awareness from the storefronts and tenement houses crowding the curb on Vine Street to watch an elderly woman position herself on the seat across the aisle facing her. Ardin tried not to stare but she felt she recognized the roundish body and tan face under the shawl that covered long graying dread locks. Ardin picked up the newspaper that had been left on the seat next to her and opened it wide. Ads about brokerage houses peered back from the financial section. Despite her attempts to hide behind the pages of The Enquirer, Ardin found her gaze consistently locking with the woman's penetrating dark grey eyes every time she bent the paper to peer over the top, or peek around the side.

Ardin was sure it was her, even though they had never met in waking life before. Ardin was accustomed to traveling through a vortex of light and energy to reach the lady guru Ardin had known in her dreams since she was a little girl.

After just a few blocks, the woman stood up and yanked at the cord running along the wall, alerting the driver she wanted him to pull over at the next stop. The bus grumbled to the curb at the next intersection. The woman barely missed striking Ardin's foot when she planted a carved walking stick loudly on the floor in front of her. She raised her free hand in the air, and she began speaking with odd tones that did not match the lady guru's voice.

"You know who I am!" Raspy words slithered like spaghetti over the edge of a pot onto a plate. "And I know who you are." The melody of the woman's words twisted sharply upward as she lifted the cane in the young girl's direction.

Thick gray dreads peeked out from under the shawl wrapped over the woman's head and shoulders. Ardin studied the coolness behind the grey eyes. Something seemed wrong. The characteristic twinkle the woman always displayed in her dreams was missing. Ardin felt pressure and turned away.

The front door of the bus banged open as the overhead speaker piped in, "Thirteenth and Vine Streets."

"Isn't tomorrow your birthday?" The woman moved her short round body toward the exit. Ardin watched as the woman stopped for a moment and appeared to be listening to something no one else on the bus could hear. The woman started to tee-hee and winked at Ardin as if she had a secret. She began to laugh, and then she started to cough. She waited next to the bus driver until she caught her breath. For just a moment Ardin thought she saw a speck of light in the woman's eyes as she continued into the stairwell, taking each of the three steps off the bus, one at a time.

The few passengers riding the bus raised their eyebrows as the old woman continued to talk, not making much sense, as she disappeared down the stairs.

"I guess we'll find out soon enough if you're ready." The old woman's voice travelled back up the stairwell. "If you're up to the task be sure and let me know!" she shouted as the bus doors closed.

Ardin felt the pressure that always accompanied taking a Math test in school. The lady guru had always told her a day would come when she would be tested and go through a rite of passage. Ardin wished she had asked more questions about what a rite of passage was, but she was certain she didn't want to miss it.

Like a crowd of race cars spinning through their last lap, the consequences of what she was about to do next flew through Ardin's mind. If she got off the bus and followed the old woman as she believed she should, the trust she had earned with Mrs. Bradford, her current foster mom and real-life teacher, would be breached. If caught, she would lose her bus-riding privileges and be grounded with no television, and forced to do arts and crafts projects after they had finished doing homework together.

Ardin had already missed her 9:00 curfew and was bound to be in trouble. She had stayed too long at the Serpentine Wall watching as the city workers set up booths for the annual fireworks display that happened every Labor Day weekend over the river. When it came right down to it, Ardin really loved spending time with Karen Bradford. She knew Karen would appreciate the importance of Ardin seeing the lady, if she just believed she really existed.

As the bus began to amble away from the curb, Ardin leapt to her feet and pulled the cord alerting the driver. "Stop the bus!" she shouted. "I need to get off!" The driver stopped in the middle of the street and released the lock so Ardin could slip through the double doors halfway down the side of the bus. Landing clumsily on the cobblestones, she looked up but didn't see the woman.

The bus blew a plume of stinky biodiesel exhaust into the air, and groaned on its way, clearing the view for Ardin to see the woman disappear through a door into an old tenement building across the street. Slipping on the cobblestones that were damp from the night air, Ardin slowed down and stepped carefully until she crossed the street.

As her eyes adjusted to the orange-colored streetlight after the bright florescent bus interior, Ardin was reminded that she was in a pretty rough neighborhood. Running to catch up, Ardin was impressed with how quickly the old woman had made it across the street. Reaching out and lay her hand on the brass handle of the door, Ardin pulled hard, but the door didn't open. She peered through the thin pane of beveled glass in the door and saw nothing but an empty foyer.

The wetness of the night air suddenly seemed to wrap around Ardin's body as she began to feel engulfed by a cold darkness. She stood very still and checked her surroundings peripherally. Her heart began to race as she realized she had left her backpack on the bus.

Ardin started to turn to see if the bus was still visible down the street, instead her eyes closed automatically as she plowed into a towering figure she recognized as a man's body. Her head was filled with the scent of a musty smelling shirt and her knees began to buckle, as she felt a large hand circle under the small of her back to keep her from falling.

As the world started to slip from Ardin's mind she heard the man's voice whisper, "There now, I've got you."

Ardin tried to see who was catching her but she couldn't open her eyes. Then she heard another man's voice that did not seem as reassuring, "There! I've got you now!"

Pause, pause, pause...

Amelia Bradford slowly became aware of her presence in the darkness of the auditorium as a clipped British accent containing holier than thou overtones narrated a video that was projected on a small screen.

'Once upon a time' is traditionally believed to be an invocation recalling events which seem to have previously unfolded. The true underlying principle is that all time is happening at once. There is no past, present or future timeframes as you shall soon see. Time, as the accumulation of seconds, minutes and hours to accrue days, weeks, months, and years, is not only an illusion, it is a gross mischaracterization of fact.

Amelia sat back in her seat. She regularly found she had dreamed herself to the small theatre to attend webinars. These webinars had nothing to do with the world-wide web, they were delivered through the etheric web during her dreams.

It had taken some time for Amelia to get used to the lucid dreaming that made what was going on inside her head seem so real and tangible. The first time she ever attended a webinar, the audience was not too fond of her confusion, as her thoughts could be heard just as though she was talking out loud.

There are different models for calculating this phenomenon known as linear time. The ancient Hindu system of time, for example, starts not with seconds but with the length of time it takes to wink one eye five and ten times.

The narrator slowed down and pronounced syllables as they crawled across the screen. *The Ma...Ha...Ba...Ra...Ta, that's Mahabharata, containing 1.8 million words and 90,000 verses is one of the longest epic poems ever written. Also known as The Great Tale of the Bharata Dynasty, this astounding compilation includes among it's discussion of human qualities such as duty, desire, purpose and liberation, the tale of time in such a way that it bridges the gap between Religion's insistence that the earth was created in 6 days with the Science's assertion that it was more like billions of years. Time, as they say, is relative.*

Amelia twisted in her seat to see how many others were in the audience. Two people were seated in the back row and four heads were visible very close to the stage. Amelia scrunched her shoulders and tilted her head to one side as she imagined a visit to the chiropractor if she sat that close to the screen.

In the Mahabharata, a Kastha, which spans the time of five and ten winks, is something like a second in western time measures. Thirty Kasthas make a Kala, and thirty of these, more or less, make a Muhurta. This is quite like an hour as thirty Muhurtas make one day including the night, with thirty of these comprising one month.

However, time takes a turn when transcribed to other dimensions. For example, the Mahabharata tells a month of time for human beings is equal to just one day and night for those who have died and are no longer living in the human time-frame. This is also, by the way, how an entire dream seems to occur in just a few minutes of sleep.

"Unless you're stuck in the Wait Zone." Amelia smirked out loud and automatically waved off the distaining shushes from the audience.

The Wait Zone was the non-denominational local term, like Limbo, for the Purgatory Amelia had been raised to expect when she died. Nevertheless, she felt totally unprepared when she showed up there unexpectedly and unable to leave just a year earlier.

Amelia understood the changing nature of time. According to the doctors and her family, Amelia had spent 135 days hovering in a coma, during which time they wondered if she would survive. For Amelia it was just 5 very busy days and nights in the Wait Zone sorting through dreams and nightmares to determine her fate. The narrator continued in a dismissive tone.

If humans would just realize their lives represent time rather than identifying life as 'self', they would have a much better time *living. When one fully embodies the notion that life is time and not an identity then one may travel time rather than attempt to carry it as so much baggage.*

Amelia smiled as her thoughts of the after-life seemed to alter the course of the narrator's monologue.

A latecomer slid into a seat a few rows behind Amelia. The scent of hot popcorn immediately produced a container in Amelia's hands. She sampled a few pieces. The snack had appeared exactly as she liked it with butter and light salt. Amelia watched as the screen switched to images touching on a variety of cultures and dynasties throughout the world.

Humans have a limited view of life-times. Some believe there is just one lifetime per soul which unfolds sequentially, in linear fashion from beginning to end. If one believes in reincarnation, one tends to view their lives as happening one after the other. While this may seem to be so, they are

8

actually happening concurrently since as we have already established, all time is happening at once.

"What is this, a school or something?" The man behind Amelia voiced confusion on the topic of time and was quickly shushed to be quiet. "I thought I was going to watch a movie on Lifetime." The man pouted as he slid down in his seat.

Amelia smiled, as she realized the man's plan to see a movie on the Lifetime channel had crossed threads with the webinar on "life" and "time". Sometimes the way threads crossed never seemed to make any sense. After an introduction to the Wait Zone during which her unconscious condition had psycho-magnetically crossed with childhood dreams, plots to do her in, and helpful guides, Amelia had grown accustomed to unexpected changes.

Sometimes people feel a previous lifetime is affecting the present lifetime and are concerned that their actions today may produce an unfavorable future lifetime. Some are interested only in living during this lifetime in such a way as to prevent the need for future lifetimes. Depending on one's beliefs, some or all of these could seem to be true or false. When it gets right down to it however, even the seemingly most enlightened being who believes he or she is moving on to completely rejoin the Absolute, is kidding him or herself as there was never any break to repair. It is unlikely a jiva or soul will master this in a single lifetime, and this is apparently what was originally intended to be the fun of it.

As she understood her studies thus far, the jiva which reminded Amelia of the Christian soul, was a collection of lifetimes expressed to collect and correct experiences with the hope of paying back what they owed to earn liberation known as moksha.

Amelia had struggled with the idea that someone else could put stains on her soul until she considered that her parents believed she had been born with the so-called original sin of

9

Adam and Eve. Either way, the Wait Zone served as people believed. The narrator's tone changed and Amelia could tell he was finishing his lecture.

Life and time are like a mystery adventure. If you want to see a movie, you would stop someone from telling you about it. Similarly time, as life and all of creation, is designed to keep everyone in suspense, always trying to figure it out yet again, which perpetuates the cycles of life regardless of the time-frame you choose. One is not better than another, nor even really that different, at most, they are all the same game by different names. The more ways you learn to look at life, the better off you'll be. As they say in the investment world, diversify!

Thank you for attending this presentation on Life-Time. We hope it will be of benefit to you in the not too distant future, which will of course then be your present and presently become your past. Come again.

The screen went black and Amelia remained seated contemplating how the lesson might be applied to her life. She came here often, not just the auditorium, but the expansive campus of what was commonly referred as The Inter-Planar University. At first arrival, she was skeptical of almost every concept that was introduced, but now she attended lectures and took field trips throughout the Wait Zone observing the way time and space shifted to accommodate and reflect the beliefs of the travelers who were arriving 24/7.

As compensation for and part of her studies at the university, Amelia spent many dream-filled nights cataloguing life histories and calculating the accomplishments made during waking life. Regardless of belief system, the results could be reviewed by those aspiring to make progress in any of the Wait Zone's various neighborhoods. In the Heavenly Realm the results were presented as The Book of Life, and observers could find out how much time they needed to stay in the Wait

10

Zone, before they could move on to their heavenly reward. Sometimes observers would find themselves bound for Hell if they didn't work out their differences, but resistance to suffering often snapped these souls back from the depths of hell so they could improve their prospects.

In the Karmic Realm of the Wait Zone the results were reported through kiosks called Moksha Meters. Even as people were learning from their progress in the Wait Zone's Inter-Planar University, their scores could be affected by alter-egos as their lifetime's contribution was registered. The more moksha a meter displayed, the more emancipated from the cycle of birth and death a soul became. The less an individual advanced, the more their beliefs would be challenged in alternate lives.

Amelia decided to go over the teaching of the webinar later, even though she knew she would awaken with only a faint feeling that there was something more than the waking life and her notes would not follow her there. She was taking steps to remember her dreamtime experiences when she awakened, but so far had not managed to find the right technique.

As she stood and began side-stepping her way down toward the aisle, Amelia wobbled on the same gold lamé high heeled shoes she always wore in the Wait Zone. They were a constant reminder of her journey as it continued to unfold.

Pause, pause, pause...

Max walked past the Moksha Meter perched on a pulpit standing in a swirl of delicate clouds outside the pearly gates at the entrance to the Heavenly Realm. He had long gotten over his fascination with the device. Max thought his

11

liberation was cinched. His life as a martyr in the early second century had landed Max extra credit. He was considered to be a Christian mystic. It ran in his lineage, he would proudly tell anyone who took the time to admire his impressive meter levels. Max's lifetime in Greece had resulted from the curiosity of a predecessor who had managed to become a divine Hindu sage after a bad start as the bastard son of a housekeeper. It had been a bit of a roller-coaster since then, what with the manifestation of a thieving court-jester followed by what ended up to be a drunken off-Broadway director, but the collective souls of his jiva were known to take big chances just to get ahead. Except for a brief downturn almost a year ago, not much had happened in the world appearance that negatively affected Max's moksha. He and the remnants of his fellow incarnations had done extra service to amend the damages done by the last ego to leave the waking life.

The Heavenly Realm seemed busy today. Max loved to toy with the new arrivals, just for shits and giggles. It was a form of weekly entertainment for Max to stop by and let himself be amused by the unsuspecting souls who waded through the clouds to meet their maker. Demonstrating a good moksha reading was the perfect way to gain the trust of newcomers just so he could pull the cloud out from under them, sending them into a veritable hell of their oftentimes first glimpse of self-awareness.

It had been more than sixteen hundred human years since Max was as naïve as the new arrivals who were expecting the Halleluiah Choir to be singing their praises when they showed up at the pearly gates. Max was proof positive that just because someone had become enlightened didn't mean that they were saintly, or even a basically nice person.

The monitor was operating in St. Peter mode so that each new arrival would instantly see his or her ratings presented as recordings in the Book of Life. Max preferred the straightforward style of the Moksha Meter view which presented a needle gauge that measured the degree to which the viewer was meeting his or her goals for development on a scale from red which was not so hot, to green which was emancipating.

Max smiled as the pages of the Book of Life format fluttered reflecting the nervous nature of a man who looked about thirty. The young man seemed to know what he was looking for as his view of the book shifted to take on Moksha Meter qualities and the needle reached the low-green range. A look of relief crossed the man's face, and Max surmised some sort of bad news wasn't taking too much of a toll on his record.

Despite his Christian heritage, Max spent most of his time in the Karmic Region of the Wait Zone. When he had crossed over to the Wait Zone around 400 A.D., Heaven was just getting started, and because his own beliefs actually predated the development of the Heavenly Realm, he found he felt quite comfortable in the Karmic Region where he initially spent a lot of time with his previous alter ego. Max found Heaven a little boring after residents got the idea they were supposed to stay forever and all they needed to do was laze around grassy fields and beautiful gardens.

Max's attachment to his belief that he had transcended bad karma indicated he had more work ahead, but he didn't care. Max liked the Wait Zone. He wasn't ready to join the great nothingness of Infinite Consciousness, and Infinite Consciousness seemed to agree. As the line to the Moksha Meter dwindled, Max stepped closer glancing around to see who might notice his stupendous read-out when his Moksha

Meter, perceived as The Book of Life would glow with a golden light while trumpets sounded.

As Max moved into range, the needle on the Moksha Meter as he saw it, quickly began dropping toward the flashing orange and red light labeled *Pathetic,* far from the green light label *Perfect.* Max slumped to a stop and stared at the meter. Swishing forward under the weight of his Greek toga, he supposed the problem could be related to a malfunction of the Moksha Meter this close to Heaven's gates, so he switched his view to the Book of Life or Peter Meter, as he liked to call it, and was horrified to see the book looked crispy as it smoked on the pulpit. Trumpets didn't toot, but a dirge started playing as dissonant chords played in the low range of an unseen piano keyboard.

For Max, it was as if the Bat Signal had been sent out to the last vestiges of ego that could still hook his attention and make his stomach (or the relative illusion of his stomach) swirl as if he was about to hurl his Post Toasties all over the Pearly Gates.

Max positioned his rotund body if he was about to spring into a series of martial arts movements. His hands and feet spread apart as his knees and elbows bent while he stared at the display in disbelief.

"What the f— "

"Fabuloussss!" a cupid-like fly-boy overwrote Max's swearing with one of the ten most popular expletive erasers used around the Pearly Gates. The job position had been developed precisely to cover the surprised and often times disappointed reactions of those who had sacrificed their whole lives just to find that they had indeed frittered away their entire vacations on earth and must now get back to work.

Max's face flashed crimson as his gaze remained transfixed on the monitor. Interpreting the color, he could tell he had accrued at least a dozen new lifetimes and most of them were scheduled as vermin, weeds, and the occasional house pet.

"How the h— " Max was cut off this time by a cupid-sized Ella Fitzgerald.

"Heaven, I'm in Heaven!" As Ella sang and flew over Max's head she was chased by a teeny tiny Louis Armstrong look-alike. Max swatted at the buzzing figures in the air and missed.

"What then?!" Max grabbed the edges of the pulpit, with sweat beads forming on his balding head like a minister's under the revival tent in August as he stared into the Book of Life. "What happened?" He started flipping through one page edged in red after another, none of which provided any information regarding the devastating decline in moksha.

"You really don't remember?" Max recognized the voice behind him as one he only heard when things were going terribly, terribly wrong.

"What's to remember?" Max replied without turning around. "There's no way this could be happening!"

"Ah Max, you seem to be mistaken." Max spun around and found the expected, characteristic cajoling countenance of the guru Tetta, dressed in her favorite caftan.

"But you always say there are no mistakes Tetta." Max knew the guru to be the supreme teacher of wisdom cloaked in the juxtaposition of seemingly contradictory concepts.

"Now Max, I think we both know you do have plenty of room for improvement." Tetta frowned. "Your mistake is your resistance to change."

When Max first arrived in the Wait Zone, Tetta was part of the team of guides and gurus who debriefed the Seven Sleepers and helped them understand the greater karmic aspects of their early Christian experience. Tetta taught Max about perfection at the same time she suggested there was nothing to which one could be compared as perfect. To Tetta, oxymorons contained truth and long wordy explanations were the veil which needed to be drawn back.

"I'm sure we all could improve Tetta." Max agreed, and held out his smoldering Book of Life. "But this is destruction. I have done nothing I know of to bring this about."

"Get thee behind me Satan!" A newcomer wearing her Sunday hat and dress that pronounced her Southern roots who had just curtsied and bowed her way to the pearly gates, pointed at Max who was bathed in the red light glowing from The Book of Life. Tetta watched Max eye the woman cautiously as she side-stepped a wide arc around him, making crosses with her fingers.

"Even she can see the remnants of your ego shining through, Max. What's going on?" Tetta wagged her finger at Max like a kindergarten teacher scolding the class clown.

Max's aged hands formed fists after he replaced the Book of Life on the pulpit and stepped away glaring at the newcomer who took up testifying right next to him.

"Why would anyone do this to me?" He ran his hands over the stubble of hair around his head.

"I believe the first step is admitting responsibility for your situation Max." Tetta sighed and disappeared against the backdrop of clouds as the bible-thumper used her Sunday-Go-To-Meeting hat to whack a young man who dared to visit the pearly gates in a Pearl Jam t-shirt.

Max tilted his head back and tried to follow Tetta through the ethers. A piece of advice was all he found.

"Try looking for Birch," he heard Tetta whisper. As if the words had been fed into a search engine, Max instantly began to surf into a vortex of light and energy. The scene spun like a game wheel at a festival as Max flew through a kaleidoscope of color until he started slowing down and the stars reorganized into familiar constellations. The faster Max flew, the slower the rotation of the vortex spun until, in a bizarre mix of spinning slow motion, Max found himself lightly floating into a relatively pin-point sized location hidden in the wide open spaciousness of countless universes.

A Banyan tree stretched below him covering nearly two-thirds of an acre with sprawling limbs that connected to the ground dozens of trunks with seemingly lopped off tops. The tree circled and twisted beneath him in a moment that shattered Max's patience then brought him smashing toward the earth issuing a yelp of fear that revealed the connection that continued to exist between him and the fear of suffering. In a burst of dust, Max landed with a thud that was absolutely painless, but full of enough allergens to bring him scrambling to his feet in a fit of coughing and sneezing.

Damned allergies, Max thought as he shook his head in frustration of the beliefs he maintained. Max looked around at the scene filled with tourists who were absolutely unaware of his amazing arrival. A middle-aged husband and wife stood next to the tree having their picture taken by their Hindi guide, a young boy. A teenage girl attracted his attention as she stood silently by the main trunk of the tree with her palms turned toward it, and her eyes closed. She seemed to be repeating a mantra or prayer. Max smiled. While he tended to pick on enlightened wannabes, this waif's intentions were palpably, whole-heartedly unlearned and her desire to connect with the tree quite genuine. While she reveled in the energetic exchange with the tree, Max decided he would grant her a bonus and stepped up next to the trunk.

Feel the space behind you. He thought spoke to the girl.

The girl's left eye peeped open as she looked at the tree with a slight amount of surprise. *Me?* She checked in to see if she had indeed heard a voice.

17

Not what's in the space, Max clarified. *Not the tree or ground or people. Feel the space behind you.*

Easily, the girl sent her awareness to feel into the space behind her and was filled with bliss. Her thoughts were still and for a moment she enjoyed this sensation.

What is this? she asked.

Contact with Infinite Consciousness, Max thought to her.

This is easier than meditation, she observed.

Yeah, meditation takes a little too much effort if you ask me, Max replied then choked back a laugh as both of the girl's eyes popped open and she bent forward to scrutinize the tree. Max remained imperceptible to her.

When you are connected with the Absolute in this way, Max attempted to reconnect the moment, *you can enjoy everything as was originally intended.* The girl took a deep breath and seemed to relax away from a state of suspicion.

It is not necessary to climb a mountain upon self-realization, Max continued. The girl smiled at the tree with a hint of understanding in her eyes. Max finished using special effects he had learned through his part-time work as an associate guide, to make the sound of his last word reverberate and echo into silence. *Rather see all that is with new eyes of dispassion and pure appreciation.*

The waif waited patiently with her head bowed, feeling into the space behind her just in case the tree had any more wisdom it would like to add. She seemed more than satisfied at the revelations Max passed along. He remained silent.

The girl bowed and smiled a last thought of gratitude to the Banyan tree for its lesson on connecting with the space behind her. She was pleased with herself for being able to connect with the tree. Giving the tree a big energetic hug the girl turned and slowly walked around under the rambling limbs.

18

Max watched the waif as she approached other visitors under the tree to make sure that they were happy and content.

"Namaste." The girl greeted a couple who did not recognize the salutation or look at her even though she stood directly in front of them.

"Let's get another picture, Mike." The girl frowned momentarily as if the woman had hurt her feelings.

"Yeah" Mike said to his girlfriend or wife, "And then let's grab a cold one, it's hotter than hell out here." Mike brushed past the waif without making any eye contact or acknowledging her existence.

"Am I invisible?" she asked after them. They did not respond. "I'm invisible," she informed herself. "Does that mean they're awake and I'm not?" she wondered. Then, reviewing her studies she added, "Or maybe I'm awake and they're not." Plus one more piece, "Or we could be in some other dimensions that center around the same tree." And finally, "which may or may not look the same or even like a tree to anyone but me."

Max was amused at the way such a young girl was working so hard to see things as they really were. He imagined she was an old soul to be so aware at such a young age.

Max remembered his own moment when he first connected with the idea of the self, and later how he had attained self-realization at the roots of this very same Banyan tree under the guidance of a divine Hindu sage. It was at that time that he realized that both the ego and the self were not personalized at all, but pools of ideas that could be dipped into and poured out as substance into limitless forms of life. Max knew life was at its best when one did not identify with it.

Max had taught his findings to thousands in the early years before he retired, even though he found t difficult to follow his own advice. The goal was to help others achieve oneness.

He had even worked closely with the subsequent incarnations of his jiva, but both of them had not demonstrated the same interest he had cultivated for eastern philosophy.

Spotting the waif walking back toward the center of the Banyan tree with its trunk measuring more than 1000 inches in circumference, Max mused at the dreamers who were imagining themselves on vacation and power journeys who had arrived on this dimensional plane to visit the oldest Banyan tree in existence. Just as Edison would later introduce the Banyan to Florida from India, this Banyan had been transferred from another universe during the reconstruction after the great flood. It was from this tree that the tree under which the Buddha would attain liberation had been born. Banyans were parasitic, always relying on a native tree to grow. Max walked around under the tree trying to figure out how returning to it after all this time connected with the condition of his Moksha Meter.

"Birch!" Max remembered the word Tetta had whispered on her way out of Heaven. "But this is a Banyan. Some would call it a Pipul Tree, or Bodhi, but never Birch. What was Tetta thinking? And why? Why does she care about my moksha? Have I landed at the wrong tree?" "Birch," Max repeated the possible clue to resolving his moksha dilemma. "Birch, Birch, Birch." Max began to chant the word. "Biiiiiiiirrrrrch." He tried it slower and looked around. *How did I end up at the Banyan when I was told to look for a Birch?* he wondered. "Birch!" Max said emphatically. "Brch-brch-brch," he repeated quickly. "Birch?" he seemed to ask.

"What, what, what?!" came an impatient reply, "I'm busy!"

"Burch?!" Max turned around, his toga swirling up as he spun in place. Before him sat a small, short man wearing a loose fitting white linen shirt and baggy pants. His fingers were clicking on the keys of a calculator placed on an overturned basket resting on the ground, squeezed between the man's bare feet.

20

"Burch, how did you get here?" Max was overwhelmed to see his accountant.

"You called me. Now, what is it Max? I'm in the middle of an assessment." Burch picked up a receipt from a stack piled on the ground beside him, and examined it through tiny bifocal lenses. Refocusing his eyes on the calculator keys, he punched a couple numbers into the machine.

"Are those for me?" Max raised his eyebrows and peered down at the mountain of receipts Burch was adding into the machine.

"Why am I not surprised you would think it was all about you, Max?" Burch spoke in a tone reminiscent of Max's last conversation with Tetta.

"Well my Peter-Meter is going crazy, so I thought you might be adding up some charges for me." Max defended himself against an assessment of out of control ego.

"I wish you wouldn't call it that Max."

"Sorry," Max corrected his tendency to use the inappropriate expression, "Moksha Meter."

"Thank you. No." replied Burch.

"No what?"

"No, I am not entering data for you."

"Oh, good I was afraid my Peter—I mean Moksha Meter was going to go crazy with all that."

"That's what I'm looking for," Burch replied.

"But what could possibly go against me?" Max stepped to his right instinctively as a couple of tourists walked between Burch and himself without seeing them.

"How 'bout four people dying before their time, Max?" Burch waved a handful of receipts in Max's face.

"Is that what this is about?" Max's face turned red with disbelief that the early passing of four less than stellar souls could reduce his moksha to nothing. "Burch, we already dealt with this, and it wasn't my doing. I'd like to stop this

21

transaction please!" Max lowered himself to eye level with Burch.

"No can do," Burch curtly replied. "Besides…your friend," Burch put his finger to his chin, as if trying to remember something. "Oh, what was his name?" Burch pulled a receipt from his pants pocket and checked it. "Oh yes, Galahad. How could I forget? You can't blame him for this one. He really isn't bad enough to reduce almost every single success your misguided jiva has managed to accrue." Burch stuffed the receipt into his pocket and shrugged. "I carry it with me as a reminder of just how screwed up things can get." Burch smirked. "Good thing you had plenty of help building it up or whatever is going on would put in the rears forever."

"Well, what or who could bring it down then?" Max felt the frustration rising in his chest. He searched through his knowledge of all the personalities with whom he shared a soul, focusing on those who were known to get in trouble. "Certainly not little Archie Armstrong. He was a thief, but like you said, what's showing up on my record is devastating, not a little foolery."

"Even as the enlightened sage your jiva was courting disaster, Max, but nothing like this." Burch picked up the pile of receipts and prepared to resume punching them into the calculator.

"Dammit man!" Max reached down and grabbed Burch by the front of his linen shirt raising him off the ground with his legs crossed in his still seated position. "Tell me what it is, Burch!"

The little accountant choked as he tried to keep his chin above collar level. "I don't know Max. No one knows."

"What do you mean, no one?" Max sought to understand. "Who are you discussing this with and who is sending these receipts you are filing against me?" Max let go of the tunic and Burch pounced back to the ground.

"I'm not filing anything Max." Burch squarely eyed Max and explained, "These receipts represent your successes as well as your shortcomings, Max. Tetta and Hrim have asked me to recalculate your entire record to help ascertain what could be this powerful and where it has leverage. So far none of it makes sense. Your moksha is going down without any help from me or you." Burch stood up and straightened his shirt from the twisted mess Max had left it.

"You're telling me the Moksha is going down even though you can't see anything I'm doing wrong?"

"Not you, or anyone else associated with your Jiva." Burch's tone was flat and matter of fact. "All I can say is that up until now your Moksha Meter has been consistently and negatively influenced by goodness in the world."

"But my moksha has flat-lined and the world appearance is in terrible condition." Max looked even more confused. "Where's the good in that?"

"I said *up until now* goodness was bringing you down. That's why I'm recalculating Max." Burch sighed and tried to explain, "By goodness I mean helping. It is the aide that follows a disaster that seems to bring you down most. Whenever humanity steps up and does the right thing, your moksha suffers a little. However, in the dualistic dream of the planet Earth, hardship is required to necessitate the goodness. I'm checking to see if what is currently happening in the world appearance is something new or just another opportunity for humanity to step up. Either way, it looks like your record will be little more than a toast, Max."

"Ya' gotta' help me Burch!?" Max begged.

"Max, your moksha is not really my concern, but if it helps our understanding of the depths of this global devastation, I'm willing to go over it with a fine tooth comb." Burch referred to his clarification of how it was happening. "From what I've seen so far, all I can suggest is the Law of Similars."

Max considered the law which stated that a problem could best be solved by administering actions similar to what caused it rather than resistance. It didn't make sense to Max.

"I don't get it Burch."

"That's just it Max." Burch sighed, clearly ready to leave the thread. "Let me put it this way, even when one of your jiva's life expressions has been solely responsible for screwing things up, direct action to fix things on the part of you and your egoic others has improved the problem. Find the hair of the dog that's biting you Max, and do the same."

Making that his last piece of advice, Burch *poofed* out of sight.

Max frowned moved out of the way of a non-seeing visitor taking pictures of the Banyan tree. Max and Burch had never gotten along very well. That Burch had come when called was a surprising favor, and Max now had a slight hint of what was making the meter melt. Max couldn't imagine where to start finding what was tilting his game, but he was intrigued by Burch's assertion that the Law of Similars would help.

Max had always been rather bad at being good. When it came to making remedies using the Law of Similars, Max new specifics were very important. Max sat down on a wooden bench and noticed the girl he had seen earlier attempting to be helpful to other visitors under the Banyan. She was offering to take a photo of a young couple. They didn't seem to notice her. Goodness was a deep subject. It could be fun and philanthropic. Max closed his eyes and wondered what specific qualities of goodness there were in giving aid to another human being that he could adapt to fix his Moksha Meter.

"Well Max?" Tetta's voice startled Max.

Max opened his eyes to see the Banyan tree had been replaced by the façade of the Himalayan Mountains as he found himself sitting outside the entrance to the Karmic Realm of the Wait Zone. "How did I get here?"

"Did you meet with Burch?" Tetta was quick to get to the point. Max sheepishly looked down at the status of his Moksha Meter which was smoldering in the low lying clouds of the Karmic Realm. The red glow of alarm had given way to a burned up, barely discernable light, and steam was rising from it as if there were coals freshly soaked with water inside the box.

"Max, you can't fix this by just looking at it."

"It still doesn't make any sense to me, Tetta. Tell me what's going on."

"I can't, Max." Tetta felt compassion for Max as she knew his future had been reduced to a millennium of lifetimes as a worm followed by another millennium as slugs. "All we can see is a teeter-totter affect that leads us to you but then the thread goes dead."

"Burch told me the same thing." Max felt frustrated. Tetta could see the anger building in Max's aura.

"One thing is certain Max, losing your temper isn't going to help." Tetta nodded her head and produced a wooden bench in the low lying fog outside the Karmic Realm. "Have a seat Max."

The pair sat down together quietly watching the very different crowd that hovered below sacred mountains. There was a mix of monk-like people wearing the variously colored robes of Tibetan, Mahayana, and Chinese Buddhists, while ascetic Hindu rishis wearing almost nothing ignored the allure of floating celestial nymphs, and New Agers from the 60's, 70's, 80's and 90's interacted through a haze of acid flashbacks and trance channeled entities to discuss existentialism and the validity of the 2012 theory applied to the Mayan calendar.

"Max!" Tetta snapped her fingers in front of his eyes and continued to explain what she knew. "Max, this is about way more than just your moksha." Tetta poked him in the arm with her elbow. "Otherwise, for all the trouble you cause, I might just ignore you altogether!"

"Is that why you're on me, Tetta?" Max acknowledged that he had put her trust to the test many times after he arrived in the Wait Zone. "Are you really just trying to help someone else?" Max bent low and tilted his head up to catch Tetta's ever smiling eyes.

Tetta, was already weary of Max's self-interest. "Max that's total bullsh— "

"Shine on, Shine on Harvest Moon..." an expletive eraser contracted from the Heavenly Kingdom floated in front of Tetta making tsk-tsk motions with his two index fingers.

Tetta was humbled before the cupid look-a-like and returned her gaze to Max. "Listen! Hear, Max! I am not *your* guru. As a mystic you have always been on your own. It's just that the world appearance needs our help, and a link to your Moksha Meter is all we have to go on!"

"I don't know how I can help save the world when my meter is such a mess." Max glanced back at his simmering screen. Tetta groaned.

"Okay Max, I'll worry about the state of the world. You just take care of yourself and see if you can find a way to be nice to someone. Burch will keep an eye on things."

"Where do I start?" Max was whining like a child now. He might be bad at being good, but he rarely enjoyed his faults anymore.

"I can take you back to where the thread drops off." Tetta offered. "Maybe that will give you a clue."

Before Max could fully cognize what Tetta was offering, the celestial nymphs along with all the monks and students in the Karmic Realm were engulfed in dense blackness. The clamor of the spiritual marketplace was stilled, and Max heard the echoing sound of water slowly dripping somewhere in the darkness as he continued to sit on the bench.

Where am I? Max wondered as his eyes kept stretching open over and over attempting to absorb some light of which there was none.

"Out of bounds." Tetta's voice gave the standard answer gurus and guides provided when they knew something their subjects were supposed to figure out on their own. "I brought you this far, now let's see if you can remember. Don't get distracted, Max." Tetta's tone was forceful and authoritative. "Find out where we go from here."

"I wish to see!" Max let go of his fear of the unknown and a soft light began to illuminate the space.

The dirt floor of a cave appeared before Max. Lying among the stones that coarsely studded the dirt were the bodies of seven men who were sleeping like babies. Max stood and began to quietly wander through the curled bodies, taking small, careful steps and examining their faces. He stopped and knelt down and reached out to touch the curly hair of a young blonde man.

Tetta softly cleared her throat to remind him touching was a no-no. Max looked with concern into the seemingly peaceful face, then looked up at Tetta who was half frowning at him as if he might do something wrong.

"How could this be?" Max looked down at the body of the sleeping young man. He ran his hands over his own balding head and pressed his palms to his cheeks giving Tetta a concerned look of commitment and respect he had not shown in ages.

The scene captured the darkest time in Max's incarnation, one of the top ten most life-altering experiences his jiva had ever produced. It had improved his jiva's Moksha Meter and those of countless others by exponential leaps. He was at once deeply moved and terribly confused by the possibility that this scene was linked to something that was producing disaster.

"I was imprisoned, Tetta. Asleep." Max searched his mind for a clue. "It's impossible that I could have done something harmful in this place. I don't know where we go from here."

Scanning Max's thought's Tetta was convinced he was completely unaware of any possible cause. She needed a back-up plan.

"Alright Max, here's what I think you should do. You need to get together with the rest of the crew here, and all of your jiva's alter egos. Perhaps they will know something that can help."

Max's fixation on the sleeping image of his younger self was interrupted by Tetta's use of the word "think". Tetta didn't think, Tetta knew. If Tetta was resorting to thinking, Max felt as if whatever came next was little more than a guessing game.

Which Way Did She Go?

Amelia waited to get a word in edgewise in the conversation as her mother ranted through the speaker on the iphone lying on the pillow next to her head.

"You have to call Miguel," Karen Bradford demanded, "and you have to call him now!" It was midnight and Amelia wasn't fond of the idea of waking her boyfriend the way her mother had awakened her, with more bad news about Ardin.

"Mom, did you try to call her?" Amelia asked in a half-hearted attempt to engage her mother in sensible conversation rather than react to the hysteria that was building up with hurricane force.

"I just told you, the bus driver answered her cell phone and told me Ardin left it behind when she got off the bus in Over-the-Rhine!"

"Does she have any friends downtown?" Amelia continued to attempt to establish a point for process.

"No!" Karen checked her memory. "Well, I don't know." It was possible. "Who knows?" She practically screamed in frustration, "The point is, she's missing Amelia and we need Miguel to find her right away. Don't you care?"

Amelia didn't feel as ambivalent as Karen perceived, she just couldn't deny Ardin's history which wasn't exactly stellar. Amelia and her mom often took different sides, like good-cop/bad-cop parents, over the kids they had in common. Amelia was usually the law enforcer which provided her mother the opportunity to be the nurturing caregiver to the youth Amelia represented on her caseload as Guardian ad Lidem to the courts.

"Of course I care Mom, but you know Ardin is a frequent runner and loves to stir up drama."

"I'm calling the police." Karen Bradford hung up the phone and Amelia used voice recognition to direct her phone, "Call Mom." The first ring was seized not with a greeting but a continuation of the argument.

"If you won't help me I'll find someone who will." Karen declared. "Either you call Miguel and we all go down there together or I'll call the police right now." Aware that another infraction could cause Ardin to be placed in detention and her mother to become unbearable, Amelia capitulated.

"Okay, I'll be there in a few minutes and I'll call Miguel on the way, Mom." She hoped she might buy a little time during which she fully expected Ardin to turn up making excuses, and creating some dramatic reason why she had disappeared.

"Well hurry," Karen demanded.

Amelia rolled over onto her back and stared at the ceiling. She was accustomed to her mother's larger than life reactions to adversity. Nine months earlier the nurses told her they

30

believed it was Karen's stubborn refusal to accept what seemed almost inevitable to everyone else that had brought Amelia back from her coma. Karen had stayed at the hospital almost full-time during the nearly five months Amelia remained in a coma often on the brink of death.

Amelia rolled out of bed and grabbed a pair of jeans and a sweater from the closet. Walking to the solarium, she softly chirped to her sleeping bird Binga as she passed her cage, and picked up her purse jiggling it to hear that her keys were inside. Proceeding into the kitchen, Amelia was closely followed by her wire-haired dachshund Zeke. Dropping the purse strap over her shoulder, Amelia freed her hands to lift the lid on a cookie jar and retrieve a dog biscuit.

"Come here puppy." She offered the treat to Zeke who eagerly snatched it from her fingertips as Amelia opened the door to leave her high rise condominium. Multi-tasking came easy to her, but even this had changed after the coma. She now felt a deep need to practice living with awareness.

As she walked down the long hallway of The Regency, Amelia thought about the strange mix of events that had changed her life so dramatically over the last year.

When Amelia awakened from her coma she found not only her mother sitting beside but also the detective on her case, Miguel Alvarez. At the same time, Amelia's employee, her step-sister Shima, and Miguel's former police partner Nick Green, mysteriously vanished causing both Miguel and Amelia to reprioritize their values from professional to personal, and kindle a relationship.

Amelia unlocked the door of her Mercedes SUV from a distance, as she walked across the parking garage. She wondered if Miguel was working or asleep. They had started meeting long before she woke up from the coma as his interest in her case led his dreams to connect with hers in the

31

Wait Zone. At the same time Amelia met Miguel's foster son, Jojo Jenkins, for the first time in the Wait Zone and the three of them continued to meet in their dreams ever since, though she rarely remembered the details.

As she turned the ignition, Amelia pulled her iphone from her purse and asked it to call Miguel.

"My mother is on the warpath." Amelia responded to Miguel's outgoing voicemail message. "Please call me ASAP, Ardin has gone missing again."

Pause, pause, pause...

Almost every culture has known its Golden Age. This is a time of tremendous growth and progress. It may be industrial or philosophical or both or neither, but for whatever reason, it's golden. These are the times when divine ideas cross over into the human realm. The gold of such times is intended to be a sort of bonding agent among cultures with the wisdom or inventions of such times transcending and melding with all other eras of gold. It just works like that. What humans do with it is another story.

Much of the lore that shows up in more than one culture is widely believed to have travelled the trade routes. The idea postulates that when people liked a story they integrated it with their own traditions and heroes. However, it is also theorized that this wasn't a tale that spread but an event that was simultaneously introduced across cultures. What is often overlooked is that these tales spread not merely through human channels but through the etheric web as well.

Jojo's eyes drooped. When Jojo was in the Wait Zone he usually played kickball with the angels and demons. Leaning his head against Miguel's shoulder he closed his eyes and hoped for a dream within his dream so he could have a little fun before he had to wake up.

The Greek and the Hindu Golden Ages overlapped and so have many of their beliefs. For instance both the Greek philosopher Heraclitus and the Hindu sage Vasistha promoted the philosophy that humanity would be better off without beliefs or thought, and that the way to release beliefs was through self-inquiry.

As soon as Miguel doubted his etheric sleuthing skills would be helped very much by understanding Greek or Hindu history, he felt the spinning of consciousness that indicated his doubt had set another experience into motion.

Jojo's head dislodged from Miguel's shoulder as the spinning stopped and Miguel watched as a neon green disc flew toward the basket of the ninth hole on the Frisbee golf course Jojo had apparently dreamed up.

"How did you do that?" Miguel smiled as Jojo turned to face him with gleaming eyes and the breathlessness that goes with a good dream.

"I dunno." Jojo shrugged playfully and waited for Miguel to throw the pink Frisbee that had materialized in his fingertips.

"Pink?" Miguel scowled at Jojo. "How come you always get the cool colors?" Miguel threw the Frisbee and Jojo went running to retrieve his own disc from the grass.

As he watched Jojo run, Miguel wondered if Amelia might be nearby. The picnic tables were empty, but he never knew when a similarity in their dream threads could draw them together. Originally Miguel thought it was Jojo that connected him to Amelia, but Miguel found there was much more to meeting Amelia than chance. There were many overlapping connections in their lives even though Amelia didn't share Miguel's awareness of them.

The clanking of chains caught Miguel's attention as Jojo threw his green Frisbee into the basket from close range. "I won! I won!" Jojo bounced up and down with his arms raised victoriously in the air.

"You are a winner!" Miguel hugged Jojo as the boy threw his arms around Miguel's waist.

"You really think so?" Jojo wanted to hear more. In his former life with his step-father, and in many of the foster homes where he had previously lived, Jojo had rarely been considered much more than a nuisance.

"Yes Jojo, I think you're great." Miguel had known Jojo all his life, and had taken the boy into his home after he showed up with bruises at school.

"Then I think we should celebrate and get some ice cream!" Jojo jiggled himself out from under Miguel's hand on his shoulder as he again began bouncing up and down with excitement.

Miguel could see an image of the local soft serve ice cream establishment grow in Jojo's thoughts, as he added a hot dog to the order. Being able to scan Jojo's thoughts made it easy to care for the boy and reassured Miguel that he had picked up very little of his step-dad's devious tendencies.

"Okay," Miguel started to pick up the pink Frisbee and stopped. "I'll take you if you give me something a little tougher looking than that." The Frisbee levitated off the ground and shifted to a deep indigo color with silver sparks shooting out of it. Miguel snatched it from the air, impressed with Jojo's ability to manipulate his dreams.

"You're a winner too!" Jojo declared as he began to run for Miguel's plain white Hyundai that was parked next to the field. "Come on Miguel! Come on!"

Pause, pause, pause...

"That girl is in so much trouble!" Amelia watched as her mother collected items from various regions of the house and deposited them on the piano bench where an accordion file containing all the paperwork Karen held for Ardin had also been deposited. "I'm going to need all this to get her things," Karen explained in exasperation.

Karen plopped her purse on the piano bench and began rummaging through it looking for her keys occasionally shaking it to follow their clinking sound while two pairs of glasses, bifocals and distance, jiggled on top of her head. She pulled a Bluetooth headset and wrapped it around her ear and then produced her cell phone which she flipped open to check for messages and to make sure the battery was charged.

"Where did I put those?" Karen started squinting around the room searching the tops of end tables and the mantel of the fireplace then ducked into her home office emerging a moment later letting her hands drop to her side with an air of exasperation.

"What are you looking for, Mom?" Amelia asked though she lacked the gene that made note of things she saw laying around so she could help locate them later.

"My glasses!" Karen put her hand to her head and knocked the bifocals to the floor.

"Mom, why don't you sit down for a minute?"

"Amelia, why don't you call Miguel?" Karen's tone squashed Amelia's helpful advice as it fell on ears that were filtering out anything that varied from the pre-approved plan. It was difficult for Amelia to support that.

Amelia picked up the bifocals while Karen twirled on her heel to locate the distance glasses which continued to lurk in at roots of her short salt and pepper hair.

"Mom, I left him a message. He must be on a case or something. Let's just go to the Metro station and get her things, by the time we do that we'll be able to talk with Miguel, I'm sure." Amelia waited for a response from her mother and started walking past the staircase toward the front door. "Does that sound like a plan?"

"SORTA," Karen replied as she lifted a newspaper on the dining room table, hoping to find her glasses.

"Sorta' what?" Amelia asked, wondering what issues her mother might have with her suggestion.

"SORTA!" Karen corrected her daughter. "Southwestern Ohio Regional Transportation Authority," she explained.

"SORTA – Metro? What's the difference?" Amelia rolled her eyes.

"Well, I looked it up so you could put the address in that thingamajig, so it will tell us the directions." Karen handed Amelia a piece of paper she retrieved from the accordion file. The address for SORTA's office was written on it in neat teacher's chalkboard script. Karen walked toward the door busily arranging items in her purse so she could snap it closed. "I wish I could find my glasses so I could make sure you don't have an accident." She wrapped her purse over her shoulder and, clenching it under her arm, turned to observe Amelia standing in the foyer smiling at her.

"What?" Karen asked, providing an uncharacteristic moment of silence. Amelia startled from the moment of deep affection she was feeling for the crazy antics that so essentially defined her mother. They'd grown closer since her dad died, and even more close since the coma.

"Hello? What are you thinking?" Karen was only interested in thoughts that would find Ardin.

"Nothing, Mom, let's get going." Amelia smiled at, but failed to point out the glasses still perched on Karen's head, choosing instead to see how long it would be before she discovered them there.

Karen pulled the door of the Mercedes open and bent down to get inside as Amelia started the engine. Banging her head on the ceiling she crushed the distance glasses into the top of her head and glared at Amelia who pretended not to notice.

"Well at least I'll be able to see where you're going" Karen dropped into the leather seat and pulled the safety belt around her as Amelia turned the key and started the SUV.

As Amelia began to back out of the driveway Karen felt the lingering instinct to check her driving as she had always done with her husband. Karen needed to be needed. Though teaching had helped in the years after her husband passed away, taking in Ardin had brought meaning back into her home as well, though Ardin definitely didn't make it easy.

Ardin had been prone to disappearing ever since she was eight. Whenever she was found and asked where she had been, Ardin replied that she had been visiting with her secret friend. Ardin claimed her friend taught her to make people laugh.

Whenever Ardin was given a choice of compliance or consequences she always seemed confused. She tried to explain that her secret friend advised her to never do anything because she was afraid. Unfortunately for Ardin, many of her caretakers based their progress on promoting a fear of consequences and expected their instructions to be followed to the letter. Ardin had a tendency to wait too long before acting, as she tried to find a moment that didn't seem as if she wanted to avoid getting in trouble, which landed her in deeper and deeper trouble.

While case workers and psychiatrists tried many methods and medications to ameliorate Ardin's antics and reported visions and voices, nothing seemed to change her behavior. Karen had watched Ardin from a distance after she moved out of her classroom into middle school. When her last foster home asked for reassignment, Karen feared Ardin might end up in a residential facility and applied to be her foster-mother.

Just as Amelia was feeling the unusual quiet that came with her mother's silent review of the responsibility she held for Ardin, Karen started pumping the SUV full of worries.

"What if someone has taken her?" The headlights from oncoming cars shone on Karen's glasses keeping Amelia from seeing the tears in her mother's eyes.

"Probably no one has taken her, Mom." Amelia attempted to be more reassuring than dismissive.

"Why hasn't Miguel called back yet?" Karen moved on to something she might be able to fix.

"I'm sure he'll call when he gets the message." Amelia kept her eyes on the road.

"What if he can't find her?" Amelia caught the glimmer of tears shining on her mom's cheeks. Such emotional expression was not the norm in the Bradford house, both women let the moment go by without further comment.

Pause, pause, pause...

"Come on, come on!" In his dream Miguel Alvarez thought he was hearing Jojo urging him to move faster toward his dream of hot dogs and ice cream, but his forward momentum was slowed as he felt a tug from behind and his arm was twisted and pulled.

"Whaaaaat?" Miguel whined in his sleep.

"Come on Miguel." Jojo's voice became more three-dimensional. "Your cell phone is ringing." Miguel opened one eye and saw Jojo checking the face of the cell phone. "It's Miss Amelia." Jojo handed the phone to Miguel who looked at the boy standing in his pajamas looking so different than he had just appeared in their dream.

"Hello?" Miguel spoke into the phone.

"Miguel? I can't hear you." Amelia's voice sounded distressed. Miguel repositioned the phone so it was not pressed against the pillow.

"What time is it?" Miguel pulled the phone away from his head and looked at the small display. "It's one in the morning."

"One, maybe one-thirty." Amelia tried to account for the time ferrying her mother to SORTA since her mother had first called "Where have you been?"

"Dreaming!" Miguel squinted as Jojo turned on the overhead light. "Turn it off!" He motioned to Jojo who flipped the switch back and plunged the room into comparatively deeper darkness.

"What?" Amelia strained to hear Miguel clearly on the speakerphone in her car while eighteen wheelers passed her on I-75.

"Nothing." Miguel let his head drop back on the pillow. "What's wrong?"

"Ardin is missing," Amelia reported.

"Missing? How?" Miguel pressed the button for speakerphone and put the cell phone on his night stand as he grabbed his jeans from the bottom of the bed and started to step into them.

"She got off the bus in Over-the-Rhine," Amelia answered.

"Tell him she didn't take her things, Amelia. Tell him something's different," Karen urged from the passenger seat.

"What things?" Miguel acknowledged the third party in the conversation.

"Her book bag, her cell phone was in it," Amelia clarified.

"That doesn't sound like her usual," Miguel agreed with Karen. "And it doesn't sound like it will be as easy to track her down."

"We're on our way to the stop where she got off," Amelia continued.

"Wait a minute. Why don't you call the police? I don't like the idea of you two going into Over-the-Rhine alone after midnight." Miguel threw his shirt on and started buttoning.

"We're not *alone*." Amelia's Irish temperament flashed. "We're with each other."

"You know what I mean." Miguel stood firm.

"Besides, you're the police!" Karen inserted.

"No, not anymore." Karen had never accepted the fact that Miguel had decided to leave the force.

"Well, you're *our* police," Karen insisted. The speakers on both ends of the conversations were thickly quiet.

"We need you, Miguel." Amelia broke the silence.

"Okay, fill me in." Miguel picked up the phone and put it in his shirt pocket. He met Jojo at the doorway of the bedroom and steered him out into the hall toward his room. Almost as if they were practicing a juggling act, the two began exchanging shirt, jeans, socks and pants for pajama tops and bottoms tossing them back and forth as the boy changed clothes. All the while, Miguel's pocket was filled with news about the quest to SORTA to retrieve the missing back pack and the address of the destination in Over-the-Rhine.

"Where are you now?" Miguel and Jojo started bounding down the stairs of Miguel's bungalow in South Avondale.

"Just about to get off I-75 at Ezzard Charles Drive." Miguel winced and put the phone to his ear.

"Stay on the main drag and wait in the car until I get there." Miguel waited for Amelia to agree. "Please?" Miguel asked nicely knowing Amelia's feminist rage could spike at any moment. A year earlier, Amelia would have given Miguel a hard time about watching out for her. Instead the silence didn't sound nearly as deafening as he expected. Even though Amelia didn't remember many details of what transpired when they first met, the pair maintained a connection in the face of danger.

"I'll be careful." Her voice had softened with a sense of appreciation for the man she believed had helped pull her back from the brink of death, and his heart felt full for the woman whom he knew had done the same for him.

"Fifteen minutes," Miguel reassured as he directed Jojo to buckle his seatbelt and closed the door of his car. "I'll be there."

"Okay."

Karen Bradford looked out the window as the call ended and listened to the hum of the highway. She wondered how she had managed to put her daughter once again into the middle of a dangerous neighborhood. She took slim comfort in the knowledge that Miguel was on the way. She said a little prayer and made the sign of the cross, in spirit, over the Mercedes SUV.

Miguel kept glancing at his dashboard as he pushed the speedometer ten then fifteen miles per hour over the limit. Swerving down Liberty Street he barely made the light as he turned onto Walnut and headed toward Thirteenth so he could double back on Twelfth.

"There's Miguel!" Amelia interrupted her mother in mid-sentence as Miguel pulled past the Mercedes and parked along the curb in front of it. He sprang from his Hyundai telling Jojo to stay in the car, holding up his hand in Amelia's direction which Karen chose not to interpret as a plea for her to stay in the car.

"Miguel, you have to find her, it's not safe down here!" Karen practically shouted as a couple of young men sauntered past holding up their jeans by spreading their knees apart.

"Shhhh." Miguel walked quickly to Karen, put his arm over her shoulder and turning her toward the Mercedes which the young men had stopped to admire. Miguel eyed them and let his jacket fall open enough to reveal the holstered gun he was carrying. The men made some grumbling sounds and moved on.

"Mrs. Bradford," Miguel began.

"Oh for heaven's sake man! How many times do I have to ask you to call me Karen?" Miguel had not been able to change the way he had always addressed Karen Bradford, school teacher, even though he had been dating Amelia for the last nine months.

"Karen, I need you to get back in the car," Miguel requested.

"But we need to go look for Ardin!" Karen insisted.

"No, you need to go home. I need to look for her." Miguel opened her car door. "You and Amelia need to help me by taking care of Jojo so I can check into this."

Karen looked up as Jojo stuck his head out the window of the Hyundai and started waving to her. "Hi Miss Karen! Hi Miss Amelia!" She frowned knowing that putting herself or even Amelia at risk was not the same as putting Jojo at risk.

"You're right. This won't work." Karen surrendered to Miguel's instructions.

"Thank you. Now have a seat." Miguel motioned as Karen climbed in the Mercedes.

"Okay, but promise you will find her." Karen waited to drop down into the seat until Miguel replied.

"Of course." Miguel looked across the seat at Amelia. "Any clues?"

"None," Amelia admitted. "Just that she was last seen here about two hours ago."

"Okay!" He motioned for Jojo to come to the car. "I'll check the whole area." Jojo climbed into the car and slid across the seat so he was centered between the two women in the back seat.

"Put your seat belt on," Amelia requested and the boy slid behind her seat to fasten up.   "See you later?"   Amelia checked to see what Miguel's plan might be.

"I will stop by after I'm through here."   He smiled into Karen's concerned eyes.   "Don't worry."

"We'll be at Mom's."   Amelia acknowledged that there was no room for the small boy at her condo.   Miguel patted the roof of the Mercedes as it pulled away from the curb.

Miguel returned to the Hyundai wondering where to begin. From what the bus driver had told Amelia, Ardin seemed to be following an old woman who appeared to be one of the local homeless.   Miguel walked to the intersection and turned right heading for the Drop-In center.   Three men were standing outside smoking cigarettes. Miguel walked past and stepped inside.

"I'm looking for an old woman."   Miguel instinctually began to reach for his badge before he remembered he no longer had one as he started the conversation with the man behind the check-in desk.   "She's probably eighty."   The man briefly looked up from his work, collected his thoughts, and squinted at Miguel.

"What for?"   The homeless were a private crowd.   It would not be helpful to this man's status within the culture if people thought he dispensed information about them the way websites sell e-mail lists.

"A 15-year-old girl is missing and she was last seen getting off the Metro following an old lady," Miguel clarified his interest in the old woman.

"So you think she's with this old lady?"

"I don't know.   I thought I could ask some questions if I could find her."   Miguel looked past the clerk to the dozens of bodies lying on thin mattresses on the floor.

"Well, she's not in here."   The man stood up to block Miguel's view of his residents.   "Why aren't the police looking into this?"   The man seemed to be questioning Miguel's motives for finding the woman, or the girl, or both.

"I'm a friend of the family."   Miguel frowned.   "Used to be in District 2.   Just looking into it before we do call it in." The man behind the desk seemed to soften, then looked more concerned.

"Listen, you know how dangerous it can be down here. You really should get more people involved."   The streets were full of predators who listed their addresses as park benches and alleyways legally due to a loophole in the county's mandatory reporting regulations.

"I will, but just think, do you know of any old lady, gray hair, shawl, crooked cane, who might be living anywhere around here?"

"Let me ask around."   The clerk left and Miguel could see him asking a few key residents if they knew anything about the old lady.   Sooner than Miguel wished, the clerk returned with little information.

"One of the guys said he saw a really tall man arguing with a little old lady a few hours ago, but he didn't recognize either of them."

"Can I talk with the guy who saw this?"

"Sure, but he's drunk and has a lot of hallucinations, if you know what I mean."   The clerk shrugged his shoulders.

Miguel followed the clerk around the desk back to a mat where a scraggly looking drunk with stubbled beard and matted hair was resting.

"Art," the clerk poked at the smelly overnight guest, "this guy wants to ask a few questions about the old lady and the man.   Art opened his eyes and raised his head a few inches off the mat then let it fall back as he groaned.

"Oh man, I can't believe you turned me over to the cops," Art complained.

"I'm not a cop." Miguel cut in front of the clerk. "I'm wondering if you could tell me about the man and the old lady you saw earlier."

"What's it to you?" Art tried to ascertain the value of his answers. Miguel kept himself from telling Art and all the rest of the men in the room, that a fifteen year old girl was lost in their vicinity.

"I'm concerned about her," he lied.

"Well, she didn't look like she needed any help," Art offered.

"Was the man her friend?" Miguel asked.

"Don't think so. She kept smacking him with her stick." Miguel felt assured the woman was the same one Ardin had followed from the bus.

"Was he trying to hurt her?"

"Nope, he was trying to help her." Art barely articulated the words as he began to nod off. Miguel was confused as to why the man was trying to help an old woman who was hitting him with a stick. He used his foot to poke at Art's mat to wake him up.

"What?" Art protested any more talk.

"How was the man trying to help the old lady?" Miguel asked.

"He wasn't trying to help the old lady." Art seemed to contradict his previous answer. Miguel looked at the clerk who shrugged as if to say *I told you so*.

"Make up your mind man." Miguel poked at the mat again. "Who was the man trying to help?"

"A girl," Art replied sleepily. "He was helping some girl."

"What do you mean?" Miguel was on his knees next to Art searching for some serious eye contact. Art pushed up from the mat and propped himself on his elbows.

"It was really cool. The bus stopped like two times. First this old lady got off and ran like a track star across the street and went inside this building. Then this teenager hops off acting like she's lost something really valuable, looking in all directions and she crosses the street to the same corner. Then, when the kid isn't looking, the old broad comes out of the alley and waves her arms casting a big spell on the girl. You could see the sparks fly, that's how big a spell it was!"

Miguel began to fear Art was losing touch with reality.

"Then this massive guy dressed in coveralls pops in out of thin air just in time to catch the girl who passed out from the spell." Art looked at Miguel who was gritting his teeth. "Really, man. He just showed up without a puff of smoke or anything, and caught the girl when she started to fall."

"And then he flew her up in the air like a super hero?" Miguel filled in the next fantastic scene in the drunk's story.

"No, he picked her up and started to carry her, and that's when the old woman started to beat him."

"Why did she do that?" Miguel queried.

"Cause the old lady wanted the girl." Miguel shook his head in disbelief that his lead was dripping in cheap wine.

"Where did they go?" Miguel would take whatever he could get at this point.

"They disappeared." Art let his elbows slip out from under him and his head hit the mat again.

"Around the corner?" Miguel hoped for an answer with substance.

"Naw. Vaporized." Art let his mouth hang open after he answered. Miguel stood up preparing to walk back toward the entrance of the center.

"All three of them?" he asked.

"First the man with the girl," Art specified. "No sparks or nothing, just sorta' faded. Then the old lady. She had lots of smoke and sparks."

Miguel paused and watched as Art easily fell into a deep snoring sleep. "I need his name." Miguel pulled out his notebook and pen waiting for the clerk to provide the information.

"Art Washington." The clerk answered. "He's clean, harmless, I'm sure. He's always on the street seeing weird stuff. I know his wrap sheet by heart. His brain is just permanently wet."

Miguel didn't doubt it. A year ago he would have bet the drunk had something to do with the disappearance of Ardin, but there was something that rang true with the story. Miguel needed the name to help him surf for traces of threads at the scene, and hopefully find out how much of the story was fantasy and how much was real.

Returning to his small Hyundai, Miguel locked the door and closed his eyes. Imagining a bright point of light above the car, he pictured it coating the car like a shield. *Good,* he thought, *there shouldn't be any interruptions.* Miguel then tipped his head back as he had learned to do in his dreams. The top of his head felt fluid and moveable, reaching out, almost like a hand, pawing into the space around the four corners for a clue as to what happened to Ardin.

Art Washington, Miguel silently recalled the name. Slowly snippets emerged from a feeling to full visual images and Miguel could see the memories as Art saw them from the shadows of a nearby alley where Art was sitting on the curb, leaning against a trash can, in a stupor. An old woman and a really large man played out the scene exactly as Art had described it. As he watched, Miguel tried to test the images for accuracy. The story held true even if it was tinged with the scent of Wild Irish Rose. When the images stopped, the thread went cold as the man carrying Ardin disappeared without a trace. For a moment before she disappeared, the old woman stood in the street. Her physical stance shouted a mixture of frustration and fear to the seasoned investigator.

Miguel was frustrated with the blurriness of Art's vision. He refocused and zoomed in on the woman. Just the same way images on computer screens pixelate, so did the woman's face but there was something unmistakably familiar about it, Miguel was simultaneously so shocked and relieved that his focus slipped, the shield of light evaporated from the car and the last traces of the web slipped from Miguel's mind. Flipping open his cell phone, he pressed 2 and called Amelia.

Amelia grabbed the silently vibrating phone off the nightstand next to the bed in her mother's guest room and whispered as she answered it, pretty sure her mother was also unable to sleep and lurking somewhere close by.

"Anything?"

"I think so, but it doesn't make me feel any better." There was nothing reassuring about what Miguel had to tell Amelia.

"What did you find out?" Amelia hated not being able to do the detective work with Miguel.

"Tetta was there." Miguel squished the words from his throat.

"What?" Amelia hissed in astonishment. The guides rarely materialized in the three-dimensional world. "Where did you get this?"

"I picked it up from a drunk who saw what happened from across the street." Miguel recounted the vision for Amelia.

"You mean this guy walked away with Ardin and Tetta just stood there?" Amelia couldn't imagine Tetta letting anyone abduct the girl she had introduced as her special project when she asked Amelia to help her in the waking life.

"Like I said, she was hitting him with a cane, and then all three disappeared."

"I've never seen Tetta use smoke and sparks before," Amelia observed, "or walk with a cane."

"I think I should go find Tetta and see what's up. One thing's for sure," Miguel added. "It's not just a runaway, and I don't think we'll find her in the waking life." Amelia wondered how Ardin could be abducted from physical life into the ethers, and how Tetta could seem powerless to stop the man who took her.

"I wish I had something I could tell Mom." It was beyond Karen Bradford's ability to accept what she would sure deem hogwash as an explanation for Ardin's disappearance.

"We'll have something by the morning." Miguel's solace offered little hope for Amelia to keep things calm the rest of the night.

"Okay, call me." Amelia sounded tired.

"Get some sleep," Miguel advised and waited for Amelia to disconnect the call.

Miguel turned the key in the ignition of the Hyundai and pulled away from the curb. Something told him there was no sense looking in the physical area even though the space between planes was fuzzy.

The best thing to do now is sleep, he told himself. Looking at his watch he noted there was time for almost two sleep cycles before he needed to face the next morning. The first order of business would be to locate Tetta and find out why she hadn't bothered to find him when Ardin disappeared. Miguel thought about the complications of the new work he had taken on. *Clark Kent only needed a phone booth, I have to get to a bed.*

Pause, pause, pause...

A ball of light floated over the center of a granite table at which Tetta sat. She lightly drummed her fingertips on the table as she gazed into the ball waiting for something to happen. The space around her was dark and cool. Not her usual hangout, but since dark forces seemed to be active, she had chosen to stay out of the plain sight of the Interplanar University where she usually spent most of her time.

Ping! The face of an elderly man appeared as Tetta gazed into the ball.

"Hrim, what have you found?" Tetta's focus intensified as she leaned in toward the ball of light.

"One moment." Hrim disappeared from the ball leaving it swirling with fog. Tetta and Hrim had been partners in spirit since the dawning of the present time. She was relieved to hear from him as almost every message she had floated to him on the ethers had bounced back unanswered.

Hrim faded into view on the other side of the granite table. "I've been looking for you everywhere." Hrim smiled at Tetta as he slid the swirling ball to one side and reached across the table to touch her hand reassuringly. "It's hard to get through," he explained. "All of the threads seemed to be congested."

"Do you think that whoever is behind the melee in the world appearance is obstructing our ability to communicate as well?"

"It seems to be so. Perhaps we could talk to Ganesha about that." As he laid a stack of newspapers on the table and sat down across from Tetta, Hrim made reference to the Hindu god with the elephant head who was renowned for removing obstacles. Tetta examined large type headlines about new concerns over conditions in the waking life as the world approached the anniversary of the financial crisis taking hold.

"What do you think we should do?" Tetta had partnered with Hrim on some of the toughest cases, but this investigation had both of them completely bamboozled.

"What have you got from Max?" Hrim inquired.

"Zilch," Tetta summarized her visit with the famous sleeper. "I took him to the cave and he was sincerely clueless that his lifetime could have anything to do with this."

"Nothing?"

Tetta let her hands take a lost looking position in the air. "I was able to survey all that he remembered, Hrim and there was no kindling for this fire." Tetta motioned toward the newspapers. "Do you continue to believe that the economic situation is connected to Max's moksha?"

"Yes, or the thread from it would not start with him." Hrim moved his hands in a stepping motion from the swirling ball toward the newspapers. "And whatever took place would have to be something Max instigated or his moksha could not be affected." Hrim paused and looked at Tetta Thoughtfully. "It is possible someone else could be involved."

Hrim knew Max could stir up trouble, but this was larger than anything Max had ever done before and just about everything Max had ever done was also something he consciously believed was amusing or helpful to the advancement of someone's spiritual journey.

To perceive the crumpling economy as potentially beneficial to humanity might be possible if it caused humans to examine their greedy desires, but the major effect had been the propagation of immense levels of distrust. It just didn't make sense that Max would aspire, consciously or unconsciously, to do such damage. Hrim kept open all possibilities, hoping to strike some vein of gold.

"What would you say is prevailing right now, Tetta?" Hrim asked. "Is it greed or avarice?"

"It's worry, Hrim. It is fear," Tetta stated with conviction. "Greed has played a role until now, but the fear of one another's greed has grown strongest."

"When I'm down there," Hrim referred to the swirling ball that was showing scenes of commentators dishing charges about the recession, "I see certain paper instruments for greed, such as stocks and bonds, being destroyed. People are fearfully hoarding resources. They are investing in commodities such as gold, precious gems and oil. Does that say anything to you?" Hrim was obviously holding back his opinion to see if Tetta might come to the same conclusion.

"Well, those are things of the Underworld." Tetta's eyes grew larger as she flattened her hand on the table and leaned in closer. "Hrim! Are you suggesting Hades...or Pluto?" Tetta named the Greek and Roman gods respectively.

"They possess control of that over which humans worry in the absence of something better." Hrim studied Tetta's expression of wondering confusion to see if his words might raise some thoughts. "Tetta, perhaps it's not someone or something other than Max that is *causing* this. Perhaps, something is missing rather than present. Something which when it's missing allows fear to reign."

Tetta eyed Hrim to see if he had any ideas, but she could tell he was just retracing the tracks of their conversation.

"So, how do we find a missing piece of unknown stuff?" Tetta looked up and relaxed a little when she saw Hrim's smiling eyes.

"First of all, dear friend, we remember what's most important." Hrim let his awareness drop into the area of his chest where his etheric heart was beating and waited for Tetta to entrain to its frequency. "We remember that this, all this swirling, twisted stuff, is just an illusion. If we forget that, we're finished."

Hrim handed Tetta one of the pieces of paper that had manifested in his hands during their conversation. "I'll be distributing this throughout the Wait Zone." Tetta looked down and read the bulletin Hrim had prepared with his thoughts as they spoke.

WANTED. IN GOOD CONDITION.
AN UNSPECIFIED MISSING SOMETHING THAT
SERVES TO BALANCE FEAR AND AID HUMANITY.
NO QUESTIONS ASKED. GENEROUS REWARD.
CONTACT HRIM.

"Do you think someone has taken this thing on purpose?" Tetta continued to study the words on the hand-out.

"It seems to be rather well orchestrated." Hrim nodded.

"Could it have been Max?" Again, Tetta couldn't comprehend Max doing much more than being distracted or rude.

"Doubtful," Hrim reassured. "If Max had taken it in Ephesus, we would have seen the results centuries ago. Burch has indicated, the preparations may have been stockpiled for decades, but not centuries, and the actual occurrence was sudden. It looks like a combination of things, but from our side I'm afraid we're seeing evidence that all this was just the beginning before the floodgates completely give way."

Tetta watched as Hrim slipped the flyer into the swirling ball and sent it posting on windows, utility poles, and the scrolling screens displayed below Moksha Meters, all over the Wait Zone. "Hopefully this will produce some hints about what's going on."

53

three

Clang! Clang! Clang!

Miguel looked through the window of the trolley car as it bustled past the brightly colored ginger bread houses lining hilly streets.

This is weird, Miguel thought, *Why would I be on a trolley?*

"To get through San Francisco?" A familiar voice from the seat behind him caused Miguel to stand up and turn around raising his knee to the seat to balance himself. Behind him was his old partner in police work, Nick Green.

"Nick!?" Miguel hadn't seen his friend since he had disappeared into the fog of the Wait Zone when Amelia was still in her coma. Miguel remembered everything that happened that early morning in his dreams. When he awakened and found no trace of Nick even after months of searching, he finally accepted the dream as true. Now, seeing Nick behind him, he had to ask.

"Nick, you're dead, right?" Nick smiled at the earnestness with which Miguel asked the question.

"Yep, deader than a doornail." Nick seemed to consider his answer. "Did you know doornails have life?"

Miguel shook his head. "No."

"It's weird like that sometimes." Nick's eyes dazed a little.

"How did you die?" Miguel wanted to know if his dream was accurate.

"Now Miguel, we don't need to go over that again."

"Nick, I haven't seen you in a year," Miguel insisted.

"A year? It doesn't really seem that long, but we need to talk about the case." At the thought of Ardin, Miguel let go of his need to catch up with Nick.

"You're investigating this?" Miguel asked

"Everyone and anyone," Nick nodded. "They've pulled in experts from every jurisdiction."

"I don't get that." Miguel slowed down to wonder why reinforcements in the Wait Zone would be called in to help Ardin.

"She's not just a runaway Miguel, she's totally gone." Nick snapped his fingers.

"So it's like the FBI up here too?" Miguel was concerned he was going to have to hand over decision-making power on his kidnapping case.

"Not really," Nick calmed, "no one is in charge. It's a mess. No one has any idea where to start."

Miguel considered Nick's reply. "So are you helping me or am I helping you?"

"Seems like you might be helping us. What do you know?"

Miguel studied Nick for a moment. The last time he saw his partner, Miguel thought Nick was going to shoot him, but stranger circumstances had taken Nick's life instead. It had seemed like a tragic end to their friendship. Miguel had been crushed to learn that Nick had been involved in illegal activities.

Miguel attempted to check the ethers to see what other threads Nick might be traveling, but kept coming up against Nick's ability to sense Miguel's intrusion into his connections and stopped short. Miguel decided to play it safe until he talked to someone else.

"Something wrong?" Nick noticed the drop in Miguel's enthusiasm for finding his old friend on the trolley.

"No. Why San Francisco?" Miguel asked as the trolley came to a halt.

"No special reason, why?" Nick replied.

"This is my stop." Miguel turned and started for the exit.

"I'll catch you later," Nick called after Miguel as he hopped off the step.

Pause, pause, pause...

Ted Galahad's head was pounding. It seemed to him that heaven should be a hang-over free zone, but that wasn't the case. His head was throbbing and he wondered if he was as addicted to the aftermath of drinking as he was to the drinking itself. It never seemed as if the twelve apostles were hung over whenever they re-enacted the last supper and the sleep-over in the garden.

Resting his forehead on crossed arms propped on his knees Galahad sat on the curb of a gold paved street ruminating over his argument with Maximian the Greek.

Max was more arrogant than usual as he inferred that Galahad might have something to do with the decline of their shared Moksha Meter. Galahad didn't see how Max thought he was so much better than him.

After all, Galahad thought, *everyone knows he's the one who started all night parties in that cave hide-out. Some saints! They were really just a bunch of winos.*

Galahad sneered as he mimicked Max's accusations in a whiney tone. "You blew it to hell last year, maybe you've gone and done it again!" Even though Galahad's lack of judgment had precipitated a nasty drop in their moksha, he had worked diligently over the last year to atone for the mishap.

Despite some personal improvement, Galahad nevertheless resorted to some old patterns of criticizing his critics. Raising his head up with his eyes still closed he groaned. "It was easy for that Emperor to imprison you so-called legendary seven sleepers. All you had to do was sleep through the whole thing!"

"What's the matter, Dumbo?" The cigarette-smoking, beatnik-wannabe, off-Broadway-producer-lush winced at the use of the name given to him just prior to his moksha fiasco. For almost a year, he had been teased and called Dumbo by anyone who heard how he had inadvertently and prematurely ended the lives of four people. He tried to argue it had been collateral damage, but the sacrificial lamb concept had been put to rest two thousand years earlier and was an illusion that didn't hold much water even in the world appearance.

Letting his head drop back to rest on his knees, he slowly pronounced his stage name. "Gal-a-had." A moment of silence passed as his awareness improved. Galahad's head snapped up sending sharp pains through the meaty part of his head which he completely ignored upon seeing the beaming face of the boy he had come to love. Their association had been abruptly ended by the Heavenly Court, but Galahad failed to remember the limits set on him as he felt his heart swell in a way it seldom did.

"Jojo!" Galahad practically cheered. The boy raised his hand and Galahad extended his own hand in a victorious high five symbolic of old friends reconnecting. He jumped to his feet and gathered the boy in his arms, stumbling as he had not prepared for how much he had grown in such a short amount of time.

"Gala---Gal-a---Gal" Jojo tried and Galahad winced at the way the name was getting twisted. Galahad forgot about all his troubles in the presence of the boy.

"How is your snail, Jojo?" Galahad glossed over trying to help Jojo master the pronunciation and changed the subject by inquiring of the boy's beloved pet which he had occupied.

"He had babies!" Jojo announced as if he was a proud parent himself. "He's back in my teacher's classroom. He had 29 babies. Does that make him a girl?" Jojo inquired and joined Galahad as he sat down on the curb.

"That makes Dumbo an hermaphrodite." Galahad began an explanation he was certain he wouldn't have the patience to finish, so he tried to change the subject.

"Why do you always use words I can't say?" Jojo wrinkled his nose at his friend.

"Learning words you can't pronounce is a part of growing up." Galahad thought about the challenge of teaching Jojo about the sexual identity of snails and decided to change the subject again. "What else has been going on for you lately?"

Jojo began to recount his living arrangements with Miguel, informing Galahad that Amelia and Miguel were dating. "And I have a new step-sister. But she ran away." Jojo shook his head and looked down at the gold pavement. He didn't know how to describe Ardin. She was like a sister to him. Her sudden appearance in his life was consistent with the many times he had been placed in foster-care. He felt a sibling-like connection with her even though his teacher, Amelia and Miguel had all tried to explain there was no *real* connection. For Jojo, it was more real than most of the relationships in his life had been. In a rare moment of sensitivity Galahad recognized the boy's sadness and asked about the step-sister.

"Why would she run away?" Jojo shrugged his shoulders and Galahad almost lost interest. Then thinking of his need to complete more community service, he thought some compassion might be a good idea. "Perhaps you could find her from this side Jojo."

"How can I do that?" Jojo's question reminded Galahad that he should check in with the ethers before he gave any instruction that could be outside Jojo's goal levels. As was his habit, Galahad chose to ignore the protocol.

"Tilt your head back." Not anticipating the physical flexibility of the boy, Galahad laughed out loud when Jojo let his head drop backward as if he had just given up the ghost. "No, that's too much." Galahad cleared his throat. "Just a little. Like this." Galahad positioned the boy's head backward just enough to put gentle pressure on the occipital ridge. "Now, reach out through the top of your head with awareness of this girl…"

"Ardin." Jojo specified the name.

"Right, right." Galahad tried to help Jojo focus, "Just see if you can find a connection to Ardin's thoughts."

Jojo remained very quiet as he had learned to do when receiving instructions from the guides at school. "I see her!" Jojo shouted.

"Do you know where she is?" Galahad inquired.

"No." Jojo frowned.

"Is everything okay?" Galahad was reminded that sending

a child out on the web included the risk of losing track of the consciousness.

"There's a man watching her," Jojo reported.

"Is she okay?" Galahad asked, ready to pull the boy back at any moment.

"Yes." Jojo's voice sounded distant. "If I go that way," Jojo gently tilted his head slightly to his right, "a big man is watching her sleep." Galahad listened carefully so he could help the boy remember any information that might be helpful in finding the girl. "And if I go that way," Jojo turned the top of his head toward his left, "she is eating ice cream in a restaurant and two creepy looking men are looking at her on a TV."

Galahad was confused as to why Jojo was seeing the girl in two different places. He started to slide onto the thread Jojo was following when Jojo suddenly gasped and launched forward off the curb toward the street. Galahad caught him and settled him back into place.

"Are you alright?" Galahad cupped Jojo's face in his hands and searched his eyes.

"Yeah." Jojo gasped. His eyes widened from bleary to excited. "I saw her!"

"So you said." Galahad's hand trembled with the fear that he almost hurt the boy. "No more of that for today." Galahad put his hand on the crown of Jojo's head, and realizing he probably would be reprimanded for helping the boy execute advanced techniques without consulting his educational liaison first, gave him a playful shake as if to rattle the experience out of his mind.

"I have to tell Miss Amelia and Miguel!" Jojo clung on to the news of his discovery. Galahad decided to let Jojo disclose what he could remember only after he wiped down the child's memory of seeing him and helping him access the web.

"Sure thing, my friend." Galahad stepped back and ran his hand through the air between himself and the boy. Slowly, Jojo lost track of Galahad's presence and their entire conversation. Jojo became fidgety in the way that often got him in trouble in school, as he wondered how he could find Amelia and Miguel. Now that the way was clear for Jojo to slide on the web his thoughts swished him from the curb. Galahad followed the thread through Jojo to Amelia, Miguel and Karen Bradford, noticing some resistance on every line when he attempted to access information about the girl.

Apparently it's none of my business. Galahad crossed the street and watched as the Moksha Meter he was linked with registered an improvement of .01 percent. *How did that happen?* It wasn't much, but Galahad wondered if he had anything to do with the ever so slight upshot, and whether he should tell Max about it. Not wishing to admit he had seen Jojo, and not at all interested in seeing Max again, he decided to keep quiet.

Pause, pause, pause...

Amelia found herself sitting in an unscheduled webinar session and wondered why she wasn't hooking up with Miguel to find Tetta. While her coursework at the Interplanar University was usually about reincarnation and dream recall, Amelia found that unscheduled classes were more about subject matter pertinent to her waking life than her studies. She surmised the reason she was in the webinar rather than finding Tetta with Miguel was because she might learn something that could help if she could just remember. Amelia imagined a pen and paper and prepared to make notes about anything relevant that she saw.

Court jesters were often also called fools. Amelia wondered if court jesters could relate to the silly pranks Ardin loved to play on her teachers and social workers. *As such, court jesters were given license to serve a very important function for the ruling classes. They put policies and principles into dumbed-down, everyday language that the average, uneducated subjects of the lower classes could understand and forget about. Jesters were not themselves stupid, but very clever as they took the incredibly complex lies and deceptions of politicians and made of them a laughable matter so that the people would not amass frustration and attempt to change things. Some jesters were not so bright, such as Archibald Armstrong who was fired from the court of King James VI for his impudence.*

Amelia quietly manifested a large popcorn container and began snacking as she watched engraved pictures of other famous court jesters throughout time give way to full-color head shots of contemporary comedians.

John Stewart, David Letterman, and Jay Leno are excellent examples of court jesters in present day times.

The Hindu have their own court jesters called vidushaka which serve the same purpose as the medieval court jester.

An image of eight men, some with animal heads, all gathered under a tree, eased onto the screen.

Rishis are ancient Hindu sages who received the word of the gods in India. This illustration shows one of their gods, under the Banyan tree, teaching the rishis.

The sage Narada is an example of a rare form of vidushaka turned rishi. After having been kicked out of the king's court for his obsession with the celestial nymphs, Narada was mentored by a group of rishis who came to stay at the ashram where he was reborn as the son of a servant girl, in India. After she died, Narada set off to follow the advice of the rishis and become a sage in his own right.

63

Narada's "own right" combined his roots as a once fallen celestial turned impoverished young man from the lower class with the rishi wisdom he attained. In this way, he was able to put his teachings into a form understandable by any human at any level of education and class, much the same as a court jester. He also enjoyed stirring up a bit of dramatic comedy by telling the secrets of one god or demon to another.

Amelia didn't hear a thing she thought might be helpful in the search for Ardin, but she had learned not to make assumptions and continued to watch as the scene shifted.

Seven young men wearing tunics and carrying bags were climbing a mountain overlooking an ancient Mediterranean city. As they started setting up camp in a cave, Amelia understood that the men were seeking asylum from some form of persecution. One man built a fire as another began unpacking some food they had brought along.

Amelia began to realize she was no longer watching the webinar. She was projecting a thread she was following through the ethers onto the screen of her own mind. She had no idea how the images she was seeing related to the topic of court jesters, and the sage Narada. The thread was so thready it seemed bizarre and disconnected.

Amelia traced the thread from the men in a cave to the men that sat under the tree in one of the last images the movie had shown. It seemed these men had existed in various forms since the world had been born into existence. She knew that the men under the tree were reincarnated as the men in the cave. Amelia was pretty impressed with the way she was interpreting the odd images.

Amelia's vision swooped back to the city below the cave, where she witnessed interrogations of the families of the seven cave dwellers until someone revealed the hiding place of their brothers and sons. A wealthy looking man, who seemed like a little Napoleon in a gown, ordered the cave to be sealed and sent his troops into the mountains to accomplish the task. Amelia wondered why the seven men didn't try to escape, and she saw that they had fallen into a deep sleep due to drinking too much.

Amelia's head snapped back and she was fast-forwarded to the future in the very same city only now there were crosses above the gates in the wall around the town. It seemed the religious persecution had ended and she was now in a time when Christianity was the dominant faith. She watched a new ruler as he prayed for the forgiveness of his predecessors' cruel habits. As part of his self-imposed penance, the ruler ordered that a stable be constructed in the mountains to help the shepherds. In a flash, Amelia was back in the cave in time to see a ray of light filled with dust, penetrate the darkness. The masons building the stable had partially uncovered the cave during their work, and the seven sleeping men awakened.

The rousing sleepers were perfectly preserved and they did not seem to be aware that more than a day, even more than centuries of time had elapsed. In fact, they just started going about what seemed to be their ordinary business. As if someone turned up the volume, Amelia was able to hear the details of their conversation.

"Get thee to the city, Malchus!" Amelia watched as one of the men gave orders to another. "And get more food than yesterday. I'm starving." The one called Malchus seemed to take offense.

"It's not as if I don't bring back more than enough, Maximian. You are just a glutton." Maximian looked at Malchus with amusement in his eye.

"My friend, that doesn't sound like service for the sake of service," Maximian teased. Malchus looked away and tried to control his anger.

Amelia's studies of reincarnation had included lessons on the four yogas of which one, Karma Yoga, was described as service for the sake of service. She wondered how these early Christians might have picked up such a term. It seemed at least the one named Maximian might have knowledge of his reincarnational status.

Amelia felt a jolt similar to a roller coaster coming to an abrupt stop and zoned in on the screen in the auditorium. The screen showed the image of a man smoking a cigarette with a stubbly beard on his chin. Amelia thought she recognized him as she caught the last few words she assumed were about the character as he faded from view.

In a world filled with jesters and rishis the fact remains, some people are just plain idiots. This concludes this installment of our review of humor and the ridiculous as a tool for both dispelling ignorance and reducing knowledge throughout the ages. Please come back next week when we will explore how saviors hinder the progress and empowerment of sinners. The screen went black.

Amelia had never considered that court jesters represented and actually promoted the common man's understanding of government affairs, or that current talk show hosts played the same role. She found herself looking forward to how the next webinar would put a negative spin on saviors. Her lawyer instincts suggested that the acceptance of a savior supplanted one's responsibility for the expression of their own divinity.

Amelia was curious about the apparent surfing she had accomplished with all the HD qualities of her flat screen television at home, and how it all passed as quickly as a dream even though it chronicled the events of more than a few centuries. She wobbled to her feet and stumbled on her gold lamé shoes as she headed for the door with the rest of the crowd leaving her empty notepad on the soft velvet seat.

Amelia exited the lobby of the auditorium into the bright cloudless daylight. She never knew where she would end up when leaving the auditorium. Sometimes she remained on the University campus, other times she ended up wherever her consciousness, often unbeknownst to her, was drawn. As she squinted in the sunlight, the familiar but blurry form of Miguel standing in front of Amelia on the corner took shape.

"Miguel." She waved as Miguel looked up. He trotted to meet Amelia as she stumbled on the gold lamé shoes.

"Why do you still wear those things?"

"I'm trying to remember." Amelia replied. Miguel's brow furrowed with concern that the shoes could also bring back memories she had not been ready to entertain so far.

"Remember what?" he gently asked.

"That I tend to forget just about everything when I wake up." Miguel laughed and put his arm around Amelia's shoulder.

"So, you're using the shoes to remind yourself to remember?" He tapped the top of her head.

Miguel thought about how close Amelia came to seeing Nick on the trolley and how much she had yet to remember of her experiences with him.

"What are you doing here?" she asked as they began to walk together on the sidewalk. "I thought you were going to see Tetta."

"I am," Miguel answered.

"Well good, now we can do that together."

"I don't think so." Miguel's remark instantly put a frown on Amelia's face. The pair had been arguing in the Wait Zone as much as they did in waking life about who was in charge of the cases they worked on together.

"She's not answering," Miguel explained as Amelia drew herself up to make her opening statement. Amelia's head tilted inquisitively. Tetta was always available and usually beat her and Miguel to the punch.

"But she knows Ardin is missing. She should be contacting us."

"It would seem that way," Miguel agreed. "But there seems to be some sort of block around her and Hrim. I can't get through to anyone." Miguel quietly wondered how he had been able to hook-up with Nick.

While Amelia seemed to focus her studies on the contracts associated with reincarnation, Miguel's work through the University tended to deal with problems associated with the duality of good and evil, and right and wrong, which he had come to understand were not the same thing.

Miguel now had a loose understanding that evil played an important role in the world appearance, if for no other reason than to motivate those humans who had no positive motivation, to hope for something better. The pair was doing the same work in the Wait Zone as they did in waking life though the goals and objectives were slightly different and the clients came in many forms, from different universes and times.

"So where did you start out?" Miguel inquired about Amelia's activity since their earlier phone conversation.

"Just my usual." Amelia shook her head. "For some reason all I'm doing is studying webinars about reincarnation.

"Maybe you're learning something that can help." Miguel looked up wondering why it seemed there were more breaks than connections in the web surrounding Ardin. "Let's head over to the coffee shop. We can compare notes there, and maybe Hrim or Tetta will show up." Not since Amelia's own experience with her coma had the two paired up on a case where the players were still involved in the waking life, and none of the few cases they handled in the past year had involved someone they knew until Ardin.

Miguel sent another request for Hrim into the ethers as he and Amelia arrived at the coffee shop. With family on the line, he wanted something more than his brief education backing him up.

The coffee shop was busy with customers in white togas as well as every night dreamers who were ordering frappachinos, decaf caramel machiatos, and cappachinos in a rush that indicated they were just stopping by between classes at the Interplanar University. Miguel and Amelia took their favorite booth in the back.

They had visited the shop together for the first time right after they simultaneously made their connection to one another in the waking life. That day, Amelia had slipped away from Miguel's protective watch and almost got them both killed. A lot had changed since then. Then again, a lot remained the same.

The waitress stepped up to the table and Amelia ordered a pot of coffee. Miguel continued to hold back the information on Nick, even though withholding information had proven to be a mistake in the past.

While Miguel had quit his job on the force to work with the guides to solve issues that crossed between dimensions, he was given enough waking life cases to keep his bills paid and take care of Jojo. He had shared the details of a number of his inter-dimensional cases with Amelia and found she often had advice and information that could help. Sometimes, without knowing it she was getting clues on threads he was following.

"So, tell me more about your lessons." Miguel wanted to see if anything Amelia had been learning could be added to Art's account of what happened to Ardin.

"Don't you think we should be talking about what's going on with Ardin?" Amelia seemed to criticize Miguel.

"Why don't you just stick to lawyering and let me handle the investigation." He smiled to try and take the edge off his statement.

"Do you really think it's fruitless to launch a manhunt?" She continued on his path.

"All I have is a drunk who says she evaporated into thin air slung over the shoulder of a really tall man." Miguel shrugged. "You think the police will buy that?"

"No." Amelia leaned across the table. "And you do?"

"I didn't just accept his word," Miguel defended, then caught himself before he validated a discussion of his detective work. "I scanned and saw the whole thing."

Amelia semi-sneered as she cocked her head trying to figure out how Miguel had learned to scan in the waking life and she was only able to have accidental experiences when she was supposed to be doing something else.

"Amelia?" Miguel noticed the blank stare which often indicated she had an idea.

"Huh? Oh! Have you tried scanning for them?" Amelia asked. Miguel blushed as he often forgot the most obvious resources himself. Tilting his head back a little, Miguel engaged a correlation between two nodes in his nervous system which usually allowed him to pick up Hrim's thread.

"What do you see?" Amelia asked impatiently.

"Nothing. I'd say the systems are down but who do you call up here?" Miguel shrugged.

"Is there some sort of utility or cable company we could check with to find out when the service might come back on?" Amelia's voice trailed off as she understood the look on Miguel's face. The Wait Zone was full of illusions of things people had known in the world appearance. Students at the university were strongly urged to not produce any more illusion than was absolutely necessary to function. Setting up corporate

entities would be strongly discouraged.   Amelia tried to erase
the thought from her head.

"It's getting kind of late."   Miguel stood and pulled his
wallet out of his back pocket.

"You mean early don't you?" Amelia joked as late in the
Wait Zone meant that it was early morning and time to re-
enter the waking life.

"Yeah, it was nice having some time with you here."
Miguel smiled at the way Amelia always seemed more relaxed
in the Wait Zone.

"Even though I won't remember it?" Amelia pointed out
her lack of ability to recall their Wait Zone excursions in the
waking life.

"Even though." Miguel nodded. "I remember."

Amelia felt a twinge in her heart as Miguel's bright white
teeth flashed beneath his neatly trimmed moustache.

"Listen, I'm going to see what I can do about the lousy
coverage we're getting on the towers."   Miguel smiled and laid
a twenty on the table. "I'm going to leave this for the bill and
I'll catch-up with you later in the morning, okay?"

Amelia nodded, amused that Miguel always manifested a
bill when they came to the coffee shop so he could pay it and
feel chivalrous.   Miguel gently placed his hand around the
back of her neck and kissed her forehead.

"Thanks," Amelia sighed.   "Even if I can't remember it,
I'm sure that will help when I wake up to my mother's
hysteria.   What should I tell her?"

"You won't remember, remember?"   Miguel teased. "I'll
have something before you wake up," Miguel tried to reassure
her.   "I gotta' go."   This time he turned and didn't stop until
after he was through the door and out of Amelia's range of
vision. Miguel didn't have a clue what he should do next.
Nick's attitude was suspicious and the guides were nowhere to

be found. Amelia appreciated the process while she was in the dream state, but once awake, she could be as unpredictable and impulsive as ever. Miguel was still learning himself, and right now he needed help. *Dammit Tetta,* he thought, *Hrim, where are you?*

Pause, pause, pause...

Amelia took her gaze off the door and looked out the window just in time to see Jojo run up and press his hands on the glass.

"Miss Amelia! I saw her!" The boy shouted through the window. Amelia strained to hear what Jojo was saying.

"What?"

"Ardin! I saw Ardin!" Jojo shouted and pounded on the glass. Amelia couldn't make out his words over the sound of his hands slapping.

"Jojo!" Amelia shouted back. "Stop pounding and get in here!" Jojo backed up and started running around the corner to get to the door. Amelia turned her head expecting to see the boy come into the coffee shop, and instead saw the shadow of her mother's head blocking the overhead light on the bedroom ceiling.

"Amelia, you're dreaming!" Karen Bradford gently shook her daughter's shoulders. Amelia twisted to reach her iphone and check the time.

"Yes mother, I am dreaming! It's four in the morning!" Amelia pulled the sheet over her head.

"I don't know how you can sleep if I can't sleep," Karen reasoned as she sat on the edge of the bed. Amelia studied her mother and became fully aware she wasn't about to get any sleep.

Karen tilted her head and masked her need for company as an attempt to seem helpful. "Maybe you can get back to sleep if you come to the kitchen and have a cup of tea with me." Amelia sighed.   She could hear both the invitation and ultimatum in her mother's suggestion.

"Okay Mom."   There was no sense in resisting.   "Give me a second to check on Jojo and make sure he's not awake too." Amelia dramatically threw back the covers exposing her sentiment that her mother was creating problems she could fix to distract her from the one that remained unsolved.

Karen frowned at the tone of sarcasm in her daughter's words and started to leave the room.   "Fine." Karen applied the disapproving do-what-you-want intonation to her words. "I'll be waiting in the kitchen."

Amelia drew back the troops of her thoughts knowing it was too early to drop into full defense mode, and tried to reassure her mother.   "I'll be down in just a minute, Mom."

As she reached for the summer robe her mother had brought to her room, Amelia remembered the instructions from the webinar.   *Shit!*   She slapped herself on the head.   *How am I supposed to stay still and remember my dreams when my mother is delivering the wake-up call?*

Pause, pause, pause...

Jojo burst into the coffee shop pounding his feet on the shiny floor as he rushed to the back of the coffee shop where he had seen Amelia seated.   The waitress turned from the empty table she had just bussed and gave Jojo the once-over.

"What's a nice guy like you doing in a place like this?" she asked.

"Where did Miss Amelia go?" Jojo asked breathlessly.

"You just missed her," the waitress replied.

73

"Have you seen Miguel?" Jojo asked, turning on his heel to see if he recognized anyone in the shop.

"You just missed him, too." The waitress sat the bus tray down on the table. "You sound like you're a little out of breath. Would you like a soda?" Jojo nodded enthusiastically and helped himself onto a stool at the counter as the waitress dumped the bus tray on a shelf underneath and grabbed a glass and a bottle of Grape Nehi.

"Oh wow thanks!" Jojo loved the drink that was hard to find on the store shelves in Cincinnati.

"You're welcome, little man," the waitress smiled. "So, do you just come here in your dreams?"

"Mostly, but I go to school here, too!" Jojo explained.

"Is that how you know Miss Amelia and Miguel?" The waitress remembered the names Jojo had asked about.

"I live with Miguel and he goes out with Miss Amelia," Jojo clarified. "I go to school with Ardin."

"Well," the waitress observed, "aren't you are just a bundle of billowing information!" Jojo took a drink form the straw in his bottle of Nehi and studied the waitress.

"Do I know you?" There was a tone of distrust in the boy's voice that concerned the waitress.

"I don't think so." The waitress laughed. "But you might. You seem to know everyone. I got the impression Miss Amelia and Miguel were looking for someone."

"Yeah." Jojo looked out the window longingly for a moment. "They went looking for Ardin."

"Where did she go?" The waitress studied Jojo intently.

"Someplace." Jojo seemed more interested in his soda than the conversation. He took another sip and let it slip down the back of his throat as he tilted his head and hummed in appreciation of the flavor. The waitress tapped her fingers on the countertop as she waited for an answer to her question.

Jojo shrugged and puffed out his lower lip as he looked up at the waitress. "I don't know where she is."

"Okay then, mister." The waitress grabbed a couple menus and a serving tray as a pair of new arrivals entered the coffee shop. "You enjoy your Nehi and I'm sure your friend will turn up."

Jojo watched as the waitress squeezed around the side of the counter with the menus as if she was going to seat the customers. He turned his head to follow her across the room but, like Amelia, she had completely vanished.

four

Who's Been Sleeping in My Dreams?

Amelia twisted and turned in the vinyl covered chair at the kitchen table jockeying for a comfortable way to sit, while her mother poured hot water over herbal tea bags in plain white mugs. Though her father's career as the CEO of a prestigious accounting firm had afforded his wife anything she wanted, she prided herself on inventing new ways to reuse junk and seldom wanted anything other than to help those less fortunate. Hence, she had continued to teach long after she no longer needed the income, and maintained the same cheap kitchen table and chairs she had purchased when she and Mike had first married.

"For heaven's sake, Mother," Amelia stopped trying to get comfortable, "do you think we could go shopping for some new furniture sometime?"

"I don't need anything new," Karen retorted.

"Well, I could give you my set and I could get something new," Amelia whined.

"You don't need anything new either," Karen replied. "You already have all the latest gadgets and these," Karen motioned to the set of four gray chairs and the table with the steel edged Formica top, "these are antiques!" Amelia chose to give up the discussion sooner than usual as she knew it was unwinnable.

"Have you heard from Miguel?" Karen started in on the case of the missing Ardin.

"No, Mom, I was sleeping." Amelia smiled to protect herself from sounding like she was smarting off to her mother.

"Maybe we should call the police?" Karen began to wonder.

"Mom, we agreed to let Miguel take a look first since it would not go well if Ardin was charged again with runaway, remember?"

"Yes, yes. Alright. But what can we do?" Karen's eyes darted around the table as if some helpful action might suddenly appear.

"Pray, Mom, and stay by the phone. She'll call, she always does." Amelia took a sip of herbal tea and looked at the paint her mother had poured into the plastic lids of saved butter containers under which newspaper had been carefully placed to protect the old Formica. Odd shaped little sponges rested nearby as her mother cut the opened flaps from a box of Ritz crackers.

Amelia didn't know, or really care, what her mom was making; the house was filled with sponge painted items. It was her mom's way of practicing the resourcefulness she extolled as a virtue everyone should possess.

As Karen hummed, Amelia's head tipped forward then suddenly shot backward where it stayed leaning toward the right or left until it dropped forward and repeated the cycle. *I'm going to need the chiropractor,* Amelia thought in between her waking and sleeping moments.

Pause, pause, pause...

"Well?" Nick Green anxiously asked as he was joined by the waitress from the coffee shop at the bar around the corner.

"Nothing," she seemed to think she was reassuring him.

"Nothing for who?" He sought clarification.

"For any of them. Nada. They don't get it." The waitress shape shifted out of her apron and dress to dawn a pair of stretch jeans and a tank top. Nick failed to take notice of her more than healthy figure. It was as if she didn't exist.

"Well I'll be damned." Nick slapped the table and picked up the mug of Irish draft still foaming at the head.

"We already knew that!" the waitress laughed then choked back into a barely perceivable smile and tried to look innocent as Nick glared at her.

"That's going to change for me, pussycat." Nick clenched his teeth and the waitress watched the small muscles along his jaw line flex and knot into place.

"For me, too." She checked in with him a slightly perceivable level of uncertainty underlining the statement.

"Sure it is, Trisha. We just have to make sure things happen in order, you know? Not like last time." Trisha nodded even as her eyes indicated to Nick she might not be wholly on board with his plan. He had reason to distrust her, but he was irreversibly linked to her due to the last ploy they had played together.

"If I can solve this case, I'll pick up points and we can move up a couple levels." Nick tried to encourage her to stay with him. "We just have to figure it out before anyone else."

"What's to figure out? That's the part I don't get. Is it money?" Nick looked at Trisha as if she was spilled coffee on freshly laid new carpet.

"What the hell woman!" The volume shot up on Nick's voice and the din of conversation in the bar went quiet. None of the locals in the dark side of the Wait Zone liked to be reminded of their circumstances. Nick lowered his voice and hissed across the table, "Is money all you ever think about?"

"No." Trisha looked around uneasily at the mix of demons, sinners, and thieves in the room. "I just don't get what the big deal is. She's just a girl."

"Not in this case," Nick grunted. "She's a hot commodity and we have insider information." Nick's eyes locked on Trisha's. She felt restrained as if he had placed handcuffs on her mind. "Don't think about it, Trisha. Don't let your mind wander on you-know-who. Things are stacked in our favor now because of the blockade. If you think about it, it might leak out of that pretty sieve you got for a brain, and any one of the kooks in here, not to mention those on the other team, could pick up on it. So don't think about it. Ya' got me?"

Trisha nodded in a way that made it quite clear to Nick, she was not thinking about it in much the same way one doesn't think of a red fire truck when told not to think of it.

"Do you think Miguel will team with you?" Trisha wondered.

"Hard to say, depends on if he gets through to Hrim." Nick looked down into the mug of waning beer. "We also have to make sure Galahad doesn't decide to suddenly show up." Nick acknowledged that their activities in the Wait Zone were supposed to be under strict observation. Fortunately for him, their guide Galahad had turned out to be a lazy drunk.

When they arrived in the Wait Zone, Trisha and Nick were assigned an intense rehabilitation plan to help them comprehend their karmic debt and establish the details of their next incarnations so they could improve their moksha honestly.

Galahad's failure to follow up with the pair had allowed them to fall in with the worst aspects of the Wait Zone, unnoticed. Without a guide to help them balance and appreciate the positive and negative forces of the Wait Zone, the pair had devised their own explanations and acted on their own rationale as to how to get back to waking life. To Nick, it was all about playing the hero. To Trisha, it was about being the winner. The differences between the two, though subtle, could easily set the pair working against each other.

Nick thought about the liability Trisha had proven to be in the waking life and grimaced at the thought that he might not have any choice other than to continue collaborating with her. If he was going to alter his situation, he had to convince her to go along with him.

Knowing Trisha didn't care about the long term effects of their situation didn't raise his hopes that someday he might attain a situation that was a little more in line with his past life hope of being a hero cop in Heaven. If he could be instrumental in solving the case that had first come to his attention on the dark side, he thought he had a chance.

Pause, pause, pause...

When you begin to understand that you can transcend time, you may find yourself arriving at a destination before you left to get there. Of course, you might have done it in a plane by flying west, but the ability to do so nevertheless flies in the face of linear time that is absolute. It just isn't. It is as flexible as the length of the day is different in Juno, Alaska from Santa Domingo in the Dominican Republic. When a changing set of diverse factors can make one thing into

81

something else entirely then none of it is absolute and
therefore not true.

Amelia tossed and turned in her seat at the webinar
whenever she nodded off in the kitchen chair listening to her
mother ruminate on the possible whereabouts of Ardin.

*When you get really good at transcending time you will
find you can be more choosy about where you want to go and
what you would like to do while you're there. It's also
possible, once you understand the passage of time is less
linear and more like a ripple spreading out from a center
created when the first thought dropped like a pebble in a
pond, that you can ride these waves of consciousness aka time,
like a surfer who jumps from one swell to the next.*

"Do you think she may be trying to find her birth mother
again?" Amelia's head rocked on her neck like a bobble-head
as she tried to not let her mother see she was beginning to
doze.

"Maybe," she managed to mutter.

"You know there's no evidence in her file of the child
being born at all," Karen commented absentmindedly as she
sponged paint on the Ritz cracker box. Amelia nodded off to
the webinar.

*When you get really, really good at transcending time, like
it doesn't exist for you anymore, then you have also
transcended ego and are no longer attached to the thoughts
that produce the swells you can ride. Then you know all the
waves of time are getting hopped by absolute consciousness.
Until then, you will continue to identify with one wave or
another for fear you might crash, and continue also to be
influenced by some or all of the past and future lives you
have ever and may ever live from moment to moment to
moment.*

Amelia snorted and was about to demonstrate a full-bodied snore when Karen looked up from her sponge painting and observed her daughter slumped in her chair.

"Amelia!" Karen expected to see her jump. "Think!" Amelia was just about beyond being startled back to awareness. She began to dream she was awake though diminished in years and trying to figure out long division. "AMELIA!" Karen's forceful shout pushed her daughter's body up stiff against the back of the kitchen chair.

"Mom," Amelia barely lifted her head, "Shushhh! You're going to wake Jojo." She repositioned herself in sleep laying her head on the table. Karen looked annoyed but let her daughter sleep, accepting even the slightest level of company was better than none as she picked up her sponge and dipped it in a combination of violet, white and green paint.

No matter how good you get, all other variations of how you travel the ethers will remain habitable depending on the performance of the lifetime you experience. That is to say, you may in some respects seem to be way more advanced than anyone else in your present time, while in another time, the quality of your life may be such that you are clinging to your ego like it's a life preserver in turbulent waters. Such a life can ripple through all other lives causing much misunderstood waves and issues.

The screen in the auditorium went black, but the overhead lights did not come on in the auditorium. Amelia felt her eyes open, and then open wider, but she didn't see anything.

Uh-oh, she thought as she continued to look around in the darkness. She was pretty sure she was surfing again.

"Who's that?" Amelia heard a cautious voice echo in the darkness.

"Who do you think? She heard another voice reply quickly.

"Maximian?" the first voice guessed.

"Yes, Malchus," the second voice answered. "Why is it so dark in here?" Maximian asked.

Amelia chose not to say anything, instead listening as the two men were joined in conversation by other men.

"We have been imprisoned." Another voice cut through the darkness before Malchus could reply. "It seems the entrance to the cave was sealed while we were sleeping."

Amelia gasped, *she realized she had somehow landed in the cave with the seven men from her previous thread surfing episode.*

"Are we going to die, John?" Another man's voice sounded a little farther away than the others.

"That was a potential risk of being Christian in a pagan society, Harley," a fifth, grumpier voice scolded. Amelia hoped that death was not a theme related to her waking dream.

"This doesn't make sense, Marcianus!" Amelia was losing track of who was which voice. "Where are the jeering throngs? Martyrs don't get socked away in caves. They are put on display to deter others from trying the same thing!"

"We must wait and see, Serapion," a younger voice offered.

"When does this charade of martyrdom end, Denis?" Amelia was sure that voice was Maximian's as he was closest to her. "I'm not going to sit around in the dark praying to be saved. That's craziness!"

The darkness was silent as the group considered their options. Amelia quietly wondered what else the men could do if they were indeed sealed in a cave. Noticing no one was scolding her for thinking too much, she was certain she was either dreaming within her dream or sliding along some sort of thread. *Damn, I wish I was better at this!*

"I'm starving," Maximian whined. The persistent silence indicated the others were also hungry.

"Well I don't think there's any hope for breakfast as Malchus, won't be leaving here to get to town today." Amelia wondered if the voice belonged to Denis, then wondered if it was important for her to keep track.

"We must pray for a miracle." A voice she hadn't heard yet seemed to make a pronouncement. "Let us meditate and pray for preservation to prove the Lord is King. Then, when the darkness is removed we shall all be proof of victory."

"To hell with meditation, Constantine!" Maximian declared. Amelia felt a trace of the energy from his hand move right through her as he reached around in the darkness for a jar of wine. "I'm going to tie one on and sleep it off! Malchus, you there?" Amelia listened carefully as Maximian lowered his voice to a whisper.

"Yes, Maximian?" Malchus softly whispered in reply.

"Do you have any morsels you could share?"

Amelia stayed for what seemed like hours as she listened to some distant voices fervently repeat prayers in the darkness, while the area closest to her was filled with the increasingly slurred speech of Maximian and Malchus. Occasionally someone would snap and strike out at another, then beg for forgiveness and the strength to bear witness to the Lord. Eventually the cave was quiet, but Amelia lingered in the darkness unable to leave the thread. She could hear the breath and snoring of the seven sleeping men. Amelia considered one of the men could be connected with Ardin. But she could only imagine a karmic thread could connect an ancient Greek with a contemporary system kid. After a long period of silence, Amelia began to wonder what would draw her back to the Wait Zone or waking life. She tried to imagine herself to Miguel, but didn't budge from the rock beneath her butt.

I hope I'm dreaming, she thought, *either that, or I'm about to become a saint.*

"Ta-daaaa!" Amelia opened her eyes and raised her head to glare at her mother. Karen was holding the now completely painted cracker box in the air as she explained the purpose of her new creation.

"I got the idea off the internet. Now I can store saved magazines upright on my bookshelves. Isn't it pretty?"

Amelia futilely tried to remember what she had been dreaming, stood up and lumbered out of the kitchen mumbling, "Max...Max...Max."

"Where are you going?" Karen called through the kitchen doorway into the dining room where Amelia had paused at the bottom of the stairs.

"Bed." Amelia set her right foot on the first step and began to shift her weight to climb the staircase.

"But it's seven in the morning! Wake Jojo! We need to have breakfast and be ready when Miguel calls."

"Jojo's asleep, Mom," Amelia argued and continued to climb the stairs.

"Amelia Anne Elizabeth Bradford!" Whenever her mother incorporated her confirmation name into a warning, Amelia knew she had better listen. "I'm making pancakes and you and Jojo better be down here in an hour."

"Yes, Mother," Amelia automatically answered as she turned the corner at the top of the stairs and headed for her room.

Pause, pause, pause...

Miguel looked at his watch. He knew that Amelia would be looking for him and she would not be happy if he came back with no information. All he had accomplished was overwhelming the ethers with alternating calls for Tetta and Hrim. He knew his calls for help were not getting through because the guides had never ignored him for any reason in the past.

In the meanwhile, he imagined the sidewalk should be developing a rut for the number of times he had walked around the block, and a depression in the pavement appeared. Stopping in front of a bar, Miguel noted the change from gold streets to gray pavement. Loud shouts from men shooting pool inside the bar expressed their challenges to the scams each was trying to play on the others.

I'm a little too close to the dark side. Miguel noted and started to move on when he recognized Nick coming out of the bar. Slipping back into an alley he watched as Nick hailed a bootleg taxi and opened the door to the back seat.

Miguel barely took a breath as he watched Trisha Jennings stroll out of the bar and get into the taxi. Nick looked around before he dropped inside and closed the door.

That was close, Miguel thought, unaware that his silent comments were still very much perceptible through his one-time close connections with Nick. The bootleg taxi started to move forward then jerked to a stop and Miguel sensed the scan that saturated the air around him. Although he had no experience dodging scans, a kind of intuition advised him to connect his mind with his heart. The scan seemed to be deflected and a moment later the taxi took off.

"Miguel!" Jojo's voice bounced off the walls of the alley and Miguel jumped as he shifted his attention from the taxi to the boy who was running toward him with flailing arms. Miguel watched as the boy's cheeks bounced with each footstep.

"I found Ardin!" the boy shouted breathlessly.

Miguel turned to make sure the taxi had not stopped again, and found himself falling out of bed.

Damn! Thoughts of Jojo sleeping at Karen's house quickly threatened to obliterate the memory of hearing Jojo proclaim he had found Ardin. Miguel climbed back into bed and closed his eyes attempting to re-enter the Wait Zone. It was too late. Too many thoughts were anchoring him to the waking life.

Miguel sat up and tried to connect with Jojo through the ethers using his body as an antenna and tilting his head backward to tune into thoughts of Jojo. He followed a thread through Jojo as if he was a needle and connected with his memories of Ardin asleep under the watchful gaze of a man nearly twice Miguel's size who was sitting bedside. Miguel recognized the large man from the drunk's street memory. Then Miguel saw Ardin in a restaurant, being watched by two men he had never seen before through a monitor embedded in a low table. The vision lasted no more than a split second before Miguel slammed into the same wall Jojo had encountered. He felt the breath of life pulled from Jojo's body, experiencing it in his own lungs.

Miguel gasped and opened his eyes. He knew the scenes were memories and Ardin might not be in either place he had seen. More troubling was not seeing Tetta anywhere in the vision. On top of that, he was worried about Jojo after having gone through that field of life-sucking energy. He knew the boy didn't know how to scan and wondered how it had happened.

Miguel flipped open his cell phone and texted Amelia rather than make the call. The longer he could stay away from Karen Bradford the better his chances of using the skills he knew from the other side to find Ardin.

"Need 2 c jj," Miguel texted and laid his head back on the pillow until he got a reply from Amelia.

Pause, pause, pause...

Amelia's iphone jiggled in her pocket imperceptible to her mother and Jojo who was relishing a plate full of pancakes Karen made.

"I'll be right back." Amelia excused herself from the table delivering her empty plate to the sink. Heading upstairs she read the message and chose to call Miguel in response.

"What's up?" she asked.

"Just what I typed." Miguel smoothed his dark hair in the mirror and for better or worse, considered himself to be street ready. "I think Jojo saw something in the Wait Zone."

"Really? What?" Miguel might have felt street-ready, but he was not ready to go over the details with Amelia.

"Amelia, can we figure out how I can see Jojo without alerting Karen?" Miguel sounded impatient.

"What do you want me to do Miguel?" Amelia was true to her waking life withdrawal of patience and admiration for Miguel. "She kept me up all night, how do you think I'm going to slip him out unnoticed?"

"Swim party," Miguel advised.

"What swim party?" Amelia didn't know anything about a swim party.

"Put it in your calendar, Amelia. Set a swim party for Jojo in an hour. Set a reminder to go off in ten minutes. Tell her you forgot." *She'll believe that for sure,* Miguel thought, then shook his head to keep his mind from wandering. "Karen will think it's a good way to take care of Jojo and free the two of you up for looking into things. If you bring Jojo to the house, I can talk to him about what he might have seen and we'll both be up to speed."

"And then what?" Amelia couldn't deny the smoothness of Miguel's plan, she just wanted more info on what was going on.

"And then... we'll see," Miguel stammered. Amelia didn't make a sound. She didn't expect him to come back empty

89

handed. Miguel couldn't help but scan her thoughts, something he had promised not to do since she wasn't equally talented in the waking life.

"If I can talk to Jojo, I might come up better than empty-handed." Amelia's face flushed with dismay for having been scanned and for not having a better plan on her own.

"Okay, I have to hang up to set the appointment. I can't be on the speaker phone, Mom will hear. I'll call you back when I'm on my way."

Miguel snapped his cell phone closed then grabbed the remote and turned on the television that sat on top of his bedroom dresser. A group of pundits were discussing the ongoing growing rate of unemployment in the country.

"Compared with a year ago, initial unemployment claims are up 30%, while continuing claims are up 82%," a man with a neatly trimmed beard and thinning hair commented.

"In August, 3.5 million people who had exhausted their state benefits were collecting benefits through extended federal programs. By year's end 1.5 million will exhaust federal benefits"

The argument was heating up as Miguel felt a strange sense of gratitude. Having given up his job on the force prior to the financial crisis kicking in the year before, he had no job to lose now. His friends on the force were worried about their future as city council sought to include police layoffs in the budget cuts, but Miguel was managing to keep things together. The lack of work had brought about a lack of tax revenue that was affecting all services at the local and state levels.

One pundit speculated that some state governments might be considering legalizing marijuana as a potential source of tax revenue. Miguel winced at the idea of Americans spending whatever savings they had left on high priced weed to get a break from the stress and strain of the financial crisis.

Miguel had never aspired to understand the politics of the regulation industry, but he found it hard to believe no one saw it coming. Nick would have said the politicians were in cahoots with the big corporations that were getting bailed out while the little guy croaked.

Miguel pressed the button on the remote and stared at the black LCD screen. There was no doubt about it, Nick was with Trisha Jennings and that didn't add up to being on the side of truth and justice. Perhaps they had just been having drinks. People tended to be very forgiving once they crossed over.

Maybe Nick was sincere about his interest in Ardin even though he had never met her. He recalled that Nick had said that all jurisdictions in the Wait Zone were being called in to deal with the problem. That didn't make sense either. Miguel wondered if the interest in Ardin was faked because Nick was after something else. It pained him to think of Nick as being that deceptive. He wished he had a chance to process the facts with Nick so he knew where he stood. His thoughts were interrupted by the chirping ring he associated with calls from Amelia.

"We're on our way," she said as soon as the ringing stopped.

"Okay, I'm here," Miguel replied and snapped the phone closed. It rang again.

"What the hell was that?" Amelia demanded. "I am not your gopher Miguel!"

"I'm sorry, Amelia," Miguel apologized, "I was distracted."

"By what?" The demanding tone of her voice had not diminished. Miguel stared at his shoes as he pondered that he couldn't tell Amelia he had seen Nick and Trisha together in the Wait Zone. He had dug his own grave when he intentionally allowed her to think that Nick was simply missing and Trisha had somehow gotten away after embezzling millions of dollars from her corporate accounts. At the time it seemed like a good choice to let it come to Amelia naturally, when she was ready. Now he felt like he was waiting for the other shoe to drop.

"Miguel?" Amelia reminded him she was waiting for an answer.

"My shoe," Miguel blurted out and wondered where he was heading.

"Miguel, could you please speak in complete sentences?"

"My shoe...lace..." he tried to go on hoping for something to change about the direction the conversation was heading, "broke." Miguel rolled his eyes at his own excuse.

"Well, get it together!" Amelia clearly had no patience left. "I'm running on about 30 minutes sleep and my mother is driving me crazy."

"Miss Amelia?" Jojo interjected from the back seat. Amelia attempted to feel a little control toward her young friend.

"Yes, Jojo?" She tried to sound sweet.

"You just missed the exit."

"Amelia, is everything alright?" Miguel worried that if Jojo had seen Nick and Trisha getting into the bootleg cab he might tell Amelia.

"Yes." Amelia gritted her teeth and switched lanes to take the next exit. "We'll be there soon."

Pause, pause, pause...

It added about ten minutes to the trip for Amelia to get off at Dana and backtrack to Miguel's house in South

92

Avondale.   As Amelia stepped out of the Mercedes onto Hickory Street, she felt the cool moisture in the air brush against her face as if to remind her she was not in a safe place.   She had come back to the house a dozen times in the past year but nevertheless, each arrival felt like the start of a countdown to that fateful moment that had questioned the sustainability of her life and thrown her head-on into the Wait Zone.

Crossing the street, she looked to the right, not for oncoming traffic but young men in long white t-shirts.   Her step was a little lighter than it was a year ago.   She wasn't carrying her heavy briefcase but now the young boy she was trying to meet for the first time then, was walking alongside her.   They had become friends in the Wait Zone before she ever knew who he really was.   Never before had she been given such insight into a case.   Jojo's imagination had been a key to understanding her own childhood which she had denied so much play.

With her right foot on the stairs, the memory of seeing Miguel on the porch came flooding over her, and she grabbed the railing tightly as she insisted she would not allow her imagination to playback any more details of what happened next.

It took her months to begin to realize that she had been consciously aware in The Wait Zone the whole time she was in a coma.   It took even longer to begin to understand that she was continuing to visit the places she saw then as a part of ongoing recovery and rehabilitation.

While she was working on remembering what happened on a daily basis between the Waiting and Waking sides of life, what she didn't know was that what had happened in order for her to return to waking life had been almost as traumatic as what put her there in the first place.   Sometimes she felt as if

93

Miguel was keeping something from her, but he and Hrim and Tetta advised her that she would know whatever she needed to as opportunities came up.

In the meanwhile she had had plenty to do. The loss of her law practice seemed as good a time as any for Amelia to move into the lesser paying work of child advocate in the courts. The SUV and her condo in Hyde Park were paid off making the transition from her life as a corporate lawyer a little easier.

As she rang the doorbell she felt the sense of safety swell over her as she had once again made it past the place where she turned and saw the face of her attacker. She had never identified the man in her waking life and though she pressed Miguel about it, he always minimized the issue focusing instead on the importance of her recovery. Amelia believed he just wanted her to be happy. It never occurred to her he would dismiss the importance of finding a killer.

Miguel swung open the heavy wooden door with beautiful inlaid lead glass and invited Amelia and Jojo into the dining room. He always waited for her to ring the bell just so she didn't know he was watching her every move from the time she parked the car. The moment in the yard a year ago had been almost as traumatic for him as it had been for her. It hadn't been easy meeting the woman he would fall in love with while fearing she might die at any moment.

"Jojo." Miguel walked around the dining room table with his hands clasped, fingertips touching the edge of his moustache. He knew Jojo had a tendency to shut down and forget details if he thought he was in trouble so Miguel had quickly established that nothing was wrong; he simply wanted to play a little game with Jojo.

"Jojo, do you remember your dream from last night?"

"Which one?" Jojo asked, kicking a leg of the table with his feet as a small twinge of anxiety nevertheless rose to the surface.

"I was wondering about a dream where you surprised me in an alley." Miguel hoped Jojo would not recount what he had been watching from the alley.

"You mean when you were watching that pretty waitress lady?" Jojo asked, then felt shy in front of Amelia who had her eyes fixed on Miguel and her eyebrows raised high on her forehead.

"I don't recall a pretty lady." Miguel smiled at Amelia and flushed slightly. "But you do remember the alley?"

"Yes." Jojo grew a little more pensive since he was sure Miguel had been watching the waitress get in the bootleg taxi with a man who looked familiar to Jojo.

"Jojo, do you remember what you said to me?"

"Sure Miguel, I said the same thing that I told Miss Amelia at the coffee shop." Miguel looked at Amelia with the same look of surprise and suspicion she had given him a moment earlier.

"And what did you tell Miss Amelia?" Miguel asked, and Jojo began to fear he was going to get Amelia in trouble.

"The same thing I told you, Miguel." Jojo dodged the answer and watched the couple stare each other down. Simultaneously they turned and looked at Jojo who was instantly certain he was now about to get in trouble.

"I said I found her, sir," Jojo tried to win points with an extra dose of respect, "and ma'am." As he watched Amelia's face grimace, Jojo thought he might have just lost points.

"Found who?" Amelia asked, and Miguel again raised his eyebrow as she moved beyond her lawyering expertise into his detective territory.

"Ardin, Miss Amelia, I saw Ardin." Miguel was now sure that Jojo remembered he had surfed the web to see Ardin.

Miguel wanted to know who had shown the boy how to access the ethers. Cutting in front of Amelia, Miguel reclaimed his place as chief investigator.

"Jojo, I followed a thread you found yesterday and saw Ardin. Do you remember surfing?"

"Yes sir." Jojo kept his answer succinct as he often volunteered information which complicated rather than alleviated his trouble.

"Jojo, who showed you how to do that?" The boy was silent. Slowly he pulled his lips inside his mouth and squinched his eyes from left to right as if he was thinking very hard but nothing came out of his mouth. "Jojo, do you know how you found that thread?" Miguel asked in another way.

"No sir." Miguel took a deep breath and frowned at Jojo.

"Jojo," Amelia jumped in front of Miguel, "do you know where Ardin was when you saw her?"

"Yes, Miss Amelia." Jojo was careful not to call her ma'am again. "She was in a restaurant and she was in bed." Jojo glanced between Amelia and Miguel who where also exchanging glances with one another and Jojo.

"It's true," Jojo insisted. Amelia let her stare settle on Miguel.

"It's true," Miguel said. "She was in two places at once."

"And neither of you know where this was?" Amelia propped tightly made fists on her hips.

"No ma'am," both replied in unison.

Pause, pause, pause…

Past, present and future are umbrella terms which seem to indicate the relevance of one moment in time to another. One moment may seem to be in the past because of a perceived relationship to another moment as present and others as future. However, when a moment is recalled it becomes present and may be used to project or actually create the future which often changes the nature of the moments accrued in the past. An example of this would be when a horrible time is recalled in the present moment and the learning gleaned from it -- which may differ each time the moment is recalled and gleaned -- produces a brilliant future the perceiver believes could not have happened without the former challenge thus making it beneficial.

Amelia squinted in the darkness as she reconciled her disappearance from the conversation with Jojo at Miguel's house with her arrival in a webinar as the screen disappeared and two men materialized along with a park-like scene out of the darkness. As if they were leaping off an invisible swing, the first man blurred into visibility dropping one foot to the ground, followed by the other and came to a stop after a few steps. The second followed directly behind him in the same form although he stumbled and reached out to balance himself by grabbing on to the first man's shoulder. Amelia recognized the two men from the seven she saw living in the cave.

It's like my schedule has gone haywire! Amelia complained. *I need to be getting info on Ardin,* she notified the ethers, but she was pretty sure the message fell on deaf ears.

"Where are we, Maximian?" Amelia connected the voice of Malchus from the dark cave with second man gripping the shoulder of the curly haired man she assumed to be Maximian.

"It must be the kingdom of Heaven, Malchus." Maximian quietly whispered as he took in the beautiful gardens and sculptures decorating the courtyard from behind a neatly trimmed stand of red cedar trees.

"We died just that quickly?" Malchus looked up incredulously examining balcony railings that dripped with gold

97

leaf and tall spires gleaming with diamonds and other precious gems against a sky so brilliantly blue it certainly all seemed other worldly.

"A second ago you were begging me for leftovers." Malchus recalled, "Now you think we've died and gone to heaven?"

"We're not in Ephesus anymore. That's for sure." Maximian nodded in the direction of a man floating overhead. "Anyway, your memory's bad, you didn't have any morsels and we drank on an empty stomach. We're sloshed, not dead, that's all."

Malchus had to agree, the scene was definitely hallucinogenic. The people who were standing on the balconies and paths in the garden were glowing as if lights filled their bodies and floated around them.

"What do we do now?" Malchus asked. "Attempt to locate the Lord?"

"It only looks like heaven." Maximian was rallying for some fun. "Let's poke around and see what there is to do."

Amelia felt herself moving deeper into the scene as its flat screen-like appearance transformed and surround her. She seemed invisible to the pair as they seemed to also be undetected by the locals in the courtyard. She had never seen anything like this in the Wait Zone and so determined she had followed the two men as they followed some sort of thread to someone else's dream.

Amelia wasn't sure what common denominator could bring all three of them to the same place. It was possible that they had followed her thread and she would have come to this place and time with or without them. On the other hand, because she had watched them in webinars while looking for Ardin, she considered the possibility that they had something to do with her disappearance.

"Let's take this slowly." Malchus pulled Maximian back as he started to walk beyond the cover of the bushes. Malchus spoke from his experience stealing into Ephesus daily to secure food for his fellow cave dwellers. He didn't want a potential dream to turn into a nightmare. It was dangerous to slip through security every day to get rations. Amelia listened to his thought process and appreciated Malchus' sense of caution.

"But the food is bound to be wonderful Malchus, and frankly, the stuff you've been bringing back from the village has tasted like hog feed." Maximian licked his lips as Amelia listened to his thoughts describe his favorite foods. "Even if it is just an illusion, I wouldn't mind feeling as if I was eating something tasty right now." Maximian added a smile to his comment to ease the criticism of Malchus' culinary skills.

Malchus frowned, he felt cheated for his service to his brothers in the cave whenever they criticized his shopping and cooking skills. Secretly though, he knew Maximian's observation was not far from the truth. He had sometimes stolen hog feed from nearby farms and presented it as stew when there were too many Roman soldiers in town. Amelia recoiled at the thought.

"Please Maximian," Malchus urged, "let's stay hidden until we know where we are. You can steal leftovers when the people rest."

"Very well." Maximian agreed and Amelia followed as the two settled in behind a large lilac bush just as those living in the quarters surrounding the palace began migrating toward what Maximian and Malchus imagined was a king's court.

As the people passed they were sharing news about someone they described as a princess of peace. One woman waved her hands in the air as she seemed to be directing a small tour group toward the palace on the far side of the courtyard.

99

"The Princess Yeshe Dawa has sacrificed for tens of millions of years and saved hundreds of thousands of people from suffering pain and fear." The woman explained. "She might become a Buddha."

Not in this lifetime. Amelia overheard the thoughts of one man in the group. She checked in with Maximian and Malchus. Neither appeared to be able to hear thought. Maximian and Malchus waited while the crowd entered the palace.

Malchus felt vindicated for suggesting the pair remain hidden in the strange land. "The *Lord* seems to be a woman."

"That's impossible." Maximian whispered. "Women don't have what it takes to be leaders." Amelia frowned as she realized the men shared a chauvinistic view.

"Apparently this girl does have what it takes." Malchus argued.

"Girl?" Maximian looked at Malchus as if he was crazy, "They said she'd sacrificed for tens of millions of years man! She's the oldest princess ever, and I bet not many men are after her hand in marriage."

Amelia became even more ruffled at the way Maximian seemed to apply the glass ceiling to spiritual endeavors, and found herself liking the way Malchus seemed to be at the forefront of what would one day become the feminist movement.

The sound of a conch shell blew from inside the palace and Malchus and Maximian moved through the empty courtyard to peer through a window and see if they could have a look at the so-called princess.

Amelia sidled up behind them and noticed that Malchus, though unaware seemed to make room for her as if he sensed her presence on some level. Through the narrow window, Amelia could see the temple was filled with wise men, soldiers, royalty while servants brought delicious food to all in attendance. She scowled as Maximian looked back and let his tongue hang loose with longing to enjoy some of the food that was offered. Malchus nudged Maximian with his shoulder to keep him in check.

On a platform at one end of the temple, a large man sat on a cup-shaped chair carved from stone. The conch shell sounded again and a beautiful young woman came into the court with her hands at chest level, held together in prayer. Bowing to the man on the platform he returned the gesture. Maximian forgot he was hungry. Malchus too felt his heart instantly open to the surprisingly young woman.

"How is it possible for anyone to live ten million years and look sixteen?" Malchus wondered aloud.

"Clearly the timeline and her deeds were an exaggeration. She's gorgeous." Maximian was mesmerized. Amelia looked past the pair of salivating men into the temple as the man on the throne spoke to the princess.

"Yeshe Dawa, it is clear you have been willing to surrender attachment to all worldly things."

"See," Malchus observed, "she *is* just like the Lord."

"Heretic." Maximian responded almost automatically.

Idiot, Amelia also automatically thought.

The man on the throne went on, "Your offerings have spared hundreds of thousands and tens of millions from suffering pain and fear." Malchus and Maximian gave each other a glance of surprise. "Though it is unusual, I have requested that the ministers and monks meet with you about your prospects as you seem to have perfected your dharma practices."

"What's dharma?" Malchus imagined it was a ritual of some sort. Maximian began slowly knocking his forehead against the wall of the palace.

"God dammit." Maximian cursed.

"Blasphemy!" Malchus pushed Maximian, "Taking the name the Lord in vain. Have you learned nothing?"

"It was a mistake." Maximian excused himself as he considered how the princess might lack attachment to worldly things. "I have just learned that the girl of my dreams probably doesn't hold a favorable position on lust." Maximian whined.

Pause, pause, pause...

The past, present and future are very nearly interchangeable depending on whom is entertaining them and what purpose they have for doing so. In this way, fond dreams become nasty nightmares and the dreamers of time may not have the slightest awareness of how this came to be.

Amelia's attention snapped into her body like a cold shower had been turned on, as the image of the young Greek explorers flattened back onto the screen in the auditorium.

It helps if one can remember their dreams. To do this, we suggest remaining still upon awakening, and having a notepad nearby to jot down images and words which may remain in the consciousness after awakening. We mention this once again in concluding yet another webinar on dream recall with hopes that you might just one day get it.

"AMELIA!" Amelia's body jumped and fell off the bed.

"SHIT!" Amelia spewed as she knelt on the floor staring up at her mother through her straggly red curls.

"I asked you to get Jojo. The pancakes are getting cold. It's late!" Amelia tried to determine which breakfast opportunity was real, the one after which she secretly met Miguel with Jojo, or the one that was still waiting in the kitchen downstairs.

"How late?" Amelia faked a response as her mother's foot tapped loudly on the floor in front of her. Keeping her eyes locked with her mother's, Amelia reached for her notepad and pen on the nightstand. She pulled the pad into her lap and started scribbling wildly across the page still keeping her eyes on her mother as she jabbered on sounding very much like the bugling school teacher in Charlie Brown television cartoons.

Princess... heaven... chauvinists... Miguel.... Jojo... swim party. Amelia glanced down and looked at the mixture of terms for which she could recall only faintly.

"What are you writing?" Karen twisted her head to see if she could make out her daughter's scribbled notes. Amelia closed the book and started to get up.

"Nothing Mom. Jibberish. I've been trying to remember my dreams and..."

"You're right," Karen had reached full throttle frustration. "jibberish! We need to get going Amelia. I will get Jojo, you get your act together." Karen inserted the kind of pause only a mother or teacher can create which although silent sounded like chalk screeching on a board as she heavily underlined her next words, "We're going to Miguel's, and he better have something to tell us."

As Karen stomped out of Amelia's room and down the hallway to rouse Jojo, Amelia reacted to the ultimatum tied up in her mother's words. She needed Miguel to have an answer too, because the one thing worse than Ardin disappearing in the first place, was not reporting it to child protective services as soon as they knew she was gone. Amelia was afraid her mother didn't understand it was now likely not only that Ardin would pay some heavy consequences, but so too would Karen in the form of having Ardin permanently removed from her care.

Amelia picked up her cell phone and checked for messages. There was a text from Miguel. Amelia looked at her feet. In the absence of the Gold Lame shoes, she knew she was in waking life and had answered the text only in her dreams. *How strange,* she thought, *How exciting!* She added as she realized she just might be showing signs of remembering her dreams, although not much information at the moment.

"Amelia!?" Karen stood in the doorway studying her daughter in disbelief as she continued to sit on the floor next to the bed holding her cell phone in one hand and the notebook in the other. "Amelia?" For a moment Karen allowed for the possibility that something was wrong with her daughter other than her priorities.

Amelia glanced up from her wandering thoughts. "Sorry." Amelia started to get up and Karen provided an impatient status report.

"Jojo is in the bathroom, I suggest you use mine and get your butt downstairs. You can write in your diary after we find Ardin." Karen's dismissive tone was wasted on Amelia, she was far too busy trying to remember what she dreamed.

Hijacked, Hysteria and Princess Peeking

When Amelia went missing from the dining room table, Miguel chalked it up to what was called DADD in the Wait Zone, Dream Awareness Deficit Disorder. It wasn't unusual for Amelia to go flying through the ethers led by one bizarre connection to the next. Miguel remembered a time when they had been sharing an ice cream cone in the Wait Zone. He was so startled when their connection whisked him away with her as she connected with a small boy who had stuck his tongue to a freezing cold metal pole. A moment later she dragged him along to the North Pole. When he finally broke free, Miguel woke up with memories of being in a pool playing Marco Polo.

In the Wait Zone a great deal of emphasis was given to classes that taught dreamers how to stay focused and recognize

105

the teasers that redirected their dreams into otherwise unrelated territory. While Amelia had not progressed much in this regard, Miguel had become skilled at holding his ground and knew better than to chase after her.

When Jojo also disappeared from the dining room Miguel scanned and saw that one very frazzled Karen Bradford had taken custody of them both. Miguel knew he had little precious time left before Karen would be calling or worse, banging on his front door.

Closing his eyes, Miguel tipped back his head and sought the thread that would lead him to Hrim. He began to move along a thread of light which, different from its usual tornadic, lightening speed was filled with static, stutters, and pixelations. Miguel wondered if traveling the web in that condition might be dangerous. Eventually he was transported to the lecture hall at the University. No students and, most importantly, no guides were around.

Taking a deep breath Miguel noticed a stack posters lying on a table. They were the same as those he had seen in the Wait Zone. He wondered why there weren't any flyers for Ardin as Nick had indicated the entire Wait Zone Authority was involved in finding her, and he knew Tetta had witnessed her abduction. There was nothing that indicated the guides were the least bit interested in finding Ardin.

Miguel read the poster again and contemplated the description of the missing something. *What could a peace-making device look like?* Miguel wondered, as he noticed copies of the New York Times and Washington Post that were strewn around the long table. He wondered if the missing thing had something to do with the devastation in the world economic markets.

"I know you guys are concerned about the safety of the world," Miguel started to talk to the guides as if they were present, "but I'm concerned with the safety of Ardin." He paused, and pictured the round woman who was always so helpful when he was in a jam. "Tetta?" Miguel waited patiently, as he hoped some thread of his consciousness might reach hers. "Tetta, I know you saw Ardin disappear. Why aren't you looking for her? Why haven't you tried to contact us?"

"Give it up Miguel." The voice of Nick Green snapped Miguel's awareness into place and his thoughts immediately angled toward distrust as he grew more suspicious of his ex-partner.

"Nick, are you blocking communication between me and the guides?"

"Miguel, how could you think that?" Nick adapted one of the guilt-laden lines Trisha always defended herself with when he suspected her of some misdeed. Nick emerged from a dark corner looking disappointed with Miguel. "Miguel, I would never get in your way." He stopped and let his chin drop as he acknowledged he had in fact very much gotten in the way of Miguel's investigation of Amelia's shooting. "Well, at least, not anymore." He tried to reassure Miguel, "I'm different now, honestly." Another of Trisha's lines converted well in Nick's defense. "I've been trying to get through for days too. Something has them blocked, but you know I couldn't possibly do that. I'm only trying to help, pal. Maybe if we pool our resources, we'll be able to break this thing."

"Break what?" Miguel asked trying to determine a way he could tell if Nick was being truthful or not.

"The raid on the world, of course." Nick picked up a copy of The Wall Street Journal from the table and held it up. "What are you thinking I'm up to?" Nick didn't seem to miss a beat, but Miguel continued to hold his attention in his heart in order to deflect any unwanted scanning.

"Nick, I thought you said you were looking for Ardin." Miguel quickly tried to test the quality of Nick's aura as the channel flowed in his direction, but was cut off with Nick's quick response.

"Ardin?" Nick seemed confused. "Who's that?"

Miguel dug his feet in as he determined he was not about to share any new information with Nick until he clarified what Nick meant in their earlier conversation.

"On the trolley you said you were investigating *her* disappearance." Miguel paraphrased Nick's words. Nick didn't bounce back as quickly this time as he tried to recall the words he might have used.

"Oh well, yeah." Nick used the heel of his hand to pop himself in the forehead as he seemed to recall what he meant. "*She*, Miguel, you know....the country. That's what I meant. It's devastating, you know?"

"What did you mean when you said she wasn't just a *runaway*, she'd been *kidnapped*?" Miguel was becoming more and more distrustful.

"I said that?" Miguel watched as Nick seemed to be scanning the conversation on the trolley for exact details. "I meant the economy Miguel. The whole economy has been snatched, railroaded, hijacked, kidnapped. And if we don't get it back, the devastation is going to be substantial because that's not the way it's supposed to be, get it?"

Miguel stayed inside his heart center and studied Nick. The two men had grown distant both before and after Nick's death. It was possible they had each misunderstood what the other was talking about in their first meeting.

"The economy has been in trouble for more than a year, Nick." Miguel couldn't figure out why Nick was acting as if it was breaking news.

"But a year in waking life doesn't take as long here, Miguel," Nick reminded him, then paused thoughtfully. "Oh, that's it!" Nick seemed to understand something that had been troubling him. "That's why you seemed so shocked to see me and it felt as if I had just seen you yesterday." Nick extended his hands and move his palms closer and farther apart as he explained, "Time passes here Miguel, but it feels different. Your year-long financial crisis has been going on here for the equivalent of about 10 business days."

Miguel was impressed with what Nick knew about the differences in time perception between the planes. Their two separate investigations only seemed to coincide.

"It's a matter of perception, Miguel," Nick commented on Miguel's thoughts as his former partner let down his guard. "Who's Ardin?"

"Amelia's..." Miguel began and felt the explanation was too complicated, "a girl who's been missing since last night."

"Oh." Nick shook his head. "No, no one put me on that case. Sorry." Miguel was slightly taken aback by what seemed almost like Nick's disinterest in Ardin. Nick continued, "The only assignments I get are petty crimes. I was only put on the investigation into the sub prime thing because, well, it's too big to fail. Miguel was amazed at Nick's concern for the financial crisis. "You mean the Wait Zone might try to bail out the big banks?"

"No, Nick clarified, "I mean the world appearance. People's dreams will go to hell in a hand basket if the economy goes down. They need to find a way to prop it up on both sides of the fence."

Miguel wished he could just ask the guides if Nick was telling the truth. It seemed to make sense. In a matter of seconds Nick had cleared up all doubt that Miguel had regarding his trustworthiness, except for seeing him with Trisha.

"Yeah, Trisha." Nick acknowledged he could hear Miguel's process. Miguel tightened his grip on his awareness as Nick explained, "We have some karma to work out, if you know what I mean. We're sort of stuck with each other. If I can forgive and forget, the next life might be a little better."

Despite the fact that Nick covering everything so succinctly should have thrown more red flags between the two men, Miguel smiled at his old friend while continuing to focus his attention in his heart. If Nick was lying, then Miguel was sure he knew more about Ardin than he was admitting and he wouldn't be able to access any more information without Miguel's trust.

"So, why do you think we can't get through to the guides?" Miguel returned to his original interest.

"I'm figuring whatever is screwing with the economy has put some sort of mojo on the web. It's never been this hard to get through. We might be on our own."

Miguel picked up one of the flyers. "What do you think this means?"

"From my side of things it seems that it's not just about what's happening, but what used to prevent it from happening. I don't think that's got anything to do with your girl though." Nick checked to see if Miguel was following his train of thought.

"One thing at a time," Miguel shrugged. "You can't help with Ardin and I can't help with the economy, at least not until I find her. If I haven't found her by the end of the day we're going to have to report her and that would set her back for years in the system. Besides, I don't think she's in the waking life."

"You think she's here?"

"Somewhere between here and there." Miguel shook his head wishing he knew more about the intricacies of the etheric planes.

"Is she a runaway?" Nick sought to clarify if she was hiding.

"No, she was grabbed by a man who, as best I can tell, carried her between planes," Miguel skimmed over the details.

"Strange." Nick seemed intrigued as he had only heard of *between planes* as a sketchy, highly volatile space that easily triggered between the Wait Zone and waking life by stray thoughts and sudden sounds.

"Yeah, and that's just part of it," Miguel replied. "Jojo caught onto her thread somehow and saw her in two different places at the same time." Nick squinted as if he was trying to understand what Miguel was describing.

"I don't get it." Nick needed more information to process.

"Neither do I. But it get's worse." Miguel's face morphed from deep thought into sudden horror. "Oh hell!"

"What is it?" Nick reflected Miguel's alarm like a mirror.

"Jojo!" Miguel completely changed the subject as Nick tried to refocus his attention. "And Amelia!" Miguel felt for his keys in his pants pocket then remembered he was dreaming and not driving. "She's probably on her way! I have to wake up or she's going to kill me."

"I wouldn't recommend it," Nick joked about death. Miguel prepared to re-enter the waking life.

"Wait Miguel, you said there was something that made it even worse. What is it?"

"Tetta," Miguel absent-mindedly replied as he simultaneously sent out one last appeal for her attention. "She was there, Nick. Tetta saw Ardin get nabbed, and she's no where to be found."

"If I see her I can tell her you're trying to reach her," Nick offered.

"That would be great." Miguel faced his friend and smiled as he waited for his mind to consciously return to the beta state. In a moment, and with a deep sigh that Nick thought sounded full of relief, Miguel faded from view and returned to the waking life.

Pause, pause, pause...

111

"Miguel!" Amelia hissed into her iphone from the master bathroom off her mother's bedroom. The outgoing voice message from Miguel's phone finished with a beep and waited for Amelia's message. "Where are you? Did you text me in your dreams or was I dreaming? Did you get the information you needed from Jojo or have I not gotten there yet? And who was that woman Jojo saw you watching from an alley?"

The last question threw Amelia off as she remembered a piece of her dream that she had not quite connected with earlier. Amelia looked at the list she had laid on the sink to help her remember, then hissed back into the phone, "And I want to know who this *princess* is too!"

Realizing she could argue with Miguel in person, Amelia tried to fill him in, "Mom is on the rampage. I overslept. I'm taking a shower. It's nine o'clock Saturday morning. Expect us in an hour. Have some answers!" Amelia pressed the button on the screen to end the call and Miguel's face vanished into darkness. *I hope he's got something,* Amelia thought as she stepped into the shower.

Amelia tilted her head back and let the water pour over her red curls weighing them down into darker ringlets. She filled her hand with shampoo and started weaving lather through her long strands as thoughts of her life before Miguel and memories of her early morning dreams swirled together in her mind. *Princess, what princess?*

The thought of another woman in Miguel's life shook Amelia to the core. Amelia had always felt competitive for the love her father held for his adopted daughter from India and she was shattered when she discovered her former boyfriend's infidelity.

Amelia inhaled the sweet scent of coconut from the lather in her hands as she wished for just a few moments of peace, then rinsed and shut off the shower. Water rolled off her face as she wrapped her hair in a towel. She thought of how much water she would save if her hair was shorter. Before she could begin to wonder if Miguel would like her with short hair, Amelia again wondered who the princess might be, then wondered why she couldn't stop thinking about this unknown woman. She wanted to trust Miguel, but she was always struggling with knowing how to trust. Her lawyer instincts wouldn't allow her to be caught off guard in the court-room or outside it.

Court room? No, courtyard! Amelia thought. *Damn, there's that princess again!*

"Amelia?" Karen's muffled voice was sounding more frantic and less chastising through the bathroom door. The shower had revived Amelia's patience for her mother's ruminating tendencies.

"Almost ready, Mom." Amelia tried to sound upbeat as she buffed the soft towel over her shins and knees.

Pause, pause, pause...

Trisha Jennings was waiting for Nick to come home. She was being more patient than was natural for her. Nick's plan to become a hero was almost intolerable to Trisha, who didn't have a compassionate bone in her body while she was alive let alone dead. On the other hand, the possibility that the hero status of Miguel and Amelia could be undermined while gaining respect for Nick and Trisha in the Wait Zone seemed slightly attractive to her.

Trisha didn't like the Wait Zone. She was stuck there, unable to get a life. As long as those involved in her past life continued to live, Trisha had no hope of gaining new life no matter how rotten it was. Unlike Nick, who wanted to move up the karmic ladder, Trisha figured if she was going to be around for awhile, it was going to be a party.

The biggest benefit Trisha found in death was the ability to manifest anything she wanted. When she set up house, Trisha modeled her living space after her former boss's condominium. Trisha didn't care if it was all recorded on her debit card. It didn't phase her at all that her continuing extravagant, self-centered ways reduced all hope she had of improving her moksha.

Trisha enjoyed setting up payment plans of 18-Lifetimes same-as-karma to roll-over her karmic debt rather than address it with good deeds to improve her moksha levels. For Trisha, that was more painful that the paybacks in lifetimes, especially since it would be awhile before she would need to work out the details.

The door of the condo flew open and Nick stormed into the solarium.

"Did you find her?" Trisha asked without looking up from the box of chocolates she gorged herself on daily without fear of gaining weight.

"No." Nick didn't sound disappointed. "But I think I have Miguel's confidence."

"So?" Trisha hated Nick's former partner. "Why do you care if he likes you?"

Nick was not nearly as resigned to accruing more suffering as Trisha was. "Because, if I look like I'm helping him I'll gain points in my Book of Life."

"And am I in your book?" Trisha teased Nick who didn't approve of her use of karmic lifetime credit cards.

"You and me in heaven together, baby," Nick promised. "You just have to help a little."

"How?" Trisha felt her body sink deeper into the couch cushion in resistance to doing anything.

"Jojo saw her." Nick started in on what Miguel had told him. "I need you to hook up with him again and see if you can follow the thread."

"Why me?" Trisha didn't feel like being nice to the little boy again.

"You don't have to see him, just pry into his mind, Trisha. C'mon, baby, you're good at it. You can get the details." Nick bent over the back of the couch and nuzzled his face into Trisha's blonde hair to bite at her neck.

"Forget it Nick. I'm not doing a mind-meld with an eight year old kid."

"He's nine now."

"He's a kid! NO!" Trisha argued. Nick grabbed the back of Trisha's neck and pinched it between his fingertips. "You can't hurt me Nick, I'm dead, remember?" Nick let go, pushing Trisha away as he stood up.

"Then I'll have to look up someone who might want to help." He walked away. Trisha didn't have to ask. This wasn't the first time Nick had played her against Amelia's half-sister, Shima, who would do anything Nick asked.

"Okay, I'll do it." Trisha agreed, afraid to lose Nick's protection in what, outside of the illusion of their apartment, was the seamiest neighborhood in the Wait Zone. "But I don't get it, you know Decius has her."

"I'm not so sure about that," Nick countered. "Miguel said Jojo saw her in two different places with two different men. I think something went wrong with his plan."

"And what are we going to do, fix it?" Trisha sometimes seemed absolutely clueless considering she had spent ten years in higher education.

"No, we're supposed to figure it out. I think we've got a shot at being the only ones who have enough information to win the prize." Nick grinned and Trisha smiled back at him. She liked prizes.

Pause, pause, pause...

The rapid-fire ringing of the doorbell was equally rivaled by pounding on the door and tweets on the cell phone beside the bed as Miguel woke up and realized that Amelia and the entourage had the house surrounded. He didn't have a story, and he didn't have a plan, but he held on to his new found hope that Nick might at least have his back.

Miguel could see the strain on Amelia's face through the lace curtains that covered the window in the front door. Right behind Amelia's face was Karen's wearing a stern frown, and beneath both faces was Jojo who looked stressed just by being in the company of the two women. Miguel opened the door and was pushed aside as Karen swept in from the back and ushered the group into the dining room. Miguel felt his house was being seized.

"Didn't you get my message?" Amelia asked looking up and down at Miguel adjusting his jeans at the waistline. When he turned to face Karen, she was also giving him the once over, but unlike Amelia, not allowing her eyes to linger on his buff shoulders.

Miguel followed Amelia's gaze downward and realized his fly was open. Quickly he turned and zipped. Miguel waited before turning back to face the two women again. He knew he was in trouble. It looked like he hadn't been doing anything. There was no way he could convince Karen of what he had seen.

Karen had never bought into Amelia's story that she had seen Miguel and Jojo on the other side in her dreams. Amelia couldn't remember enough of the dreams to be convincing. Jojo claimed to have ridden on a giant elephant with Amelia,

116

but Karen attributed his story to having over heard Amelia's and urged her not to talk of such things in front of him.

Amelia had argued vehemently that rejecting her story of life after death was inconsistent with the family's Catholic views. Karen reminded Amelia she hadn't died. "It was like purgatory." Amelia tried one last time several months later. "Did you see your dad there?" was Karen's only response.

Miguel shrugged his shoulders. "It looks like just another runaway, Karen."

"Impossible," Karen added her insights, "Why Over-the-Rhine then? It's so far from everything. If she wanted to hop a Greyhound and run, she would have made it somewhere closer to the bus station."

"But it's not that far, Karen. Less than a mile."

"Through Over-the-Rhine?" Karen couldn't believe Ardin would willingly get off in a strange neighborhood when she could have chosen a bus stop less than four blocks from the Greyhound station.

"Maybe she decided after she got off the bus," Miguel suggested.

"What about the old woman who taunted her on the bus? The driver said she took off after her." Karen was pacing the dining room, alternating between Amelia and Miguel as if she was asking questions but not necessarily of them. Karen was processing the information she had already stewed all night long. Like cooking in her kitchen, she had reduced most of the liquid and was coming to one conclusion.

"She's been kidnapped," Karen decided. Miguel looked at Amelia who did not recall their earlier dream conversation in the dining room with Jojo.

"She sure has!" Jojo chimed in. Amelia watched Miguel start to move in Jojo's direction then grit his teeth and pull back. Karen sighed and tilted her head as she looked at Jojo who was playing with his favorite Transformer toy on the lace tablecloth.

"You know what happened to Ardin?" Karen's tone was doubtful and Miguel relaxed a little to let the scene play out as it always did when Jojo divulged secrets from the other side. Amelia listened intently to find out what she may have forgotten from the Wait Zone to see how it fit together with her dream record.

"Yes, ma'am," Jojo stopped to see if Karen would like or dislike being called a ma'am. She didn't seem phased either way. "It's like I told Miguel and Miss Amelia." He looked back and forth between the pair to see how his helpfulness was faring with them. He second-guessed himself for a moment as there seemed to be little encouragement coming from them.

"You have told Miguel and Amelia about what you saw?" Karen forgot for a moment that Jojo had been fast asleep when Ardin disappeared, and invited Jojo to continue. The boy felt suddenly awkward having no large measure of reassurance or discouragement from anyone in the room.

"Yes ma'am." Jojo chose to continue. "Ardin is getting watched by a man on a table and she is in bed with a big ugly man watching her." Karen shuddered in horror.

"Miguel! Where does he get stuff like this?" Karen switched from interest in Ardin to accusing tones. "What sort of television programs are you allowing him to watch?" Amelia was just as shocked by Jojo's revelation as Karen. It was unconscionable for the boy to be imagining the 15 year old girl in bed. Miguel wanted to jump in and adjust the boy's tale to clarify the man and girl were not seen in bed together, but Jojo started to fix it without even trying.

"The big man is very worried about Ardin," Jojo continued.

"Worried?" Karen lowered her temper and wanted to know more.

"Karen." Miguel shook his head as if he didn't want her to encourage such story-telling.

"Yes ma'am, Ardin is sick in bed and he was taking care of her." Miguel was impressed with Jojo's observations from an image he saw for just a few short moments. Karen pleadingly looked up at Miguel.

"I'm sure she's alright," Miguel lied. "There have been no reports of any accidents or anything like that. She'll turn up." He tried to soothe her concerns.

"Apparently that's what you're expecting." Karen raised her eyebrows to indicate she would appreciate an explanation as to why Miguel was half dressed. Miguel passed the pleading look on to Amelia, begging for intercession.

"Mom," Amelia thought fast, "I called Miguel earlier and asked him to take a nap so he would have a little energy left to help us when we arrived." Amelia waited to see how her mom would take the explanation.

"You're right Amelia," Karen observed. A manhunt – or girlhunt – is too much for one man. We are going to have to call in back-up." Karen waved her hand in the air simultaneously dismissing the hope for trying to find Ardin by herself and summoning more troops. "I'm calling the police. Sorry Miguel." She acknowledged her disappointment in his investigation. "They will be able to search the entire area where she was last seen. For a moment the room was quiet.

"Mom, it hasn't been 24 hours." Amelia spoke up first.

"Right," Miguel added. "They won't search yet, especially considering her background."

"I'll see if I can find her, Miss Karen," Jojo offered, and tilted his head back just a little. Miguel jumped forward and to straighten the boy's head, and then tried to seem nonchalant about his actions.

"I think you should just hang on to that idea and we'll talk about it later, little guy." Miguel broke the rule and

119

scanned Amelia's thoughts to learn what she was thinking. Amelia looked at him and thought, *I'm thinking he is way too young to be surfing the web when I can't.* Miguel's face blushed for having been caught breaking the rule again.

"Well, then, what's the plan?" Karen interrupted the silence that was threatening to erupt in an argument there wasn't time to entertain.

"I'll go back to canvassing the sidewalks downtown," Miguel began. "You keep a look-out for her at home."

"Oh no you don't, mister." Karen was done taking a back seat. "I'm going out there too." She stopped Miguel's argument at the expression on his face, with her finger in the air. "Uh-uh-uh! Amelia and I will go together."

"What about Jojo?" Miguel argued.

"We're going to drop him off at the pool. He's a big boy now. He'll be fine. Let him enjoy the day Miguel, while we get this taken care of." There was no argument that would surpass all of Karen's points.

"Okay," Miguel capitulated.

"Alright!" Jojo jumped up from the table and shot up the stairs to change into his swim trunks. Miguel smiled half-heartedly at Amelia who hadn't been able to get a word in edgewise. If she was thinking something to him, he wasn't going to get it, the estrogen in the room was already overwhelming his senses to the point that he felt stuck between poorly performing elementary school boy and equally poorly performing teenager trying to get a girl to like him. Life seemed so much simpler when it was just him and Jojo.

After dropping Jojo off at the pool outside Amelia's condominium complex, Amelia took the back seat and let Karen sit up front with Miguel. The thirty minutes of sleep Amelia had managed to catch last thing in the morning were not enough to get her through the ride to Over-the-Rhine.

Miguel had insisted on driving Amelia's Mercedes following a lengthy discussion on whether the car would be safer from break-ins in front of his house or in Over-the-Rhine where they would at least be closer to the vehicle. He watched in the rear view mirror as Amelia's head bobbed from shoulder to shoulder as she rocked in and out of sleep. Karen was still going strong, acting like a bizarre noise machine keeping the interior of the car filled with constant sound. Amelia wasn't hearing any of it. She was fast asleep.

Pause, pause, pause...

"Isn't she beautiful?" Maximian whispered over his shoulder as he peeked through a window to watch the princess gathering offerings of precious gems and beautiful clothes. Malchus frowned at Maximian's fixation of the princess with disgust.

Amelia connected the pair with the word "chauvinist" on her dream list. *Oh good,* she thought, *I was afraid that was for Miguel.* She peeked over Maximian's shoulder and looked at the princess. *Double good,* she added, *'princess' is not a pet name for Miguel's secret girlfriend.* Amelia frowned at the thought of the unnamed woman Jojo saw Miguel watching from an alley then turned her attention to the scene into which she had entered without benefit of her usual seat at an auditorium webinar. *That's strange,* she thought, *maybe I am getting better at this.*

"You shouldn't stare like that," Malchus chastised Maximian. "She is more than beautiful. The princess is brilliant." Amelia snapped out of her wandering thoughts.

Pay attention, if you don't figure out the link with these two you'll have to keep on visiting them. Amelia was certain there was a connection between the pair and Ardin.

121

"She is gorgeous, exotic, and perpetually young!" Maximian's words almost slurred with drunkenness over her beauty. Amelia rolled her eyes at his lusty regard for such a young girl. Amelia followed the thread to the first time she visited the scene, it had been nearly two months since the pair had arrived in the courtyard.

Maximian and Malchus had found it impossible to reveal themselves to the people of the kingdom even after they found them to be peaceful and kind. The pair had imagined themselves a fairly opulent dwelling just outside the courtyard without being detected. Amelia imagined their invisibility to the villagers was due to the fact that they were from a different time.

Amelia was determined to find out what the common thread was between the two young Greeks and herself. She set her intent to stay on the thread of the two men to learn more about their activities and the possible connections.

"Do you think we have died yet?" Malchus asked Maximian.

"No. If we were dead, we would have to move on to heaven," Maximian decided. "When we can't be here anymore, then we are probably dead." Maximian turned away from Malchus and looked back through the window to investigate something he perceived in the courtyard. "Uh-ohhh."

"What?" Malchus joined Maximian as he went outside and peered through a lilac bush to see what was happening with the princess.

"Visitors." The two men watched as a group of monks and sages approaching the princess who bowed with respect.

"What do you think they want?" Malchus didn't sound as if he liked the monks very much. Amelia honed in on his thoughts and felt his dislike for the way the monks talked down to the princess about her spiritual prospects. He felt the princess's faith rivaled any he had seen among the Christian martyrs, whether they were women or men. The monks who attended to the princess acted like they were being helpful, but Malchus felt all they ever seemed to focus on was her shortcomings as a woman. He wished he could help her gather her offerings as it seemed the more the monks criticized her, the harder she worked to prove them wrong.

"I think they want her, just the same as any sane man would wish." Maximian's comment irritated Malchus, and drew Amelia out of his thoughts. Teasing Malchus was one of the few pleasures Maximian could enjoy in his dreamlike state.

"Maximian, you will surely go to hell for your disrespect!" Malchus scolded.

"But I'm not of this world," Maximian argued.

"Have you not learned a thing by watching her practice her faith all this time?" Malchus pushed Maximian as though he was trying to knock some sense into him.

"I am not watching her faith!" Maximian growled and pushed back.

"There is but one faith!" Malchus tried to stay on topic.

"That of my Lord, not this girl!" Maximian temporarily redirected his attention to his religion. "Are you defecting to her dharma and losing your faith, Malchus? Because you're not dead yet and you can go to hell just as easily as I can." Maximian warned.

"But the Lord said we were all one. Why can she not be one with us?"

"I would love to be one with her," Maximian let his side of the discussion deteriorate once more.

Malchus slugged Maximian and wrestled him to the ground. Both men grimaced at one another holding their breath as they exerted pressure in ever tightening grips. In the silence of that rough and tumbled embrace of aggravation and frustration, the two men could hear the monks complete their business.

"Therefore Princess Yeshe, we will mentor you in the formation of your next lifetime so that you may be reborn as a man and attain Buddhahood."

Malchus and Maximian rolled over onto their stomachs and peered beyond the trunk of the lilac to see the ministers looking very pleased with their teaching.

"Kind sirs," both Malchus and Maximian melted at the soft sound of the princess's voice. "I have listened patiently to your admonition that I aspire to be born again as a man so that I may attain the highest levels of spiritual development."

"Shit, don't tell me," Maximian lamented, "she's going to turn into a man. It wouldn't be the same."

"Shut up!" Malchus smacked Maximian in the back of the head slamming his chin into the dirt. Amelia felt a stroke of victory every time Malchus corrected Maximian.

The princess went on, "However, Holy Ones, I refuse to agree to such a ridiculous suggestion." Maximian smiled with relief as the monks and sages started to tremble at the impudence of the princess who seemed to be growing more vivacious as she continued her discourse.

"I intend to be born again, but not in the manner, or for the reasons you have prescribed. I will come again and again until all sentient beings may freely experience nirvana, and I will become a Buddha, but I will do it all as a woman." Amelia jumped with excitement at the princess's boldness.

"YES!" Maximian shouted and Malchus pounded him with a stone knowing the cheer was for lustful reasons.

The monks and ministers drew themselves into poses of arrogance and judgment as the princess finished her declaration with a short bow to the monks. She turned abruptly and left them standing alone in the forest.

"What the hell is a Buddha anyway?" Maximian's chin rested in the dirt as he watched the ministers also leave the scene.

"It is like the Christ." Malchus began to explain. Amelia got a feel for the way Malchus had been hovering around the monks as they taught the princess. While he learned about the religion that seemed closely connected to her karmic studies, Amelia saw Malchus come to the conclusion that the princess was teaching her teachers more than they were teaching her. He was impressed with her humility as she didn't lay claim to the knowledge she was imparting. The princess was pure and without egoic complication.

"Nothing other than the Lord can be like the Christ." Maximian dismissed the comparison Malchus made.

"Are you saying you don't believe she can accomplish her goals?" Malchus wondered if the princess's aspirations had finally alienated Maximian.

"Oh trust me, she could accomplish her goals, but she needs to find out what they are." Maximian did nothing to hide his lingering sentiment for the princess. "Beautiful women can serve a man, but they shouldn't seek to be served. I lust after her in a way that could keep me out of heaven. But there is no way in hell the things she aspires to do are possible."

What a pig! Amelia swatted at Maximian wishing he could feel the slap of her hand.

"I believe she can." Malchus felt his heart swell with love and support for the princess's mission. "She doesn't seek to be served like a man... like you do!" Malchus took the towel wrapped around his waist like and apron and threw it at Maximian. Clearly Maximian was continuing to expect Malchus to cook and clean for him. "I believe the princess Yesha Dawa can accomplish her goals, and I would go to my death protecting her right to pursue her faith."

"And I'd bet my life that you won't ever have the opportunity, because she's going to forget all about it, Malchus," Maximian bantered back. "Eventually she will be distracted, just like those monks have said! She's just a woman. Take her for what she is."

The area behind the bushes went quiet as Malchus delivered food to Maximian and the pair silently sat on the ground and ate. Amelia listened to their thoughts and considered how her own faith had diminished over the years as Malchus sought to reconcile his feelings about the princess with his faith.

Malchus believed the princess was better able to fulfill the teachings than any man and reasoned that this was why she would be able to return again, just as the Lord had promised he would. As far as men went, Malchus had to agree with Maximian, there was but one Lord. But he also agreed with the man who sat in the big chair inside the temple. To Malchus, Yeshe Dawa was a goddess of extraordinary potential and Amelia agreed.

Amelia's eyes opened as the Mercedes rolled across the cobblestones near the place where Ardin had disappeared. Miguel was smiling at her in the mirror wondering what she might have dreamed. As usual, so was Amelia.

Pause, pause, pause...

At nine-years old, Jojo didn't understand adults much better than he did at the age of eight, but he had developed a conscience that kept him from thoroughly enjoying himself when others were not equally able to do so. Ardin had taught him that this was the way of the Bodhisattva. He liked the way she pronounced the word that Ardin had learned from Tetta. He couldn't wrap his tongue around it.

In some ways Ardin reminded Jojo of his mother. Like Ardin, Jojo's mother was very encouraging and forgiving. Since his mother lived in the Wait Zone, Jojo was able to see her only in his dreams, usually on special occasions. No matter what the occasion, Jojo would produce an etheric version of his report card to show her how good he was doing in school. To Jojo, both Ardin and his mother had a strange kind of inner glow that got brighter when they talked about the things that seemed important to them. Sometimes he checked his own dark skin to see if he glowed whenever he talked about football or Transformers, but those things didn't seem to have the same affect on him.

Jojo sat on the edge of the pool and watched his feet rise and fall with the waves as other children jumped in and played. Jojo had given up on the idea of trying to find Ardin with the grown-ups. They always seemed to make things so complicated.

On more than one occasion Jojo had awakened to find Amelia and Miguel furious over something he did in his dreams. Jojo always seemed to say something that would make Amelia look upset with Miguel, and there didn't seem to be any clear rules to indicate what he should say. On top of that, Amelia didn't always remember her dreams the way they happened and Miguel always seemed to be worried she would.

"Hey, Jojo! C'mon!" a boy who lived in Amelia's condominium building called from the water. Jojo barely seemed to notice as he got up and moved toward the chaise lounges that were lined-up poolside. As he wrapped his towel around his shoulders and lay back, Jojo peered deeply into the clear blue sky.

I know you're out there Ardin. Jojo waited for a reply. Jojo was sure he could find her easily. Ardin and Jojo often dreamed together. He knew all of their favorite places.

Jojo reached for his sunglasses from beneath his chair. Water from his swimsuit that had dripped through the chair danced and wiggled down the lenses as he placed the shades over his eyes and lowered the back of his chair. It didn't matter that the people in the pool were looking a little fuzzy; he wasn't going to be watching for very long.

Jojo closed his eyes and tilted his head back the way Galahad taught him to do in the Wait Zone. He set his intent to find Ardin and let his hands hang limp over the edge of the chair arms. In a moment, he was spinning through the ethers.

Jojo followed the theme of water from the pool to the river where he liked to rollerblade with Ardin on the Serpentine Wall. Jojo only dreamed places he knew and since he was only nine and hadn't travelled outside of Cincinnati, his venues were largely limited to places he liked to play locally. He really didn't know how to get to the place on Vine Street where Ardin disappeared, but he knew, as he listened to the waves of the Ohio River lapping at the concrete shore behind him, that the only place it could be was forward.

Jojo started scrambling up the sloping eighteen inch steps where people were starting to gather to watch the annual Labor Day fireworks explode over the river in one of the top ten public events in the country.

It's your birthday! Jojo sent Ardin another silent message as he arrived at the top of the Serpentine Wall. It had taken Jojo quite awhile to be happy that Ardin got fireworks on her birthday when he couldn't have any on his. Miguel said it would be dangerous for Jojo to try it himself.

Jojo knew that Ardin would never miss the birthday bash the city was about to throw for her. If he couldn't find her in Over-the Rhine, he would come back and start searching for her in the crowd that was sure to top 500,000 by nightfall.

Don't worry Ardin, Jojo thought as he pictured her sleeping in the big bed and sitting in a restaurant. *I'll find you and put you back together in time.*

Jojo crossed Third Street and found Vine Street in just a few minutes. Heading North on Vine, Jojo remembered Miguel repeating the intersection where Ardin had disappeared, Twelfth and Vine. Quietly in his head Jojo attempted the math to ascertain how long it would be before he arrived at the spot, while early arrivals for the fireworks occasionally bumped into him as the streets were beginning to fill.

With a flash of guilt, Jojo glanced around as if Karen Bradford might be keeping an eye on him, then he resorted to counting the difference on his fingers. Waiting for the walk signal at Fifth Street, Jojo surmised it would be seven streets before he made his destination. He wasn't sure what he would do when he arrived.

Jojo allowed himself to be distracted from his mission by the activity on Fountain Square. A large screen was showing images of the Serpentine Wall at Sawyer Point which was quickly filling up with blankets as people claimed their space for the big show at 9:00pm. Jojo thought of how his stepfather, Darius, used to take him to the fireworks, though he barely kept track of the boy. Sometimes Jojo would get lost and one time it took hours for police officers to locate Darius. When they did, Darius was put in jail and Jojo went to a foster home.

Jojo startled out of his memories and looked up at the beautiful copper woman who was at the center of the fountain in the square. She seemed to be looking directly at him as she gazed down over the water. She reminded him of his mother, the first time he saw her in the Wait Zone after she died. Jojo felt his eyes sting and he drew a quick breath as the walk signal changed and he continued up Vine Street.

At Eighth Street, Jojo passed the Main Public Library.

"Dude, wassup?" a tall boy in a group of gangsta' wannabes called after Jojo as he passed and kept his eyes on the sidewalk as he walked faster. In the space between Central Parkway and Twelfth Street, Jojo's heart started to race. He had forgotten that he had once lived on this street. He had not realized that the memory of the shooting that would take his mother away would come through in vivid detail through the dreamscape.

In his waking life, Jojo had no recollection of the incident. He was only two when it happened. Darius had often told him that he had been standing right next to his mother when she took a stray bullet in the doorway of their apartment building. Whenever Darius recounted the event, his voice changed and it sounded as if he blamed Jojo in some way.

Jojo started running as Darius' voice chased after him on the sidewalk. He thought he also heard his mother's voice faintly gasp his name as he saw her take her last look at him in his mind's eye. The sound of police sirens filled his head and Jojo felt himself crying like a baby deep inside his heart. His feet pounded to a stop and his hands wrapped around his ears. Jojo was having a nightmare in his dream, and had no idea how to change channels.

"Jojo?" A gentle finger rested on his shoulders followed by a hand that instantly felt soothing. The noise and images that were wreaking havoc in Jojo's imagination quieted and the boy opened his eyes to see the pretty waitress from the coffee shop.

"Are you okay?" Trisha actually felt some compassion for the boy who was so thoroughly suffering she had to get out of his thoughts due to the vicarious pain she was experiencing.

Jojo's features were tense as Trisha took hold of his other shoulder. He was stiffly leaning back. His dazed stare caused her to give him a little shake.

"No!" Jojo raised his arms and knocked Trisha's hands free from his shoulders. "Don't touch me!"

Trisha let go and carefully backed away, afraid the boy might hurt her. She could see that he didn't seem to see her. Jojo stood still for a moment, his chest heaving in great pangs of tears that never made it to his eyes. Then, without much indication he would do so, Jojo took off running so fast Trisha could only follow him with her eyes until he rounded the corner at Twelfth Street.

Nick stepped out of the alley and joined Trisha near the corner of Twelfth and Vine. "What did you get?"

"Nothing." Trisha touched her temples gently with her fingertips. "Except a migraine."

"Couldn't you get in?" Nick didn't trust Trisha and she could tell.

"He was having a nightmare Nick. All I saw was you, and the kid's mom." She felt Nick shrink back in resistance to the memory he knew so well himself as he had been there that day, in the midst of a heated exchange of gunshots between gang members and the police. He hadn't seen the boy. He couldn't have guessed Tonya Lovelle would step through the door to try to rescue him. Nick had acted in self defense, but that didn't change the lifelong affects of the incident.

Trisha let up on the memory of the frightening scene and remembered something she thought might prove helpful. "This is it, Nick."

"What?" Nick was feeling shell shocked. It was easy to forget his past life in the afterlife, only to have it come up again without being prepared. He imagined that was his personal Hell.

"This is where the girl was last seen before she disappeared. This is where she was taken."

Nick regained a little awareness as he processed the possibility of finding a thread back to Ardin. He tilted his head back and felt around for clues thinking the name, *Ardin.* Better than sifting the memories of a drunk from the etheric plane to waking consciousness, Nick was able to tap directly into the memory of Ardin. Instantly, Nick felt the coldness that enfolded her as she was unable to get the door open. Then quite unexpectedly, Nick also felt a large man slide into the scene and catch Ardin's body as she fainted. A loud bang blasted Nick off the thread and he opened his eyes in time to catch Trisha also getting bounced off the trail.

"Damn migraines." Trisha started rubbing her temples and pretended she hadn't been spying on his connection.

Nick slipped his awareness into his heart space, knowing Trisha had no awareness whatsoever of her own heart and would not be able to sense his distrust for her or any theories that might arise from this new information. As far as he could tell, Decius hadn't even been present when the girl disappeared. Someone else had beaten Decius to the punch. Quietly, Nick contemplated the image of the young girl and wondered what she could have that was so attractive to more people than just the slimy Roman Emperor he had met in a bar in the Dark Side.

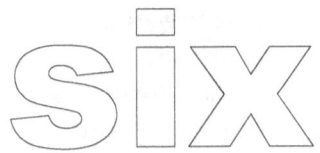

Reunions and Defections

Pluto the Lord of the Underworld was having the time of his life. Although he didn't really have a life, Pluto had believers. Every culture had gods, demigods, and demons believed into being by various cohorts within each culture. The gods served the needs of the people, though it appeared the other way around. Through the invention of the gods, humans established authoritative explanations for the values of the community, how they were established, and what would happen to anyone who went against the acceptable protocol.

Once believed into being however, the gods were not limited to the reasons they were born on the thoughts of men, which always kept things interesting. For decades Pluto and his ilk had been piling up a treasure of bad business practices by infiltrating the dreams of investors, regulators, and policymakers, luring them with desire and greed.

Pluto incorporated the latest technologies, setting up virtual trading floors in the underworld where he trained and advised those who gave in to his temptations, all from the comfort of their own dreams. He implemented every bit of evidence he could amass that there was every reason to behave in ways which otherwise might have been considered irresponsible and unfair to future generations.

Through news of global warming and rumors concerning the Mayan calendar, Pluto had been able to convince many that the world would not last long enough to truly experience the devastation such greed and hoarding would cause. In a single moment, all of Pluto's plans were fulfilled. In a well orchestrated moment of exactly calculated pros and cons, someone cried "wolf" and brought about a mass panic which shifted the same system that had been doing the same thing for more than fifty years into a riotous tizzy.

The confidence necessary to keep the monstrous economy that conceived consumerism on the back of selling out industry and extolling the virtues of egoism, was undermined and the fear spread like wildfire among investor, creditor, business owner, and Wal-mart customer alike. The dollar was weak, gold was rising, major players were toppling, and Pluto was laughing all the way to the *under*world bank. He was thriving on the fears that were as valuable an asset as any for a god believed into being.

The skeleton-filled closets of every politician who was on the take were technically, as a closet, under the jurisdiction of, and benefit to the underworld. Every time a government official was doubted, Pluto grew stronger. The sudden news that the economy was in ruins had caused the closets to be emptied more suddenly and Pluto was swimming in the riches born of greed and conceit.

And that was just the beginning. With fear unchecked, Pluto had freely conjured one failure after another to maintain the cycle of fear which caused humanity to worry for fear that they would be worried if they did not worry.

"It is genius, pure genius!" Pluto complimented himself as he watched reruns from the earliest moments of the crisis. He laughed out loud as he watched the Treasury Secretary sweat during congressional hearings.

"Yes Lord, pure genius." A small troll-like character dressed in a red toga placed a platter with a large goblet filled with wine before the lord of the Underworld. Under the platter, the surface of the table appeared like a flat screen monitor. The frenzy that had been set loose in the world appearance unfolded in high definition color as the tabletop played it like video trailers for newly released movies.

"The drama is delicious, and the comedy is hilarious!" Pluto pointed as a newsman chased a member of the Federal Reserve under the platter. "Look Decius, they are so afraid." Pluto licked his lips and made a slurping sound as his own spit was sucked back inside his mouth. "Vermin." Pluto chuckled.

Decius tried not to take Pluto's dismal view of humanity personally even though he was an ancestor of said vermin. Choosing to make a compliment to some of those who had successfully delivered the infrastructure for Pluto's success, Decius tried to point out some promising human contributions to the event. "I'd say the Secretary did pretty well."

"Idiot," Pluto snorted. "He was an idiot!" Pluto looked up in time to see the look of frustration on Decius' face. While it was more possible that Pluto would smash anyone in his presence that showed the weakness of wanting validation, the god attempted to compliment Decius in recognition of the good work the former emperor had accomplished.

135

"But he was the perfect idiot, and we have you to thank for that." Decius had studied the system masterfully and become adept at crossing the aisle to draw legislators over to Pluto's camp. He had developed the ability to cross between planes disguised as highly respected financial advisors and powerful investors, and convinced the CEOs of big banks and analysts to recommend and take the huge risks that were currently backfiring on them.

As Pluto's thoughts turned to the ingredient so very crucial to finalizing the formula for his potpourri of decadent delight, the flat screen coffee table morphed and zoomed in on an image of a young girl.

"Is everything in order?" Pluto drummed his heavy fingertips on the table screen.

"She is secure and oblivious, Lord," Decius reassured Pluto.

"Good." Pluto rarely used the word. He tilted his head back and looked down his long crooked nose into the restaurant scene. "Make sure you keep it that way." Pluto adjusted a wreath of leaves atop his head as he observed the girl. "What did you say they call her?" The Lord of the underworld dialed down the temperature and refocused his attention on the teenager.

"Her name is Ardin, you know, a variation of green." Pluto ignored the research Decius had poured into finding the girl.

"As in the green of money," Pluto slobbered. Decius rolled his eyes the way an underappreciated wife regards her husband when he ignores her good housekeeping.

"Did she dream all this up?" Pluto wasn't accustomed to entertaining his captives in restaurants.

"Yes Lord, she's quite good at manifesting whatever she sets her mind on."

"Make sure she doesn't set her mind on going home. She stays right here and nobody gets through." Pluto ordered.

"With her there, I am free to wreak havoc on the Earth, and I am ready for a great time." Pluto slid his finger across the screen wiping out the image of Ardin as the screen filled with thumbnail images of financial reports from around the world.

"The world economy has been a party. I can't wait to see this through." Pluto roared with laughter as he poked a thumbnail of Wall Street and the scene filled the screen.

Decius tried to hide the fact that he was feeling increasingly underappreciated and undercompensated for his efforts. It was only because he had put in the last 1800 years studying and trying one thing after another to gain the girl's trust that Pluto was finally able to enjoy the benefits.

"Lord?" Decius interrupted, "How long do you think such devastation can go on before other gods and demigods develop an interest in shutting down the melee?"

"What?!" Pluto stood and towered over Decius wondering what news the emperor was revealing. "What do you know about who would be so stupid as to shut this down?"

"I don't know anything Lord," Decius defended. "I'm just saying, the noise and all the complaining is sure to irritate someone and they might wish to drown it out they way they did with the great flood." Decius tried again as Pluto failed to relax his position. "The scientists say the earth is overdue for such destruction."

"This *is* a flood, Decius," Pluto dismissed the concept. "If it continues, they will annihilate themselves, so there is no need for concern." Pluto sat on the couch and started flipping through images as the heat in the room reduced to a simmer. "Emperor, it's time you get back to work!" Decius jumped to standing from his nearly kneeling position on the floor.

"Yes Lord." Decius replied and bowed repeatedly as he backed out of Pluto's chamber.

Pause, pause, pause...

Ardin picked up the pot that held hot water for her tea and felt its emptiness as the pot rose higher in the air than expected. Looking around for the waitress from her booth in the diner, she noticed that the place was empty. She had missed the din of business as it died down around her. Ardin stood up to see if she could find someone to fill her teapot.

"Can I help you?" Ardin turned to the tune of a voice that didn't quite match the face that greeted her.

"Tetta? Where have you been?" Ardin sat down in her seat. "I've been waiting and waiting for you."

"Well, there are a lot of details to be taken care of my dear. And I am of course observing your progress."

"I've been doing great up until now." Ardin frowned. "All of a sudden, things seem to be slowing down."

"Okay, let me help." Tetta picked up the teapot and poured a fresh cup for Ardin and filled a second cup for herself.

Ardin felt comforted by Tetta's appearance. She had been fixated on the learning more about the rite of passage she was sure she was there to accomplish. "Is it time?" Ardin asked, half afraid that if it was time, she might not be prepared to demonstrate the abilities needed to make the passage.

"Time for what?" Tetta asked. Then, seeing the concerned look in Ardin's eyes, corrected herself, "Oh not just yet, Dear." Tetta smiled, but Ardin didn't feel reassured.

"People here aren't able to be able to see me, Tetta." Ardin started to explain how she had been spending her time under the Banyan tree trying to boost visitor's attitudes. "Is this a sacred place?"

"One of the most sacred places in the universes." Tetta glanced back at Ardin and nodded. "It's good that they don't see you. Kudos on the ability to remain invisible." Ardin thought of blue bunnies to cover the thought that she hadn't been trying to be invisible and hoped Tetta didn't find out her invisibility wasn't a skill but an inability to be seen.

"They don't have to see you," the still strange voice reassured Ardin. "Just work on bringing them peace as you encounter them." Ardin nodded.

"Tetta, do you have a cold?" Ardin asked with hopes that she could help and make some extra credit for her test.

"I don't have much time to visit today." Ardin was surprised as Tetta stood up and began to conclude her visit. "But I am always present, keeping track of you." She magnanimously waved her hand toward Ardin. "You will stay here until the time is come."

Ardin sought to clarify the instruction. "I will return here every night?" Ardin wondered if she would be through the rite of passage by the time new classes started in the Wait Zone.

"Day and night," Tetta clarified. Ardin frowned as her guru uncharacteristically swiped her arm under her nose and rubbed at an itch.

"I will be sleeping all day and all night?" Ardin wondered how Karen Bradford would allow her to sleep all day and night.

"Yes," Tetta said forcefully, looking deep into Ardin's eyes, "it has been arranged. It will be alright. Just trust me."

Ardin studied the lady guru's grey eyes. Something seemed different but she couldn't figure it out. Not wanting Tetta to register her doubt, Ardin bounced her attention off thoughts of blue bunnies to keep her mind from being afraid.

Tetta was Ardin's most beloved teacher. She had introduced Ardin to the Wait Zone before she was able to walk. Ardin had always been able to understand think-speak, even before she could talk. Tetta would sing the Vedic hymns to Ardin through her thoughts. Even as a teenager, Ardin preferred thought-song to verbalization unless, of course, she was listening to her favorite waking life band.

139

All in all, Ardin lived a fairly well-balanced dual existence as waking teenager and dreaming seeker on the path. Tetta always commented that Ardin didn't need to learn, she needed to remember. Ardin believed the rite of passage would connect her with her memories. One thing Ardin had never been able to do was remember any past lives, or even the circumstances of her birth in this life. It never seemed to bother Tetta. Tetta had simply insisted that Ardin was different and that what was most important was for Ardin to be a good student.

"Ardin?" Tetta's voice peeked through the fog in which Ardin had become engulfed. "Ardin!" The girl's deep thoughts about Tetta stopped suddenly. "You are going to be just fine. I must go now, but I will return in good time."

"When will you be back?" Ardin asked quietly.

"Soon enough." The words failed to reassure Ardin. "This is a special time for reflection, dear. You must do this on your own."

"What must I do, Tetta? Why am I so special?" Ardin had never heard of anyone else going through a rite of passage in the Wait Zone.

"Ah, my dear, this fear of the unknown is ego driven. Contemplate this, and be patient until our next session." In a flash of sparks and smoke, Tetta disappeared.

Ardin blinked and sniffed the smoke as it dissipated in the diner. *That's new,* she thought.

Looking around at the empty diner, Ardin imagined the reason no one was around was because it was waking time for most people. She stepped outside and imagined a small hut where she could take a nap. As Tetta had instructed, Ardin set her intent to dream within her dream rather than return to waking life. She liked dreaming while she was dreaming. The plots and potential were doubly good.

Ardin heard the song of a nightingale as she slipped onto the small cot she imagined was appropriate for a seeker sleeping under a sacred Banyan tree. Ardin was grateful for the company of such lovely music as it resonated in her mind.

Pause, pause, pause...

In a fit of smoke and sparks, Decius threw himself off the vortex to arrive at his favorite bar on the dark side. Decius slid through the door and approached the bar that came up to his chest.

"Give me a Mavrodafni, Mac." Decius ordered a glass of Greek wine that was similar to Portuguese Porto. The bartender rolled his eyes at Decius and waited for the former emperor to change his order. The bar was on the dark side of the Wait Zone and served only common stock and otherwise distasteful combinations of liquor.

"Okay, I'll take a shot of Ouzo." Decius often dragged out the ordering process thinking he was making the bartender look like an idiot. "And a beer." Decius rubbed his hand over his face, comforted by the presence of his close cut beard.

The bartender set the shallow mug of beer on the counter and put the shot of Ouzo next to it. Decius liked to think he was a superior being, but everyone in the bar knew he was a bottom feeder at heart. Decius picked up the shot glass and dropped it into the beer creating an explosion of suds as he eagerly gulped licorice tainted brew.

Bleck, the bartender observed.

"Don't knock it until you've tried it," Decius retorted and took his mug from the counter to a small table in the corner. He needed time to think, and he was running out of it. If the plan was to be fulfilled before midnight, he needed to figure out how to get the rest of the package. As long as some portion of it remained in the 3-D world, the deal would not go through and then, he was fairly certain, Pluto would eradicate any evidence of him ever having existed, sending him to the sub-basement of the worst imaginings any human ever held for their version of Hell.

"I've been thinking about you Decius." The chair on the other side of the tiny table pulled back and Nick sat down.

"Do I know you?" Decius looked at Nick suspiciously.

"Nick, Nick Green. Remember me?" Nick held out his hand and accepted Decius' small hand with short fingers into a warm if not bone breaking grip. "I have a feeling you weren't too successful with your little venture to secure a certain fifteen year old girl. What happened?"

"You must be mistaking me for someone else." Decius kept his eyes from meeting Nick's as he tried to figure out when he could have met this man. He didn't remember the night in the bar, when, in a drunken stupor he had spilled the plans for abducting Ardin and taking over the world. He had been working on it for fifteen years, from the moment the girl had been reborn into the waking life.

He had watched and waited as Tetta earned her trust and went about the same work she had always done, coaching the girl how to keep fear at bay, and help humanity elevate their prospects through levity and selfless service.

This was the perfect time for things to turn out one of two ways. Either the girl would accomplish her goal under the most difficult of circumstances, having been born into the consumerist culture of the western world, or she would fail and hardship would endure.

"I hear you Decius, but I think Pluto isn't going to enjoy hearing the news from me." Nick was bluffing his way to success as Decius was sure Nick, whoever he was, knew of the plan. Nick pushed back from the table spilling a little of the Ouzo over the rim of Decius' glass as he rocked the table.

"Wait." Decius was thinking fast, which for him was a major undertaking. "I don't know where you got the idea that I don't have the package, but I have it right where I want it." Decius hoped Nick would disclose more about what he knew, but Nick kept it short.

"I really don't think so," Nick reasserted his position. "If I'm wrong, Pluto will have me whacked." Nick curtly tilted his head and let his eyes burn into Decius. "And if I'm right, we'll be watching you get toasted on the spit."

Decius caved. "Who are you and what do you want?!" He growled in low tones that could only be discerned through the mug of ouzo fizzy draft beneath his slitty lips.

"Why, I want to help you, Emperor." Nick shrugged. "That's all."

"How can you help me?"

"You tell me." Nick played his last card. He bet the emperor would pick it up. Once in with the other cards Decius seemed to be holding, Nick would be able to discern the usefulness of working with Decius. If the emperor really had nothing, then Nick could leave him to Pluto and move on. But if Decius knew who had the girl, then he would play along, long enough to find her and then steal her for his own.

"How much time do you have?' Decius picked up the card.

"I got all night, Emperor." Nick leaned forward resting his elbows on the table.

"That's about what I'll need." Decius glanced right then left partly to make sure their conversation was secure, partly to make sure no other helpful hacks were going to come crawling out of the woodwork.

"So what's the story, Decius?" Nick wanted to push things along so he could get home before Trisha got suspicious.

"I'm finished with Pluto." Decius took a hard right from the direction he thought he was going. "I have the girl and he is absolutely clueless as to her whereabouts. I want what's due to me, and I will compensate you quite well for your assistance in getting it."

Neither of the two men breathed while each observed and calculated the galvanized texture of the other's energetic field. Neither was letting anything slip. It was a draw, and until one of them blinked or both agreed to work together, neither was leaving and the conversation was going nowhere.

Pause, pause, pause...

When he got home from the bar, Nick found Trisha sleeping off her migraine on the couch in the solarium. Quietly he opened the desk drawer and pulled out a piece of note paper and a pen, looking over his shoulder to make sure he wasn't disturbing her. He knew she had become a liability in his plan to become a hero. He needed to throw her off, make her think he was continuing to work with her on the plan to find Ardin first. Nick reasoned it was eye for an eye payback after Trisha deceived him in their previous life together. *I'll be rid of her once and for all.* He thought.

The hell you will. Trisha kept her thoughts close to her chest as she listened from behind a one-way shield she had learned to construct at a webinar.

In his note, Nick explained he was going to hook up with Miguel and see what his former partner may have found in the last few hours, and promised he would be home around midnight. He placed the note on the desktop and faded from

144

view. Trisha kept her eyes closed and locked on to his thread as Nick flew through the ethers to a physical address in Over-the-Rhine.

The room into which she peered through Nick's mind's eye was dark and drab. Under a blanket on a high bed with an iron frame, lay the sleeping body of a teenage girl. Trisha agreed, as Nick surmised, that the girl was Ardin.

Suddenly Trisha felt Nick's throat constrict as he began to gasp for air. The image of a face, gnarled with age and decay moved into view. The face was as ancient as the cliffs in the Grand Canyon, etched with lines that ran so deep, the man's eyes were barely discernable. His lips parted and revealed a stench that Trisha could hardly bare.

Trisha felt herself starting to choke and knew whoever this man was, he was seeing more than Nick, he was seeing her too. She struggled to disengage, sure that the man was going to kill Nick. Then, remembering that Nick was already dead, Trisha cut lose from the scene and sat up on the couch gasping for breath, losing all track of Nick.

It was still difficult for Trisha to remember that everything was just an illusion. Had she not remembered that Nick's loss of breath was little more than a notion, she may well have allowed herself to be choked to death and could have been lost for a long time in the mirage of what she thought might follow. Trisha stood up and walked over to the bar where she imagined a bottle of rum and started to pour it to a mix of ice and Coke which magically appeared in a short glass in front of her.

I'd rather be dead right where I am, she thought. Trisha appreciated the way the quality of life in the Wait Zone, although completely imaginary, was often perfect, as the rum-laced carbonation of the drink stung at her nose and eyes just before it warmed her throat.

145

It was quite possible she had lost Nick. She sure as hell wasn't going back to find out and possibly wrestle with that creature again. He was huge, at least six feet tall, and decrepit. *Nick can have him,* she reasoned, *that's what he gets for stabbing me in the back.*

Trisha started to plot on the first drink, and three glasses later, thought she had a pretty good plan. Calculating her options it took practically no time for Trisha to come to the conclusion she needed someone bigger and badder than Nick, if she was going to get any of the benefits Nick believed were attached to rescuing the girl before anyone else could have her. But unlike Nick, Trisha wasn't interested in becoming one of the good guys. She knew who she had to see, and being careful to positively apply her imagination to her devious plot, Trisha believed she would easily be able to persuade him to collaborate with her.

Pause, pause, pause...

Someone has got to know something, Max thought as he bent over a low table to center a bowl of fruit and a pitcher of ice tea centered among neatly laid out place settings of cup and saucer. He stood up and groaned. Max may have died young, but his body felt ancient. He wondered if it was the weight of the ever-mounting additional lifetimes he was mysteriously accruing as his Moksha Meter continued to decline that was making him ache. Of all the incarnations his jiva had entertained, Max had invited just three to help him sort out the problem: the comic Archie Armstrong, wise sage Narada, and, in Max's not-so-humble opinion, the incompetent idiot, Ted Galahad.

The setting was Turkish. Max had chosen it for its similarity to the palaces Archie and Narada were accustomed to while imagining Galahad would not be opposed to sitting around on pillows and smoking out of a bong. It was the best non-denominational scene he could imagine while still producing something more inviting than a picnic bench for the meeting. He had not seen his predecessor Narada, since he had first arrived in the Wait Zone.

Narada had been Max's greeter when he crossed over. The sage explained to him that every recently terminated life meets with a previous life attributed to the same Jiva. Of course, Narada also had to help Max understand that the Jiva was his name for what Max considered a soul. Max disagreed that it was the same thing, but they had decided not to let differences stand between them. Narada had shown Max the history out of which he had been born. Narada was a divine sage in the Hindu tradition. He explained how he had not understood his divine nature when he was born as the illegitimate son of a servant girl in an ashram. Narada explained that this was not a life he would have consciously chosen had he been given the opportunity. The lifetime was created after an irate king complained about Narada's inattentiveness in the king's Court.

"Actually," Narada had confided to Max, "I was plenty attentive, just not to the king." Max recognized the mischievous energy Narada emanated as similar to his own. "Those celestial nymphs were to die for," Narada had explained, "and I nearly did."

Max listened as Narada told the story of the rishis who visited the ashram when he was a boy. Narada was impressed by their wisdom and respectability. He wanted the same for himself. The sages stayed for a long time and taught Narada. After his mother died, Narada left the ashram and eventually became a divine sage himself. Though he maintained a bit of a reputation for causing trouble among the deities and demons,

Narada was able to stay out of trouble by always using the circumstances he created to teach and help others.

"That was my saving grace," Narada told Max. "Still is, as it was yours and several others who came from our Jiva. Humor, and plenty of it. That's what got us through, Max." Narada smiled. Max didn't understand how he could be born again as a Christian from a pagan in India. Narada had been very patient with Max as he explained that the same rishis who taught him how to be a sage, were Max's friends in Ephesus.

"That's impossible!" Max shouted as the egotistical walls that sheltered his belief that he was the one and only life his soul would ever know, were crumpling under the power of Narada's words.

"Not impossible, Max. But very important." Narada tried to reel Max in by letting him know his life did indeed have some unique features. "You see, Max, after we, the rishis and I, were all retired to the celestial plane, Christianity presented us with some questions we wished to have answered. And so it was that we explored the life of martyrs, to comprehend how."

"How... what?" Max didn't understand what Narada was talking about.

"How humans actually missed the meaning of the teaching." Narada eyed Max to see if he was just playing dumb as Max puffed up his ego and refused to accept that his life had been merely about exploring some misunderstanding. "The part about dying in order that you should have eternal life, Max. Did you really think being stubbornly attached to your beliefs and getting slain in the name of the Lord would win you a spot in heaven?"

"They were still working on the details," Max justified the changing scene of the second century mystic.

"Well, we didn't get it either since we saw the teaching as recommending *de*tachment," Narada clarified his position.

"But we were demonstrating our faith," Max defended.

"To us that is identifying with the ego," Narada countered, then went on to explain, "It doesn't matter Max.   You did perfectly well as one of the seven sleepers.   It's not important that you agree with me, though your experience was quite helpful to me.   I understand what you're saying, and I am grateful for your lessons."

Max had eyed Narada carefully as he processed the divine sage's explanation of reincarnation.   Narada had taught Max everything he needed to know to work with the Jiva to produce new life and welcome it home on its return like a prodigal son.   Of course Max was none too thrilled with either of the prodigy he had been responsible for greeting.   Archibald Armstrong was a lousy court jester in the 17th century and Galahad didn't seem to be able to get anything right.

Max had not taken much time to consider why he had been saddled with the responsibility of creating personalities who would compensate for the idiot factor in their Jiva. Today he was wondering that if he had been a little more considerate, might he not be in the mess he was in.

A gong sounded in Max's holographic scene and he went to the door to greet his first visitor. Being host to anyone felt a little awkward to Max, he was more the party animal than the party planner. He hoped his first visitor would be Narada, and that he would be able to help figure out if Galahad and Archie were part of the problem. Unfortunately for Max, the eyes that locked with his on the other side of the threshold belonged to Archibald Armstrong.

"Max, old boy." Archie glad-handed his way across the threshold pushing Max aside as he headed for the low table to see what food Max had prepared. "Fruit? Max, my friend, I believe a little scotch would be in order. It's been a long time. And what's with these digs, my friend. Don't you think a pub would be a better place to... to..." Archie Armstrong didn't know why he had been summoned away from his happy cottage on the cliffs of Dover. "...to do whatever it is we're about to do," he finished and looked at Max as if he thought he was some sort of a sissy. "You couldn't get a good fight going here," he complained.

"I don't want a fight," Max started to answer when the gong sounded again and he turned to answer the door.

"Well, you won't get anyfing out of me in this place any way you look at it!" Archie hollered to Max as he absentmindedly opened the door for Ted Galahad. Cigarette smoke wafted across the threshold and snapped Max out of his concern that Archie might leave before Narada arrived.

"Hiya' Max." Galahad seemed cordial though smelly.

"Welcome." Max stepped back and invited Galahad inside.

"What ya' cookin' Max?" Galahad asked in his upper crust accent that was neither too strongly American nor British. Max had forgotten how confused he remained about why subsequent manifestations of his Jiva tended to be western. He made a mental note to add that question to the list he had prepared for Narada.

Max turned around to see Galahad and Archie getting along just a little too well. He could tell they were conspiring, and as they put their wills together, the scene began to shift from one bar scene to another, eventually settling on a country pub filled with beer guzzling men.

"Hold on there!" Max walked over to the pair, still wearing his toga which was capturing the attention of a rather large man playing a game of darts. "No other guests," Max demanded. "Besides, they could kill me." His eyes darted around as several drunkards started moving in his direction.

"Alright," Galahad sighed and the crowd disappeared.

"Hey, wait a minute!" Archie started to complain, but Galahad wasn't too fond of the rough pub patrons either, so he sided with Max. "Alright, then," Archie consented, "a round for everyone, on the house." Archie poured himself a tankard of ale and hopped up on a bar stool.

"So, what's up, Max?" Galahad asked, just as the gong, which neither he nor Archie had remembered to turn off, sounded. Max walked briskly to the entrance of the pub and opened the door to Narada.

"What the hell?!" Archie exclaimed as Narada, dressed in silk pleated pants and a vest over a shirtless torso, entered the room. "It's a bloomin' genie!"

Max's eyes rolled as he greeted Narada, "Wise sage, thank you for coming." Narada looked around at the pub with a mixed look of dismay and confusion. "Their choice, Wise Sir," Max apologized.

"Hot Damn!" Narada exclaimed and waltzed into the pub to meet Galahad and Archie. "I've heard a lot about you boys, and you sure don't disappoint."

"But, wise sage?" Max was now wearing a look of surprise. "I had prepared a table of fruit and tea."

"What's up with you, Max? I do that everyday." Narada walked over to Max and laid a reassuring hand on his shoulder. "Relax Max, we can have our cake and help you too." Max gave up the notion that he needed to impress Narada and walked to the other side of the bar to start mixing a pitcher of Martinis while the unlikely threesome took their seats.

"Where'd you learn that?" Galahad happily waited for his drink to be poured.

"Some webinar," Max dismissed a potential conversation. "I guess you're wondering why I invited you all here."

"I imagine it is because of the devastation you have somehow brought to the Moksha Meter," Narada stated point blank.

"Perhaps." Max nodded as he poured the pitcher of martinis into three glasses. "And maybe I'm wondering if any of you have played a part in it." Max placed triple olive martinis in front of Galahad and Narada then picked up the third martini for himself while Archie manifested his preferred scotch straight up.

"Why would we have anything to do with it?" Galahad asked, "We never had that spiritual part you had." Galahad eyed the sage, "And his Eastern roots."

"Well, someone did something that changed the Moksha." Max clarified, "Not the downturn. I mean, there's a blip, a moment of improvement. Have any of you done anything out of the ordinary lately?" Max looked across the three faces to see if any registered a hint of knowing what he was talking about. Galahad's nose dived into his Martini glass.

"You?!" Max asked incredulously, bringing the attention of the other two on Galahad.

"What did ya' do?" Archie jumped down from his stool and walked to the other side of Galahad as if surrounding him, while Narada started in.

"What could you have done?" Narada waited for a response as Galahad's lower lip trembled with the knowledge that to share what he did would be simultaneously admitting he had not followed protocols.

"Never mind man," Narada advised. "We're not about to turn you in, we are already paying heavily for the buck that stops at Max." Galahad looked at Narada quizzically, "How does an ancient sage pick up such expressions?"

"Oh, I still show up in countless ways to the people of India, especially since they started taking on the outsourced work from the States. Turns out I have quite a good business acumen." Archie grabbed Galahad's collar.

"Okay, okay," Galahad surrendered. "I saw Jojo." He looked up at Max, thinking he was the only one in the room that would comprehend the error Galahad made, but Archie clenched the collar tighter.

"What the hell you peasant!" the former court jester yanked. "We're just starting to dig out from under your mistakes and you start setting up new ones when we're so far under we may never get out?"

"Wait," Max interjected. "Whatever he did with Jojo, helped."

The threesome of a different configuration silently looked at Galahad waiting for him to fill them in on the details. He shrugged.

"Okay," Max filled them all in on Burch's advice, "Burch told me that I needed to apply the Law of Similars if I was going to begin turning the Moksha Meter around. If we know what Galahad did, we can all do it and gain points back. The threesome continued to look at Galahad expectantly.

"I helped him?" Galahad doubted helping Jojo could be the cause. The threesome continued to wait silently until Galahad finally began to fill them in on seeing Jojo in the Wait Zone and helping him get on the web in search of his step sister. After he finished, the threesome continued to look at him with perplexed expressions on their faces.

"So, our Moksha got better," Narada began.

"By 0.01 percent," Max clarified.

"Because you helped a little kid across the ethers?" Archie finished the sentence.

"It doesn't make sense to me," Galahad replied. "I mean, having anything to do with Jojo should have gotten me in deep," he shuddered, "deep, trouble."

"Well then, what was it?" Max asked helplessly.

153

"I think it was the compassion Galahad exhibited for the boy." Narada sensed for the truth and nodded. "He was in need and Galahad tried to help. Yes, it feels like that's it."

"Just being nice, or being nice to Jojo?" Archibald asked.

"That, I cannot tell." Narada shrugged and finished off his Martini. He nodded at Max. "That was good."

"The Martini or the compassion?" Max sighed.

"Both," Narada replied.

"There's just one thing," Archie added, "if the Law of Similars, something I know a bit about as I have taken a few webinars from Merlin, is requiring *compassion* then that means whatever is turning our Moksha Meter to mud is *nice*. How the hell does that work?"

The four men looked blankly at one another. "Maybe it's not about being nice." Narada considered an alternative view. "Perhaps it has something to do with the boy?"

"So we should find him and see if it's niceness or Jojo that moves the Moksha," Max recommended.

Not wanting to seem as though he would take orders from Max, Galahad looked around nonchalantly ignoring the obvious.

"Galahad," Narada bridged the differences between the two men, "could you please take us to Jojo?"

"I'd be happy to, sire." Galahad overdramatized respect for Narada to spite Max as he tilted his head back to get a fix on Jojo while Archie ran around the bar and started pouring himself another scotch just as the four men faded from the pub.

Pause, pause, pause...

"I don't listen to little twits like you, now get out of my way and let me through!" The sound of Trisha Jennings

154

plowing through security distracted Pluto's attention from his flat screen coffee table. Pluto didn't really need security since he was the primary malevolent force in the region, but he liked having guards, and someone to polish his trident for him when he made appearances at important events.

Pluto squinted at the young blonde, wearing a low-cut blouse under a short jacket and matching black slacks, as she burst through the doorway to his game room.

"What could you possibly think was so important that you would sacrifice your life this very moment?" Pluto was willing to listen before he pointed his finger at her and blew Trisha into the next dimension.

"I have information about your plans to hi-jack a girl named Ardin," Trisha began.

"That's already been taken care of. You are a waste of time." Pluto started to point his finger and Trisha could see it smoking with sparks.

"Wait!" The finger hesitated for only a moment then continued to take aim. "You have been deceived. Decius does not have all of the girl." Pluto stopped drawing his finger and eyed the girl suspiciously starting to scan her consciousness. *You can scan all you want,* Trisha thought to him as he slid his mind around inside her slight figure, b*ut I'm happy to tell you what I know.*

"Who are you?" the Lord of the Underworld bellowed. "How do you know these things?" Pluto usually didn't do his own dirty work, but with Decius watching the girl, he decided to lay back and listen to the new arrival until his other henchmen recovered from her rude entrance.

"I am your new partner in crime," Trisha started to explain how she was a much more trustworthy accomplice that Decius but Pluto wasn't biting.

"My dear," Pluto dismissed Trisha's helpful act, "there is no way you could possibly have found me and gotten in here if you had one drop of innocence in that etheric body, so cut to the chase." Pluto sneered and shot his smoking fingertip into the air blasting a hole through the ceiling, revealing nothing but darkness above them.

"Okay, so I'm not so innocent, but I'm smart." Pluto huffed. "Your man Decius only got half the package. The rest is still 3-D and you can't fulfill your plan without it."

"Where did you get this information?" Pluto considered how insane the idea was that Decius would attempt to deceive him.

"Part of it comes from a boy who saw her, and part comes from the very man who has her now." Trisha felt Pluto try to follow the thread through her to where she had left Nick. "Wait a minute. I said I was smart. Do you really think I'll show you where before I know we have a deal?"

"What did this man look like?" Pluto asked skeptically.

"Damned ugly." Trisha allowed Pluto to surf the image of the face. *Not nearly as handsome as you,* she added in thought.

"Can it!" Pluto ordered Trisha to be silent. "I'm not buying cheap compliments." Trisha felt a little drag on her confidence that she would be able to make arrangements with Pluto and took a deep breath to help regain her strength.

Pluto was convinced Trisha believed she was speaking the truth, a rare activity in the Underworld. He scanned for a thread to Decius and was surprised to find his right hand man appeared to be out of the office. Tonight was the night. The plan had to be completed before midnight EST where the girl resided. If not, then millennia of waiting and the whole plan that had been put into motion would be wasted. Worst of all, Pluto's flat screen coffee table would be showing signs of economic recovery. That was something he just couldn't bare.

"What do you want?" The lord of the underworld was willing to listen to Trisha's ransom demands before he cracked open her psyche and took it without paying.

Trisha knew she could manifest all the riches she could imagine; she had always known that. But there was an element of power she had never grown tired of, and which, when she engaged it, made her feel like the most powerful person in the world. She believed that her response would not only catch Pluto off guard, but endear herself to the old bastard in the best way she knew of to get a man to put the world at her feet.

"I want to be your consort." The slobber that rose to Pluto's lips let Trisha know her dart had struck hard and, for the first time ever, she questioned the sanity of her decision.

Pause, pause, pause...

Following Jojo's thread was a bit of a bumpy ride for Max, Galahad, Archie Armstrong and Narada, especially since each had his own unique way of doing so. Nevertheless, they appeared, one by one, in Jojo's Over-the-Rhine dream just as he ran through Washington Park. The four men sat on the steps of the Music Hall looking like a combination of Greek statuary, a peculiar looking Buddha, and two homeless men. The sight stopped Jojo at the curb. The men watched as all of the worry and fear slid off the boy's shoulders when he recognized Galahad.

"Dumbo!" Jojo yelled and threw himself full throttle into Galahad's arms. Galahad looked at his peers as the boy refused to ease his gripping hug on the slacker beatnik wannabe. Max, Narada and Archie watched as Galahad's expression turned first to one of confusion then unexpected compassion as Jojo's shoulders heaved under the weight of heavy sobs and tears.

"There now," Galahad patted the boy's head then wrapped his arms around him and gave him a comforting hug pulling the boy onto his lap. "What's going on, my man?" Galahad looked down to see if Jojo showed any signs of easing up as he felt tears seeping through his linen shirt, as his three amigos looked on out of respect for the intimate moment.

"Sir Gala-," Jojo started the name into the director's belly.

"...had," he finished for the boy. "What is it?"

"I want my mom." Jojo looked up, still holding on to his friend for dear life.

"Well, now." Galahad cleared his throat and pulled the boy up so he could look in his eyes. "You know your mommy loves you." Galahad tried to sound reassuring. Jojo nodded, then sniffed. Galahad resisted showing any disgust for the snot that Jojo wiped from his lip and onto Galahad's shoulder as he repositioned his arms around his neck. Archibald Armstrong stifled a laugh as Jojo turned to check out Galahad's companions.

"Are they your friends?" Jojo asked, continuing to wipe his nose with his hand until Max produced a handkerchief from inside his toga and handed it to the boy.

"Yes, we are all friends here, Jojo," Max answered. "My name is Max. Is everything okay?" Max wanted to know what had happened to make such a small boy cry so hard. The Wait Zone was generally very supportive of its youngest visitors.

"I had a bad dream." Jojo explained his experience coming up Vine Street. "I have to find Ardin. It's her birthday today." Narada mentally nudged Max and sent him the image of their Moksha Meter.

"Just a moment Jojo, my associate has something he wants me to look at." Max closed his eyes and saw that the meter

158

showed a definite improvement coinciding with their arrival in Jojo's dream, then a second bump partway through the upward trend, which Max realized was when he helped by producing the handkerchief. *Perfect,* Max returned the thought to Narada, *but which is it, compassion in general or just with Jojo?*

In general. Narada pointed to the evidence. *You could have let Galahad struggle with the snot, but you had compassion for* him *when you produced the handkerchief. It's any of us demonstrating various forms of compassion including kindness or being helpful to anyone.* Max let go of his mental hold on the Moksha Meter and observed Galahad continuing to be kind to Jojo as Archie joined in with a couple coin tricks and a little juggling.

"Will you teach me how to do that?" Jojo asked.

"I thought you had to find your sister," Narada interrupted the fun and games.

"Can you help me look for her?" Jojo asked. The foursome checked in and agreed any help offered would be good for their moksha.

"Archie and Galahad will help you Jojo," Narada delegated the responsibility. "Max and I have something to do, but we'll check back later." In thought only, Narada gave Galahad a warning, *Our moksha is improving man, don't risk it with any stupid maneuvers.* Then to Archie he added, *Keep an eye on them and let us know if anything gets out of hand.*

Max looked at Narada quizzically; it seemed he was taking more than just a passing interest in Jojo.

"Okay," Jojo dropped off Galahad's aching knees to the steps and joined hands with him and Archie as he proceeded to lead them down the steps to the sidewalk. "I think we have to go back this way. I'll show you where she was last spotted."

Narada and Max waited as the threesome crossed the cobblestone street and started across Washington Park. "I think

159

it's time to check in with Tetta," Narada commented. Max winced. He knew Tetta would not be happy if she found him working on anything other than discerning what he had to do with the demise of the world economy.

"She'll think I'm just concerned about my moksha." Max protested.

"Well you are," Narada agreed, "but I'm sure there's a deeper connection. I don't know what it is, but it feels very old. I know Tetta will be able to help."

Max decided Narada held out what little hope he could grasp. That small measure of acceptance was all that was needed for Max and Narada to evaporate from the pavement leaving Jojo, Galahad and Archie on their own.

Pause, pause, pause...

The poster in Hrim's hand dissolved into thin air as he and Tetta listened to the story Narada and Max told of meeting with Jojo in his dream.

"How could we not know about this?" Hrim looked from Narada and Max to Tetta with a slight hint of skepticism in his eyes.

"What?" Max felt instantly defensive. "I'm telling you the truth, Hrim. This boy, Jojo was upset because his sister is missing and when we were kind to him, the Moksha Meter improved."

"I saw it too, Hrim," Narada supported Max's version of the story. "He's telling the truth Tetta."

"That's not it," Hrim corrected. "I'm not talking about the economy and the effects of compassion on your Moksha Meter." Hrim stopped and reconsidered. "Well, perhaps I am. There is a related situation. It appears you are telling us the worst possible thing has happened." Hrim turned toward Tetta. "Do you know where Ardin is?"

"I've been standing here trying, Hrim." Tetta's eyes pleaded for help. "The web isn't congested Hrim, it's blocked."

"Tetta, when was the last time you saw her?"

"Not for days." Tetta looked around, wildly turning and pacing and turning, as if Ardin might be hidden in the room. "It's my fault, Hrim. I am responsible for this!"

"Tetta..." Hrim took a step toward her, but the lady guru held up her hands refusing his compassion.

"No! She's my responsibility, Hrim! I have taken care of her for more than 2,000 years and I have lost her!"

"But, Tetta!" Hrim reached out again. Tetta dissolved at his fingertips. "Tetta, don't do this!" Hrim urged into the air after her, then dropped his hand into a clenched fist at his side.

"I've never seen Tetta like this, Hrim," Narada observed. "What is it about the girl that makes for such a disaster?"

"Think about it, Narada." Hrim suspected the Hindu sage would be able to figure it out for himself. "Her name is Ardin." Narada shrugged. "Translated it means Great Forest." Narada's eyes narrowed then opened wider.

"It can't be," Narada whispered in astonishment.

"Yes," Hrim nodded.

"In America!" Narada declared.

"Whaaaaat???" Max whined.

seven

Déjà vu

"Oh for Heaven's sake!" Karen offered vociferous back seat commentary from the passenger side of the car as Miguel navigated the SUV through the downtown streets filled with people on their way to the riverfront and ready to party all day through to the night. "Why don't the police put up barricades, Miguel?"

"Then we couldn't get through either, Mrs. ..." Miguel checked himself, "I mean, Karen." He looked at Amelia in the back seat and wished she didn't look as if she was enjoying the respite from her mother.

"Not across the streets, Miguel." Karen was sounding more and more stressed the more often Miguel had to apply the brakes. "They should put the barricades on the sidewalks to keep the people out of the streets!" Miguel looked

163

pleadingly into the mirror and locked eyes with Amelia who rolled her eyes.

"Where do you think we should start Miguel?" Amelia weakly attempted to empower Miguel's expertise over her mother's tendency to micro-manage.

"I think we should all go back to sleep and start over." Miguel was clenching his jaw. Amelia understood his dual meaning, but also felt the smack of his frustration over having to entertain others' opinions in his investigation.

"It's Ardin's birthday." The far away tone of Karen's voice uprooted the growing irritation between Miguel and Amelia. Karen didn't express sadness or disappointment very often.

"Mom, are you alright." Karen didn't answer and Amelia was pretty sure that meant she was on the verge of tears. Then again, her mother also became insufferably silent when she was angry and couldn't think of anything positive to say. Amelia caught Miguel's eye in the mirror and raised her eyebrow in a gesture expectant of some help from him with her mom. Karen tended to be demanding, but she also on occasion needed encouragement to keep up the fight.

"Karen," Miguel started in, "I'm not even sure she's in the neighborhood anymore. Perhaps she got a bus ticket and headed south like before?'

"No." Karen went no further.

"But Mom, if she has run," Amelia started.

"No," Karen said again. Then, turning, she addressed both of them in the best information-turned-ultimatum tone she could produce. "It's her birthday. Ardin would not run on her birthday, at least she would not run anywhere but here, to see the fireworks. Even if she didn't want to be with us," Karen took a breath and Amelia could see the possibility of rejection was tearing at her mother's heart, "she would not leave town." Karen made a fist and struck the armrest of her seat. "She's here, and if she's not on her way to the fireworks, then someone is keeping her away." Her lower lip trembled. Karen couldn't allow herself to think of the potential harm a fifteen year old girl could run into on the dark city streets. She threw open the door of the SUV, and slipping out of her seatbelt, landed at fourth and Broadway.

"Karen, get back in the car." Miguel shouted as Amelia's mother backed away and started to mix in with the crowds.

"Mom!" Amelia unhooked her seatbelt and was out of the car as Miguel watched her disappear from the rearview mirror.

"Amelia!" Miguel shouted, but she was lost in the crowds. Miguel stayed behind the wheel, unable to park and unable to move, and unable to get any cooperation from the two women in his life.

Miguel wished this had happened in the dreamtime so he could just abandon the SUV and go after Karen and Amelia, but it was 3-D life and he needed to find an open parking lot before he could even start to track the two women.

I could track them from the Wait Zone and continue my search from there. Miguel considered the possibility that he could monitor threads to Amelia and Karen while also trying to find Ardin's trail. *Damn! It sounds good. I wish Hrim or Tetta or someone could tell me what was best.*

Miguel thought about Karen's theory that Ardin wouldn't run on her birthday and wondered if it was possible that desire to be at the fireworks might help her awaken from the sleep Jojo described. *Damn, it's all too complicated!* Miguel wished he had taken more webinars like Amelia.

Pulling into the Alright Parking Lot at the corner of Main and Eighth Street, near the Justice Center, Miguel was glad it was one more cool day in the coolest summer the city had known in a long time. He parked and paid the attendant then returned to the SUV. Using the controls at his fingertips, he cracked the windows open and locked the doors.

Without a second thought, Miguel sent his awareness across the ethers to the Wait Zone while maintaining consciousness in the 3-D world as well. First he threw a thread to Karen. She was walking aimlessly now not only looking for Ardin, but Amelia and himself as well. He threw a thread to Amelia and found her looking pretty much the same as her mother.

Miguel set an intention to receive a message if either of them turned up any evidence and hoped it would work like receiving a text message. Then Miguel set an intention to locate Ardin and found himself banging against an etheric brick wall.

Okay then, let's try Nick. Miguel decided two heads were better than one, and since his was a little busy tapping the threads of two women, he figured he could use a little more testosterone on his side, even if it was only etheric.

Pause, pause, pause...

Amelia tripped over the electric wires that ran from a booth near the main stage at the public landing. She was wearing white Sketchers. *Just checking to make sure,* she thought, as she had often mistaken dreams for 3-D life in the past. Whenever the gold lamé shoes were on her feet, she knew she was dreaming. Amelia also never dreamed with Karen. Amelia guessed having her mom in her dreams would be a little like being Facebook friends with her. Amelia couldn't bear to imagine what embarrassing reminders and requests her mother could write on her wall.

Dreaming felt like one of the few places Amelia could get away from everything. She thought it would be the ultimate way to take free vacations. She sometimes daydreamed about visiting the hottest destinations. Of course, being able to remember when she had visited them would be helpful.

Amelia knew she had been dreaming a lot, and it hurt that she didn't seem to have anything to contribute. If she had been learning anything of value in the search for Ardin, she needed to get a grip on it.

The stage speakers blared and Amelia squinted at the crowd knowing there was little chance of finding Karen, and hoped her mother hadn't decided to notify the police of Ardin's missing status. Amelia hated the crowded environment that came with the annual fireworks. Even when she was the same age as Ardin, she had never enjoyed coming to the riverfront for the celebration as most of the spectacle was not in the air but on the ground as the crowd, weary of waiting and full of beer, became increasingly pushy and stubborn as they tried to keep the space they had claimed from latecomers who were trying to find a good spot.

The city had done its best to practically child-proof the fireworks by banning coolers and containers, but she preferred to view the fireworks from the comfort of her law offices where she used to hold a party every year. Those days were over when she moved her office home. From her condo on Erie Avenue, she might hear the booms, but not see even a hint of light in the sky. Last year, to please her mother, they rented a room at the Ramada Inn across the river, where they celebrated Ardin's first birthday with the family. She knew her mother was right. Ardin wouldn't miss the fireworks if she could help it.

Where the hell could she be? Amelia's thought of Ardin was answered loud and clear by a voice she had been longing to hear.

I'm afraid your question answers itself.

Tetta? Amelia ventured to converse in thought even though she couldn't figure out how it was happening.

"I'm right here." The robust character of Tetta's voice seemed flat, but it didn't stop Amelia from twirling on her heel and grabbing the lady guru almost before she could see her, as she simultaneously stumbled. She looked down at her feet and was surprised to see the gold lamé shoes firmly attached.

"I'm dreaming?" Amelia checked in with reality.

"Not exactly," Tetta corrected, "you are between planes." Amelia didn't know much about the transitional state of consciousness between waking life and the Wait Zone.

"Where have you been, Tetta? What happened?"

"Amelia," Tetta replied, "I have failed her."

"Tetta, Miguel said that guy was huge. You couldn't have stopped him. What have you been able to do since then?"

"What are you talking about?" Amelia was taken aback by the surprise in Tetta's voice as it turned suspicious. "What do you know about Ardin's disappearance?" Tetta demanded.

"You were there when she was taken."

"I should have been but I wasn't."

"But you were," Amelia insisted, and then remembering that Miguel got his information from a drunk, she added, "You hit him with your cane."

"What cane? Amelia, I don't need a cane!" Tetta held out her hands in frustration. "Please Amelia, tell me what you know!"

"Okay, calm down." Amelia ducked her head to catch the soft brown eyes of the somewhat shorter woman. "Tetta?" Amelia put her hand around her shoulder and felt Tetta's long salt and pepper braid as it ran down her back. She wasn't accustomed to her teacher seeming so helpless. "I'll tell you everything I know."

Amelia recounted the story of Ardin's disappearance. Tetta paced and waved her arms in the air as she listened to the description of how she taunted Ardin on the bus and beat on the man who had carried Ardin into the ethers.

"This is all my fault, Amelia."

168

"So you remember this?" Amelia hoped Tetta wasn't losing her mind.

"No! I wasn't there. I should have been more careful this close to Ardin's birthday."

"Are you saying that this man knew it was Ardin's birthday?" Amelia considered a biological relationship between the man and Ardin.

"Yes, the man and the woman knew of her birthday, but they are not related," Tetta noted having heard Amelia's thoughts.

"It seems someone posed as me to lure Ardin away." Tetta cried out in pain as tears flooded over her cheeks. At once Amelia ceased to be a student and became a skilled lawyer in need of extracting the truth from a witness, or the lack thereof.

"Tetta, I need you to tell me what there is about Ardin that could make her a target for an etheric kidnapping." All Amelia knew about Ardin said she had been abandoned at birth and relegated to the system ever since. Anyone who ever applied to adopt the girl changed their mind within a month. If someone had waited until Ardin's sixteenth birthday to take her, then there must be some payoff, a trust fund or something they were seeking to gain.

"Amelia, there's more to Ardin than what is apparent in this world." Tetta replied to Amelia's thoughts. "There is a trust fund of sorts, but not the kind these people want to acquire. They want to prevent it being delivered."

Tetta took a breath. The tears had stopped and she was returning to her guru nature. "Ardin is an integral part of a system that will disintegrate if we cannot find her."

Amelia couldn't wrap her mind around how Ardin could be a part of any system other than child welfare, but she felt the level of tension in her beloved teacher and she wanted to do whatever she could.

"Help me understand, Tetta."

Tetta looked at Amelia intently until she was sure she had her full attention. "The people you have described were operating between planes just like we are now. In this state they were able to glide between waking and dreaming life using the alternating presence of subatomic particles to move from one to the other without changes to consciousness. It is the essential Limbo state. It is how ghosts appear and cause physical disturbances. It is where eyeglasses go when they disappear. This is how these people were able to disappear and take the physical as well as the spiritual nature of Ardin."

"Jojo said he saw Ardin in two places at the same time Tetta. Is this possible?"

"I'm afraid it is, and that makes things much worse." Tetta walked away and Amelia waited while the guru collected her thoughts.

"Amelia, I need you to become proficient in your ability to work between planes. It is vital to getting Ardin home. The threads to her on both sides of this Limbo line are blocked. It is only by working in this field that we have any hope of accessing her consciousness, and body."

"You say that as if..." Amelia's voice trailed off trying to comprehend the possibility.

"Her consciousness has been separated from her body," Tetta explained. "It seems the man took her body but I believe the woman has her soul."

"But how did this woman know Ardin would trust her if she looked like you?"

"I have been in service to Ardin for thousands of years," Tetta explained. "Countless evil spirits and hooligans have attempted to derail the special role she plays for the universes."

Amelia recalled how Tetta encouraged her to help her mother become a foster parent for Ardin. She wondered at the

170

time, why Tetta thought it would be a good match. When Tetta explained that Ardin was almost sixteen and needed a caregiver with a strong, but supportive hand, Amelia never dreamed someone might try to take Ardin from that hand. She couldn't imagine how the girl she knew could be so important to the world.

"Come with me and I will show you everything." Tetta took Amelia's hand and the pair was enveloped in a vortex of swirling light.

Pause, pause, pause...

Miguel was frustrated when he set his intent to find Nick and landed in the Wait Zone short of his goal, just like it was his first time getting there. All around him, happy, and some not so happy souls were being escorted to ride on shafts of light that acted as elevators in the Wait Zone. Miguel decided to give it one last try and built up a strong intention to connect with Nick.

Miguel felt himself drawn into a vortex of energy that had been swirling since he first put out a call for Hrim. The velocity ferociously tossed and turned his dream body. As he came across an intention to see Tetta he was flipped one way, then he was turned in the opposite direction as he reconnected with his intention to see Nick. Miguel felt nauseous as he flipped head over foot whenever he came across one of his earlier pleas for Hrim. Miguel's mind went black and he felt his body, etheric as it was, crumple to a hard surface in a pile that was frozen still, like a 'possum playing dead.

"Miguel!" Hrim's voice rang out in the darkness. "Narada! Max!" Miguel felt Hrim's hands grip his shoulder to raise him from the floor. "This is the man I was hoping for. He can tell us about Ardin."

"Not really." Miguel opened his eyes and squinted at the aged guide. "You mean you don't know either?" Resting his hands on his knees as he stood, Miguel remained doubled over trying to catch his breath. "Where have you been, Hrim? I can't even find you, let alone Ardin."

"There's a blockade," Hrim explained. "It has been somewhat circumvented, now that we are aware of it, but the thread to Ardin remains cut." Miguel looked up at Hrim and his two companions, allowing his eyes to rest a little longer on Narada as he wondered if he had come out of a lamp.

"Miguel, let me introduce you to Narada and Max." Miguel nodded to the strangers. "They have seen Jojo and brought news of Ardin's disappearance to Tetta and me." Miguel wondered why the two men would be interested in Ardin and Jojo.

"We met Jojo in a dream," Narada volunteered. Miguel became even more suspicious.

"Where is Jojo?" he demanded.

"He's okay." Max held out his hand to indicate he meant no harm. Miguel did not seem to be on shaking terms. "We left him with …" Max hesitated and looked at Hrim, realizing the arrangements he made might not sit so well with Miguel.

"You left him with who?" Miguel glared at Max who offered no more information.

"Galahad," Hrim finished.

"Are you crazy?" Miguel flared. "That guy gets people killed."

"It will be okay," Hrim tried to reassure Miguel. "Galahad has been going to training." Miguel was silent. He had never questioned Hrim's judgment before.

"Miguel, these men found Jojo in Over-the-Rhine looking for Ardin. What can you tell us about this?"

Miguel studied Max who wore a tunic that reminded him of the Greeks he had seen briefly in his webinar dream, the memory of which corresponded with Narada's similarity to the Hindus shown during their golden age. *I'm supposed to trust these two?*

"Narada is an ancient sage of wisdom," Max offered. "He thought it best not to leave Jojo alone, so he is in the company of Galahad and our friend Archie Armstrong. I assure you, he is being well looked after." Miguel's eyebrows raised briefly in acknowledgement of both Narada's impressive sounding role and his resignation to Jojo's status.

"Why are they so interested in the kids?" Miguel returned his attention to the waning opportunity to find Ardin.

"Well, they're not exactly interested in the kids," Hrim explained, "They have a different interest. Jojo and Ardin came up as they were investigating another matter."

"Yes," Max interjected, "We came across some excellent news as a result of Galahad's attempt to help Jojo surf the web for this girl, Ardin." Acknowledging Galahad's presence in Jojo's thoughts just moments after Hrim reassured Miguel Jojo was safe, didn't exactly inspire confidence in Miguel.

"Honestly, Miguel, Jojo will be just fine." Hrim glared at Max who quietly motioned a closed zipper over his sealed lips.

"So where is Ardin?" Miguel demanded assuming Galahad knew where she was if he helped Jojo see her.

"That remains out of bounds." Hrim recaptured Miguel's attention.

"Hopefully not for much longer!" Tetta's voice preceded her arrival with Amelia into the room.

Hrim swelled with relief as his dear friend appeared. He hurried across the room to embrace Tetta and hugged Amelia with his other arm. Amelia looked over Hrim's shoulder at Miguel, Narada and Max.

He seems familiar. Amelia studied Max.

Who, Dear? Tetta couldn't imagine that anyone in the room other than Miguel could ever have been seen by Amelia.

Amelia started to walk toward Max.

"Hello, I'm Max." He stepped forward and offered his hand to Amelia. Amelia studied the flabby frame of a balding man who looked old enough to be her father as she realized this appearance established his age more at thousands than tens of years.

"Max?" Amelia felt there was more. She waited for it to come, and as it arose in her mind she felt her hand squeeze his tighter, then release with a push. "You mean Maximian?"

"Well, yes." Max blushed at the idea the lovely lady before him knew of his reputation.

"You're damn right I do!" Amelia read his thoughts as she raised her hand and slapped Max hard across the face. "You perverted chauvinist!"

Tetta, Hrim, Miguel and Narada watched in surprise, as Amelia looked at her smarting palm as if it had overtaken her, while Max backed away, soothing his stinging cheek.

"Have we met?" Max couldn't imagine the circumstances under which a contemporary woman could so well know his underlying personality quirks.

"No, but I've seen you, you, you...voyeuristic creep! Salivating over the princess! You should be ashamed of yourself. She was just a girl." Amelia raised her hand and was ready to chase after Max, but Tetta caught her by the wrist and pulled her back.

"Amelia, tell us what you have seen. What *Princess*?" Tetta tried to peer into Amelia's consciousness but the same block was there which had surrounded Max's situation from the very start.

"Yeshe Dawa." Amelia reeled as she remembered the dreams that escaped her in waking life. Tetta took Amelia's face in her hands and searched her eyes.

"You saw Max with Yeshe Dawa?" Tetta wanted the details in order.

174

"He watched her for months." Amelia began to recount her memory of the visions that came to her during the webinars. Her dispensation of what she'd witnessed popped to Amelia's lips in short bursts, faster than she could think about what she was saying. "Malchus was better than him. He was rooting for the princess."

As she described them, the scenes Amelia had observed in her dreams were poured forth into the ball hovering over the granite table in the center of the room. Everyone gathered around and witnessed Max's lust for the princess and Malchus' devotion to her. Narada smacked Max in the back of the head.

"Malchus said he would gladly die to protect her right to become a Buddha." Amelia felt dizzy and her knees buckled. Tetta helped her to a seat at the table.

"Max, are you remembering this?" Hrim asked. At that very moment Max was completely reunited with his memories of the three divine months he lived outside the courtyard while he slept for 208 earth years sealed in an Ephesian cave.

"Yes, I remember." Max's eyes glazed over as his mind's eye filled the foggy ball with the memory of the day he and Malchus returned to the cave.

"We didn't want to leave. Malchus wanted to protect her, and I wanted ..." Max blushed, "...to stay. But we couldn't. So we made a bet to keep track of how she did. If she did well I would lose. If she did poorly Malchus would lose."

"You bet on Yeshe Dawa?!" Tetta practically screamed and Hrim placed his hands on her shoulders to keep her from interrupting Max's memory. "No wonder your Moksha Meter is in the dumps." Tetta mumbled and sat down next to Amelia at the granite table.

"Who is Yeshe Dawa?" Miguel asked.

Amelia and Tetta replied in unison, "Ardin!"

175

"You knew this?" Miguel was insulted that Amelia would keep something from him.

"I didn't keep anything from you," Amelia replied to his sentiment. "It just clicked now. I just remembered my dreams. They don't look alike, but I can see it now."

"Your Ardin is an incarnation of Yeshe Dawa, also known as Green Tara," Narada filled in.

"And it is her sixteenth birthday today," Tetta added.

"If the forces that have taken her prevail," Hrim brought the conversation to one possible conclusion, "she will not be able to go through the rite of passage and become fully empowered to balance and heal the world."

"Which would kill our Moksha Meter," Max said to Narada.

"Which is inconsequential!" Tetta was really mad at Max.

"But of unbelievable consequence to the world appearance." Narada agreed his karma was much less important than the welfare of the planet onto which his jiva may need to extend a few more lifetimes.

"But if we find her?" Miguel asked with the slightest sliver of hope in the room.

"Before midnight," Tetta qualified the conditions, "then we can perform the ceremony and get things back on track."

"How can I help?" Max shrugged as everyone in the room looked at him suspiciously. "The Law of Similars indicates I need to do good deeds to turn this thing around."

No one said a word. Though they now knew what peaceful thing was missing and how it was affecting the waking life as well as Max's Moksha Meter, they felt no closer to bringing the situation to a positive conclusion.

"Maybe this Marcus guy took her?" Miguel suggested.

"Malchus," Max corrected, "But he would not harm her or keep her from her purpose. He would only protect her."

"Maybe he did protect her." As Miguel remembered the disappearance he picked up from the drunk in Over-the-Rhine, Hrim checked in and made it so everyone was able to see Miguel's thoughts as they materialized in the swirling globe.

"Is this man Malchus?" Miguel asked. Miguel pointed to the man who caught Ardin as she fainted. Amelia and Max nodded simultaneously.

"The question is, who is the woman?" Tetta wondered.

"It's you," Miguel replied matter-of-factly.

Hrim reached out and tapped the ball zooming in to the scene. He tapped and tapped each time waiting for the scene to enlarge and sharpen until they had a good close up shot of the woman.

"That's not Tetta." Hrim pointed at her eyes. "These are grey. Tetta's eyes are brown."

"You're right." An unexpected voice added to the discussion. "That woman is Emperor Decius!" Everyone turned to face Nick Green as the counterfeit Tetta beat on Malchus until the two finally parted and disappeared.

"How could you know this?" Miguel stepped forward and grabbed Nick by his collar. Nick Green offered no resistance as Miguel noticed his disheveled and shaken appearance. Nick held his thoughts close as he quickly tried to rework his strategy. After he had found himself unable to retrieve the body for Decius, Nick decided to return to his original plan of shared heroics. Someone with more experience with spirits and monsters was needed to take on the animal that was protecting Ardin's body. Whatever that thing was, it had nearly killed him before he remembered he was already dead.

"I met this guy named Decius at the Dark Side bar last night." Nick looked down, hoping his previous meeting with the rogue emperor and knowledge of the plan to nab Ardin well in advance of her capture would not be apparent. Keeping a watchful eye on the swirling ball, Nick made every

177

attempt to keep his fears from going public. "He said he took Ardin."

"We know that." Max started to dismiss the newcomer who obviously hung out in the wrong part of town. "Now go back to your little hole in the wall."

"Wait." Miguel looked at Hrim, "Nick has been helping me with this."

"Nick?" Amelia looked at Miguel in astonishment. Miguel looked to Tetta for help as Amelia realized Miguel had been lying to her. "I thought you didn't know where he was?!" she asserted.

"Hello, Amelia." Nick smiled weakly. "Long time no see."

"Nick, I don't think you ever met Amelia." Miguel tried to keep Nick from telling Amelia more than she remembered.

"We may not have been properly introduced..." Amelia's voice trailed off. Her body seemed paralyzed, the pressure building up inside was palpable to everyone in the room.

"Amelia, please!" Miguel started toward her.

"You knew!" Amelia started toward Miguel.

"Excuse me." Hrim waved his hand and froze the pair in mid-stride. "You'll have to catch up on this later. We need to find Ardin first."

Amelia stood locked in place fuming at Hrim and Tetta. "You knew too?"

"Yes, Dear," Tetta replied, "but you may be sure, there is more than you now know, and when you recall it all everything will be clear to you."

Amelia took a deep breath and stared at her most trusted teacher. "I'll take you at your word, Tetta."

"I'm sorry, but we must return to the matter of Ardin's whereabouts," Hrim continued. "Nick, what more can you tell us?"

"Well, he said he had a problem with a girl and I thought it might be something about the girl Miguel was looking for. So, I worked him, ya' know?" Nick swallowed, hoping the holes in his story would not be too obvious.

"After a few drinks, he told me where Ardin's body was. Said this guy Malchus had taken it. When I dialed in and surfed to the location I couldn't see much because some sort of attack creature was guarding her." Nick revealed the bruises on his neck which he imagined developed when he feared he might lose his not so real life.

Hrim finished weighing the information Nick shared and determined that though the completeness of content was questionable, the part about seeing Ardin was absolutely accurate.

"So, Malchus has Ardin? That's good, right?" Amelia ventured.

"Partly," Tetta sighed. "But as I suspected, Malchus only has the physical part of Ardin. Decius has the spirit."

Amelia was distracted as she noticed Max was fixating on the image of Ardin's disappearance in the swirling ball. Max kept rotating a close-up image of Ardin back and forth, obviously trying to get a better look.

"I really think that you're being inappropriate," Amelia chastised him. Max looked up bewildered.

"What?' He looked around at everyone, including Narada, who was giving him the evil eye. "I'm not doing anything wrong. I think I've seen her before."

"You're probably just picking up on the Yeshe energy," Tetta surmised.

"No. Really. I saw her recently." Max waited and scanned his memory. "I saw her under the sacred Banyan tree!"

"When?" the whole group asked at once.

"Yesterday," Max remembered. "She was communicating with the tree."

"That sounds like Ardin," Tetta murmured and Amelia nodded. "But how could you connect with her when the rest of us could not?" Tetta wondered.

"I wasn't looking for Ardin." I think the connection was to Burch. Or maybe I'm not on the bounce list because there was no known connection."

"So, you just bumped into her?" Miguel was skeptical. Max didn't seem like the innocent type.

"Yes. I said hello, and that was it." Max glossed over teaching the current embodiment of Yeshe Dawa how to feel into her heart space.

"So you know where her mind is," Hrim concluded.

"I guess so," Max agreed, "But where is her body?"

"I can help you find that," Nick offered and Amelia fumed as she was reminded of the deception surrounding him. Hrim scanned Nick's memory and plucked the location from Nick's experience.

"Alright then." Hrim prepared to assign tasks and jobs to the team such as it was. "First things first. Miguel and Amelia, you are about to be taken back to waking life."

"No!" Amelia started to argue. "I'm a part of this now."

"Indeed you are, but I assure you, your mother is just a few feet away from finding you sleeping on a bench at the riverfront." Hrim raised his eyebrows and cocked his head in a warning gesture to stave off more arguments that would waste time.

"You will join your mother and meet Miguel at this address." Hrim deposited the location in Amelia's mind and repeated the invisible act with Miguel.

"Miguel, Jojo is also about to be awakened and since you have the car, you must meet Amelia and Karen and go get him." Miguel nodded.

"Max and Narada, you will go with me and Tetta to the Banyan Tree to hold off Pluto and Decius as Tetta prepares the sacred rite."

"How will we find you?" Miguel didn't like the idea of splitting up with Hrim after it took so long to find him in the first place.

"You will find the way." Miguel looked at Nick feeling a little jealous that he might be allowed to go.

"Nick won't be going with us." Hrim surprised the slain police officer with the announcement. "You will wait here and watch the crystal ball in case someone needs help."

Nick started to argue. "You want me to sit back and watch?"

"That's the only way you get to attain hero status," Hrim seethed, and Nick caught the unmistakable message that Hrim had indeed seen through the holes in his story.

Tetta turned to Amelia. "Remember you are traveling between planes, Dear. You will hold space for the reunification between the physical and spirit."

Like iridescent bubbles meeting with some unseen pointy object, Miguel popped out of the room, followed a moment later by a rather surprised looking Amelia.

Hrim looked at the empty space where the two had been standing and took Tetta's hand as they dissolved into the ethers with Max and Narada.

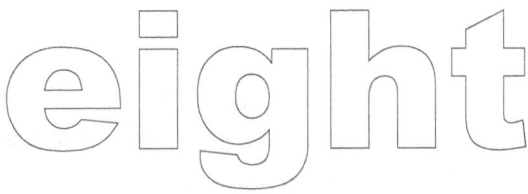

eight

Smack! Thwack! Splash!

Malchus was dying. He held back a moan as he reached around the body he had placed on the bed not even 24 hours earlier and tucked the blankets under her arms and legs. It was September, and rather warm, but the princess felt cold. Even if he had experience surfing the web, there wasn't a shred of consciousness in the body to follow as a thread.

When the seven sleepers awakened in Ephesus, Malchus had chosen not to cross over to the Wait Zone. He had no notion of the life he was missing as a martyred saint in the heavenly realm. Instead he had chosen to live between planes, following Yeshe Dawa wherever she materialized in the world appearance. For more than 1600 years he had maintained his youthful appearance, ever ready to protect the princess from

183

evil entities, but Tetta had always helped the princess and he had never needed to intervene until last night.

Staying present with her in the physical realm for less than a day was nevertheless bringing about the reconciliation of the youthful age at which Malchus died with the years he had been between planes invisible to the illness and aging of the physical plane. He was decaying now, he smelled horribly. He would be embarrassed to finally meet his princess in such condition, but he would gladly do so if she would only open her eyes.

He had been watching over the spirit of Yeshe Dawa, known as Ardin in this lifetime, through a most difficult set of circumstances. He recognized Decius gained her trust disguised as Tetta who had taught Yeshe Dawa one lifetime after another. He had been tracking the evil emperor and Roman idol, Pluto, through all of their escapades as they plotted to undermine her contribution to the world. He thought they were enjoying a bit too much fun prematurely when they raised oil and gas prices to record highs more than 2 years before Ardin's rite of passage. But everything was about timing, perfect timing, and he was worried they had managed to get away with it.

Every lifetime since Yeshe Dawa began her quest to help all sentient life attain Nirvana, Malchus had watched as the lady guru Tetta, had trained the princess and helped her make her passage into power upon the occasion of her 16th birthday. Over and over again, Malchus never recognized anything different about the princess, but he understood now, that the difference was in the people she sought to help. Sometimes, she never seemed to become fully aware of her role in the world, but without her the people had become engorged with fear.

Through many lifetimes, Decius and Pluto had waged war on her and those who believed in her ideals. This lifetime had been battered with genocide and terrorism that surpassed the combined deeds of centuries before. He recalled a time when he heard Yeshe Dawa argue with the monks that people could not be saved by fear. She said fear of harm was neither an effective deterrent nor motivator for behavior. If it was, she had argued, there would be no more wars.

Malchus felt his heart ache and wondered if he could find a way to save her before it quit on him. He dared not leave her for fear Decius would be able to access her body.

Malchus? He heard a voice in his mind which, though it was strange to hear, was also gentle. *Malchus, I can help you.*

"Who is that?" Malchus mustered all his strength to protect Ardin if need be.

I have been listening to your thoughts and recognize your good intentions. I am the guru Tetta who has taught Yeshe Dawa for many lifetimes. She is in need and I am asking for your help.

"Show yourself," Malchus requested.

I cannot. You are in the physical realm and I am in the etheric. If you will come with me I will provide protection for the body until we return.

"Where will we go?" Malchus wanted to do whatever he could before he died and imagined going between planes might give him strength.

We must find the essence of her heart and soul and return it to the body. The voice said everything Malchus needed to hear.

"Granted," Malchus agreed, and allowed himself to fade from view.

Pause, pause, pause...

Smack! The sound of a hand slapping on the window woke Miguel in the SUV as it was accompanied by shouting. "Sir, Wake up! Sir? Are you alright?" Miguel opened his eyes to see the pores in the parking lot attendant's face as he nervously peered inside the SUV. "Open the door sir. Are you breathing?"

"Of course I'm breathing." Miguel opened his door, bumping it into the attendant. "What's the matter with you?"

"Me?" The attendant looked offended. "You're the one who is cooking yourself in your fancy SUV."

"It's not mine," Miguel acknowledged absentmindedly.

"Whose would it be?" A police officer the attendant called to the scene walked up to the Mercedes just in time to hear the suspicious looking Latino man turn into a suspect. "Let me see your license and registration please."

"Officer, I used to be an officer." Miguel tried to explain as he produced his wallet. "The registration is in the glove box." Miguel informed him. The police officer unlocked the vehicle using the controls inside the driver door and walked around to the passenger side of the car.

Pulling the registration from the glove box, the police officer drew his weapon and ordered Miguel to put his hands on top of the Mercedes.

"You don't look like an Amelia Bradford, do you?"

"No sir." Miguel gave the office all the respect he could muster knowing he was missing out on a really big assignment and also missing Jojo. "But you better believe I'm going to be making my one call to her." The officer handcuffed Miguel and guided his head in through the back door of the police cruiser.

"This is a mistake." Miguel offered little protest knowing it would make no difference. In his mind, he recalled the frantic excuses of many collars he had made when he was a beat cop with Nick. Miguel settled back and hoped Jojo and

Amelia would be okay as he watched the growing crowd for the fireworks through the fence barrier behind the front seat.

Pause, pause, pause...

Thwack!

"Ouch!" Amelia opened her eyes to see her mother's 100% organic hemp purse flying back for another attack on her shoulder. "Mom!" Amelia raised he hands to catch the purse. Karen glared at her daughter.

"I assume if you're sitting around snoozing that you have found Ardin?" Amelia held on to the purse and kept her mother from taking another swing.

"Jeez Mom! I was looking for you!" Amelia stood up so she could have the advantage in height commensurate to that her mother possessed in seniority.

"You weren't looking for me!" Karen adjusted her glare to look up into her daughter's face. "You were sleeping."

"I only sat down for a minute Mom. If you hadn't kept me up all night..." Amelia's attention diverted to the almost imperceptible chirping at her side. Frowning at her mom, she rummaged for her iphone in her purse and answered.

"Hello?" Amelia listened, and then shot a sharp look at Karen as she mouthed the word "police" to her mother. Before she could be sure Karen had reported Ardin missing, a look of disbelief swept over her face.

"Yes. Yes, officer, I did." Amelia listened. "He was doing what?" Amelia listened some more and was growing impatient. "Yes, I can. Where?" Karen struggled to remain quiet as Amelia covered her ear to listen over the noise of the crowd on the public landing. "Thank you." Amelia pressed the button at the bottom of her phone and the screen returned to the springboard view of apps ready to be launched.

"We have to go, Mom." Amelia dropped the phone inside the front flap of her purse and started walking away from the landing.

"Did they find Ardin?" Karen was eager to hear why the police called.

"No." Amelia couldn't believe the call.

"But what about Ardin?" Karen protested. Amelia stomped her foot and postured the attitude that she was about to start making the decisions.

"Mom, look around. The wall is full. How will you find her here?" Karen's shoulders slumped with exhaustion at the lack of progress that had been made. Amelia was right, she hadn't found anything yet and she had no idea of how to make that any different.

"Well, what did the police want?" Karen retraced to the phone call.

"We need to meet Miguel at the station." Amelia turned and stomped up the ramp of the public landing toward Third Street.

"Where's the car?" Karen trotted to keep up with Amelia's obviously aggravated pace.

"At the police station," Amelia grumbled.

"We're walking?!" Karen knew the closest station was more than a mile away.

"Yep." Karen understood Amelia's monosyllabic response was intended to end not invite any more conversation. Breathlessly she quietly puffed up the incline after Amelia glancing at the crowd just in case Ardin was close by.

Pause, pause, pause...

Splash! As the water beat down on Jojo's body near the pool the last of the 3-D players was awakened from the dream state.

Archie and Galahad watched as the three balls Jojo had been juggling with them on Main Street dropped to the ground and Jojo disappeared.

"Uh-oh!" Archie looked up at Galahad.

"We're in trouble now," Galahad agreed. "Quick! Follow that boy!" The two jumped on Jojo's thread and followed it to the pool outside Amelia's condo complex. Jojo was in a fury, chasing a boy who had dumped a bucket of water on him.

"You dummy," Jojo yelled, "I have to find Ardin!" Galahad was proud of the level of commitment his friend displayed.

"Get him, Jojo!" Archie cheered as Jojo plowed into the boy and knocked him into the pool.

The boy came up coughing and yelled at Jojo, "What you doin' sleeping at the pool if you're looking for your girlfriend?"

"She's my sister!" Jojo jumped into the pool and proceeded to dunk the boy underwater.

"Should we break this up?" Galahad wondered if he should move from between planes into the physical for a moment.

"I think we should be careful not to pull any heroics, Dumbo. You know how that can backfire." Archie nudged Galahad who frowned at the ever present knowledge of what had become known as The Snailing Vessel Debacle.

"Don't call me Dumbo, okay?" Galahad insisted. "We'll just keep an eye on him then, and make sure he's alright?"

"Yeah, just watch." As quickly as the pair agreed on their ongoing role with Jojo, he gathered his things and stomped out of the gated area around the pool.

"Let's move!" Archie motioned for Galahad to follow him. The pair went through the glass door that had just closed behind Jojo and found him talking to the Concierge. Archie attempted to throw a link to Max and Narada to find

189

out what was happening as Galahad listened to Jojo's conversation.

"I need to talk to Miss Amelia." The Concierge picked up the receiver on his desk phone and dialed Amelia's cell number and waited for the call to go through.

"Miss Bradford, this is John at the front desk," the concierge began. "I have a very wet young man who is in need of speaking with you." John looked slightly dismayed as he handed the receiver to Jojo and motioned for one of the valet's to get a mop to clean up the water Jojo was dripping on the marble floor.

"Miss Amelia?" Jojo shivered in the air conditioned foyer of the Regency. "Can I please come help find Ardin now?" Jojo requested.

"Oh, Jojo, we've run into some trouble." Amelia slowed the pace of her stride which had rendered both her and Karen breathless as they neared the District 1 Police Station. Stopping at the corner of Ezzard Charles Boulevard. and Central Parkway, Amelia focused on Jojo. "I have an idea. Would you be willing to visit with Miss Jason until we can get there?" Amelia hoped the promise of joining them would help Jojo remain patient.

"Ok," Jojo put a little pout in his voice to convey his disappointment as he stepped around the mop pushing at his feet. "It's Ardin's birthday, Miss Amelia."

"Yes, Jojo, I know, and we're going to find her and have a big celebration." Amelia tried to sound reassuring as she walked through the front doors of the police station. Amelia recognized the officer at the front desk and reached with the phone toward Karen.

"Mom, will you talk to Jojo while I take care of this?" Amelia shoved the iphone into Karen's hands and turned to face the desk officer.

"Hello Amelia, that was quite a mix-up wasn't it?" The desk officer said of the rookie cop arresting Miguel. "He just didn't know who Miguel was." The police officer shrugged. "They're bringing him up now."

"Good." Amelia wondered what Miguel had learned during his nap in the car. She intended to get it out of him before Karen's curiosity could make conversations difficult.

"Officer," Amelia started.

"Jim," the officer reminded her of his name.

"Could I meet Miguel in another room?" She nodded over her shoulder attempting to let Jim know she didn't want her mom to be involved. Jim was well aware of Karen's meddling ways as he had made more than a few calls to her classroom during the school year. He opened the gate next to the counter to usher Amelia through.

"Mom, I'll be right back," Amelia whispered to Karen without waiting for a reply.

Miguel looked frustrated when he came into the room. "I'm sorry Amelia. Did you make it to the destination before they called?"

"What destination?"

"You don't remember?" Miguel observed the characteristic amnesia that followed Amelia's dream sequences. He sighed, "Well, maybe it's a good thing I got picked up."

"Did you find something?" Amelia asked.

"Yes. Hrim gave us a location for Ardin's body." Miguel left out the part that the information had come from Nick.

"Is she alright?" Amelia worried at the use of the word *body*.

"I think so." Miguel explained, "Her mind or soul or something like that has been taken to another location. Hrim wants us to find her and wait for instructions.

191

"But how do we do that with Mom?" Amelia imagined her mother would be calling an ambulance upon finding Ardin.

"Well, first we have to get Jojo." Miguel retraced his agenda back to picking Jojo up from the pool.

"He's going to stay with Janet." Amelia explained getting the call from Jojo as she arrived at the station.

"Okay, well, we'll figure out something for Karen," Miguel offered, "but let's get moving." The pair exited the interrogation room and found Karen listening to Jojo on the phone.

"Okay, Mom." Amelia reached out for the phone. Karen gave her the eye and responded to Jojo.

"Okay, so we have a deal?" Amelia clenched her teeth as she anticipated the deal her mother was making. "We'll make some popcorn and watch together." She paused. "In just a couple minutes." She looked up at Amelia and Miguel. "I promise." Karen disconnected the call and handed Amelia the iphone.

"He needs someone," Karen declared. "You're right Amelia, we will never find Ardin at the wall and Jojo is so sad. I think we should tell the police what is happening right now and go home to the child that wants our help."

This was typical Karen Bradford as far as Amelia was concerned. It took her a moment to compose herself and not bring up the residual frustration of every other time her mother had decided to detach with a vengeance.

"Mom, I agree, Jojo could use our company, but Miguel thinks he has a lead. What if I take you up to the condo and then bring Miguel back downtown." Amelia could see that Karen was emotionally drained and being with Jojo would be the best solution for both of them.

Fortunately Karen was missing every other word that Amelia said. "Fine," she accepted the conditions. "Do you have popcorn?" Amelia nodded. "And Miguel has filled the police in on the details?"

"Yes, Mom, everything is in motion." Amelia let Karen think the police would be following through.

"And they don't need anything from me?" Karen had forgotten to bring the paperwork that qualified her as Ardin's foster mother.

"No, not yet." Amelia steered her mother into the front seat and opened the back door as Miguel got in the driver seat. "Home, James." She said rolling her eyes with relief that the anticipated altercation with her mom had magically been avoided. *If there's a guide or guru helping with this,* Amelia sent out a broad-based, *thank you.*

Pause, pause, pause...

Tetta, Hrim, Max, and Narada arrived under the Banyan tree that was the parent to the Bodhi tree under which Siddhartha had found enlightenment. Narada spread his arms and walked around breathing deeply under the tree that had descended from the mythical fig tree which was filled with all sentient forms of life on Mt. Meru. He looked as if he had returned to his long lost childhood home. Hrim looked around. There wasn't a soul in sight.

"It seems pretty desolate, Max," Hrim commented.

"I'm telling you, Hrim, it was like a tourist vacation yesterday and that girl was walking all over the place trying to make people laugh.

"That sounds like her, but I don't see her, do you?" Hrim acknowledged that it was possible that Max could see things he couldn't see due to the unique way he was tied to the situation and the nearly seamless blockade Decius and Pluto had managed to produce.

"No, I don't see anyone," Max admitted, sighing in disappointment.

"Nothing," Tetta sadly agreed, "but this is new." She peered through the door of the small hut Ardin had imagined and saw a simple cot, but no one inside. "Empty."

"Well, well, well!" a booming voice announced the arrival of another entity under the Banyan tree. "Look at all the pretty guides gathered for this auspicious occasion." Pluto walked out from behind the banyan tree ducking under the branches and winding between its trunk-like roots as he zeroed in on Max. "I have a little surprise for you, Max."

Pluto pulled his arm back and moved as though he would deliver a bowling ball to the ground. Instead, Malchus rolled into visibility and tumbled to a stop in the dust at Max's feet. Malchus looked up and locked eyes with Max. Even as he suffered, even after spending more than a millennium following Yeshe Dawa, Malchus' eyes were filled with contempt.

"You selfish bastard!" Malchus pushed up on his elbows but he twisted and fell flat on his back.

Max dropped to his knees to help his friend. Malchus grabbed Max by the front of his clean white toga and jerked him closer to the mass of collapsing skin and muscle that hung from his skull. "How could you destroy her?"

"Malchus, I did not." Max begged his friend to listen as Malchus raised his hand weakly striking him in the face. "You tricked me into coming here. She will surely die now." Hrim and Narada reached down to separate the two men.

"Are you enjoying this, my Lord?" Trisha's sexy voice announced her arrival as she stepped up under the branches of the Banyan.

"You would deceive someone like Yeshe Dawa for a tramp like this?" Malchus squeezed his hands into fists and staggered to his feet.

"I don't even know who she is!" Max defended himself. "Malchus, my friend, I have not deceived you. I swear!" Malchus saw tears of joy and concern as he looked at Max who seemed to be telling the truth. He turned his attention to Trisha.

"You deceived me into coming here. What have you done with her!" The decay that had made Malchus look like a beast in the 3-D world was resolving under the Banyan, as was Malchus' ability to move. With all the same ferociousness he had gone at Nick, he lunged for Trisha and felt his body caught in the grasp of Pluto's large hand.

"You lose." Pluto squeezed the newfound energy out of Malchus. "Your little girlfriend remains an empty carcass where you left her. And so she shall forever remain.

"NNNNooo!" Malchus struggled to break free then fell still from the exertion.

Max wanted to tell Malchus Ardin would be okay, but tried not to think of Miguel and Amelia's assignment to find her.

"Fool." Pluto laughed at Max. "Did you think I would leave that room unprotected? Whoever spends more than a moment in there will be put to sleep. The twain shall not meet." Trisha sidled up next to Pluto and leaned against him, smiling at Max.

"We don't want to hurt anyone," She added. "We're just making sure you all maintain a little healthy distance." Pluto threw Malchus back to the ground at Max's feet and put his arm around Trisha.

"My Dear, you have done fabulously at circumventing Decius' stupid errors. Now all we need to do is seal off the consciousness for good."

"No problem," Trisha offered. "Where is it?" Pluto's face went flat, then began to transform into fury. Pluto thought

195

Trisha knew where Decius had stashed the mind. If she did not, his victory was not yet fully established.

"You must think me the fool." Decius seemed to have been waiting for the perfect moment to make his presence at the tree known to the rest. "I guess you thought you were through with me." The Roman Emperor bristled as he approached the stupefied Roman god. "Don't overheat yourself Pluto. I alone know how to access the consciousness, and, make no mistake, I will set it free in an instant unless you do as I say." Decius showed no doubt or concern for the wrath emanating from Pluto in the form of steam rising from his head and shoulders. Decius continued, "First. That vamp. Get rid of her."

Pluto raised one hand and, with a flick of his wrist, pushed Trisha across the dirt to land next to Malchus.

"Now, for me..." Decius began to recite his laundry list of demands.

Pause, pause, pause...

"This is it?" Amelia and Miguel stood outside the building on the corner where Ardin had first disappeared. "Couldn't you have figured this out before?" Amelia asked. Miguel winced.

"There was no thread." Miguel didn't feel like he had time to defend his actions to Amelia again. He thought about the beast that Nick had described guarding Ardin. He touched the gun in the holster under his left arm and hoped it would stop the creature if needed. "We need to go downstairs, to the basement."

The tall wooden door opened easily as Miguel pulled on the brass handle. Walking past the stairs to the far end of the foyer, Miguel opened the door to the basement and started down the steps. Amelia followed closely behind trying to

196

remember all of the details he had told her about their time together in the Wait Zone while they both napped. It didn't seem to make sense.

As they made it to the door marked Maintenance, Amelia made up her mind to just trust Miguel and hope to go over everything again later. Miguel tried the door knob which wouldn't turn. With a flash his foot flew up to make contact with the door and kicked it in. Miguel drew his weapon and leveled it as he entered the room. Looking completely undisturbed on the bed was Ardin, asleep under a blanket.

Amelia peeked in through the door behind Miguel. Seeing Ardin, she ran to the bedside stopping short of touching her as the teenager was so still it seemed unreal. Amelia held her breath and touched Ardin's shoulders. She was cool to the touch. Amelia squeezed the shoulders gently. "Ardin?" Quietly Amelia inquired, "Ardin, can you open your eyes please?"

"No use." Miguel placed his hand on Amelia's as Ardin seemed to sleep peacefully. "She's not in there, Amelia."

Amelia demonstrated the protective nature she usually saw in her own mother. "We've got to help her. She needs to go to the hospital."

"No, Amelia." Miguel remained steadfast in his execution of the instructions Hrim deposited in his mind. "If she doesn't stay here, her consciousness may never be able to find its way back."

Miguel left Amelia for a moment as he made sure no beast was hiding in the closet. Closing the broken door to the room, he came back to the bedside and held Amelia close. "We need to make sure she is okay on this end and hope the others will be able to work it out at the Banyan tree. All you can really do is hope and pray."

Oh great, Amelia thought, *Two things I'm really bad at.*

Miguel took Amelia's chin in his fingertips and kissed her. *I heard that.*

As Miguel moved two chairs together he wondered where the beast had gone and if it might come back. Amelia took one chair and Miguel sat down next to her. As Amelia's head began to nod forward into sleep, Miguel yawned and put his arm around her shoulders. *She needs a break,* he thought as he struggled to keep his own eyes open.

Pause, pause, pause...

Carbohydrates, even light carbs, but especially those heated in butter, can make a person very sleepy, especially when one is already sleep deprived.

Karen Bradford pressed the channel down button on the remote control assuming she was somewhere up in the public television channels. She was looking for the pre-fireworks show anticipating that Jojo would be able to learn how fireworks are made. "What channel are the fireworks on Jojo?" Karen's innocent question was answered by a number of hissing shushes coming from the dark room around her.

Where am I? Karen wondered and the shushes became more insistent as Karen asked, "How did you get in my daughter's living room?"

"Listen, lady!" a voice from down front shouted back, "This ain't your daughter's house. It's a weight loss webinar. If you don't want to be quiet so the rest of us can watch, then get out!" Karen blinked in the darkness trying to comprehend what was going on.

"Mrs. Bradford," Jojo whispered in her ear, "you better come with me." Karen was surprised to see Jojo standing in the aisle next to her seat in what looked to her like a movie theater. The boy's warm hand wrapped around hers and she let go of the armrest of the chair. Standing, she tried to keep her head down so she wouldn't obstruct anyone's view. "Don't worry about that," Jojo advised her. "They can see right through you."

Jojo led Karen to the lobby outside the auditorium and imagined a box of Raisinettes for her. "Miss Amelia loves to eat these when she's here." Jojo offered her the box.

"She does?" Karen accepted the candy and opened the end of the box, looking around at posters for upcoming webinars as she did. "Jojo?" Karen ventured to ask, "Where are we?"

"We're in the Wait Zone." Karen barely recalled hearing Jojo talk about such a place a long time ago. "This is where we have our dreams and last year Sir Galahad fell…"

"Greetings!" Galahad and Archie approached the pair before Jojo could give away much more information that would surely put Karen over the edge. "Jojo, who have you brought to the dreamtime this day?"

"Dreamtime? Day?" Karen repeated as she gave the once over to the straggly looking Galahad and his equally straggly looking -although from a different era- companion.

"Yes madam." Archie reached out to shake her hand. "You are dreaming and we are your guides. How may we be of assistance?"

Karen's mouth just opened and closed for a moment before she managed to form words. "But this is so real," she whispered. "Can I touch you?"

"Excuse me." Jojo sounded more like an adult than Karen did at the moment. "Before we can go out and play, I think we better find Ardin, don't you?"

"Ardin?" Karen repeated. "We can find Ardin here?"

"I think so." Jojo kept talking even as Archie and Galahad tried to interrupt and steer the conversation toward a more usual dream topic. "I saw Ardin here in a dream. I bet we can find her at the fireworks!"

Before Karen could begin to tell him how unlikely it was that they would find Ardin at the Serpentine Wall, he ran through the exit of the lobby.

"Stay with her!" Galahad ordered Archie and ran out the door after Jojo.

Karen locked eyes with Archie. "You're crazy if you think I'm staying here while that guy goes chasing after Jojo!" Karen made a break for the door.

The daylight was waning as they went through the doors and landed amid the noise and crowds of the fireworks celebration. Karen stopped so suddenly Archie plowed right into her. "Watch where you're going!" a lady shouted as she pulled her little boy out of the way of their falling bodies.

Karen and Archie sat up and looked around. Jojo and Galahad were nowhere to be seen. "Listen here, buddy, you better start talking fast or I'm calling for help," Karen threatened.

Pause, pause, pause...

Decius finished his list of demands with unlimited vacation days and a throng of worshippers ever at his side. "Now, if the *Lord* will be so kind as to agree to all my wishes, I will be happy to collect the package."

Hrim attempted to insert doubt into the former emperor's psyche. "Decius, you know you can't rely on him to hold up his end in any bargain."

"You will be granted special dispensation if you give up this evil agenda," Tetta urged.

"You know there are no shortcuts." Max kicked in from the ground where he was holding Malchus.

"Enough!" Decius screamed maniacally. "Give it up people!" Decius strode around the circle of onlookers as he spoke. "You are not going to reform me. So why don't you all just have a blast imagining whatever your little hearts desire until this day is over, then you can all get back to work."

Decius anticipated Pluto would stab him in the back in less than one second after midnight. He needed to nail down a deal that would keep his life in tact. Could I speak with you privately, Lord?"

"What choice do I have?" Pluto seemed resigned to making a deal. The pair moved away from the tree and Decius prepared to deliver his final offer, if necessary.

"Pluto," Decius began, "May I just call you Pluto?"

"Yes, Emperor," Pluto growled.

"Pluto, can I trust you?" Decius inquired.

"No Decius, you cannot." Pluto truthfully revealed his intentions. "You are finished."

"But you're worried. Admit it. You gave up that trollop." Decius eyed Trisha jealously, then returned his attention to the advantage he still believe he held in knowing the location of Ardin's consciousness.

"Decius," Pluto seemed almost to coo the name, "May I call you Stupid?" Pluto put his pointed finger beneath the emperor's chin and bobbled it up and down to make it look as if Decius was nodding. "The trollop is right over there. I have given up nothing but my faith in you now that I have seen how you would betray me."

"But I can tell you where the consciousness is," Decius grasped at straws.

"I don't need to know, Emperor. The mind can not find its way back to the body from wherever you have stashed it. All its helpers are present and accounted for except for those two

201

who are too inexperienced to make a difference. I saw your plan a mile away. It is so flawed. You are a dead man."

Decius acknowledged his long-demised status. "Well, that goes without saying, but..." He faltered. "Dammit anyhow! Now what?"

"Well, ..." Pluto allowed the pause to lengthen just to torture Decius a bit. "I couldn't ask for finer, more deceitful stock than you to continue carrying out my every wish and desire, could I?" Pluto slapped Decius on the back and plowed the emperor to his knees in the dirt.

"No, Sir." Decius was restored to his sniveling, subservient self. "As ever, I am at your service." Decius conceded the failure of his plot.

"Good, now go and fetch me the mind."

"But you said you didn't need it," Decius complained.

"I don't Decius, but I want her, right here." The Roman god seemed to be tasting something delicious as he slobbered a smile toward Tetta. "The energy I will gain from watching her suffer when she cannot confer the blessing upon the girl will give me such a powerful jolt nothing will ever be able to block my power again!" Decius quivered with anticipation of Pluto's unrestrained empowerment.

"And then, can I take a vacation?" Decius opted for another shot at some prize.

"Perhaps." Pluto smiled in a way Decius associated with imminent danger. Bowing his head, Decius dropped the issue and dissolved from the site in a weak hail of sparks and ash.

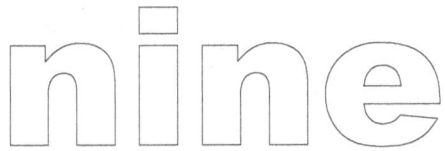

Bing! Bang! Boons!

"This is better than a dream!" Ardin found herself seated in lotus position on a thick sleeping bag in the middle of the growing fireworks festivities at the serpentine wall. She started to reach for her back pack then remembered she had left it on the bus.

"Excuse me!" she called to a passerby to see if he could tell her the time, but he didn't seem to notice. Ardin stood up and looked around making some notes about the scenery in her mind so she would be able to find her spot again, and began walking toward the a refreshment booth to get a drink.

"Excuse me, do you know what time it is?" Ardin asked the woman in front of her in line. The woman didn't seem to hear her.

"Even here?" Ardin looked up as if she was asking the angels for an answer. "I'm at the fireworks, but I'm not really at the fireworks?" She felt a little miffed and a little perplexed at the way the test Tetta was giving her was playing out. *That's not fair!* Ardin pouted. *You mean I'm not going to get to celebrate my birthday with anyone?*

For as long as she could remember, Ardin had looked forward to her 16th birthday. She never knew what had been the impetus for her enthusiasm for reaching this milestone in her life. Her classmates in school looked forward to getting their learner's permits so they could drive. Strangely, Ardin felt no interest in driving. But she longed to be sixteen.

When she came to live with Karen, Ardin was startled by how soon her new foster mom had started looking forward to her birthday. None of her other foster parents had ever made a big deal of her birthday. In fact, most of them avoided inspiring hope as they immediately recognized Ardin was more of a challenge than they had bargained for. But Karen had proven to be different, and promised after the fireworks last year, that the fireworks for Ardin's 16th would be even better.

Ardin wondered if Karen and Jojo and Amelia and Miguel could be in the crowd. She wondered if they would be able to see her or, like everyone else, they wouldn't notice her.

She realized she was not advancing in line as people who couldn't see her kept getting in line in front of her. Finally Ardin stepped aside, held out her right hand and manifested an orange strawberry smoothie absolutely free of charge.

Well, there are some perks. She smiled, and started strolling around listening to the mixture of radios blaring mixed with excited conversations along the walkway. The Delta Queen steamboat was positioned at the public landing and the big stage had great music blaring through the speakers.

Ardin imagined herself levitating to the top of one of the scaffolds holding the enormous speakers and lifted off as she drank her smoothie on her way to her high perch. Looking around to see if she recognized anyone in the crowd, Ardin saw the river was already filled with boats from the Ohio side to the Kentucky side.

On a whim, Ardin blinked herself from the Public landing across the river to the Newport Levy and back again imagining that it could be great fun to shout out from both sides of the river as the MC prompted the crowds to do just before they launched the fireworks. *It would be more cool if I could be with my friends,* she quietly complained in her thoughts.

Ardin wondered if she could surf the web to find Jojo. That way she would be able to find out what the plans were for her birthday without letting the adults know that it was important to her. Even though Karen Bradford had spent the last year attempting to reassure Ardin that she was one of the family, Ardin sometimes worried she could do something that would alienate herself from the best home she had ever known. Picturing Jojo in her mind, Ardin tilted her head back and hit her consciousness on something hard.

"Ouch!"

"Excuse me, but it seems you were about to wander out of bounds." Tetta appeared beside Ardin on the speaker scaffolding.

"But it's my birthday," Ardin started to explain.

"I know!" The twinkle remained absent in Tetta's grey eyes which grew stern as she focused on Ardin. "It's more than just another birthday, Dear. It's *the* big day."

"Is there going to be a party?" Ardin never worried about concealing her feelings from Tetta, she had always been in her dreams to keep her company, even on the worst birthday.

"Trust me. There will be a celebration to beat all celebrations." The guru held up her index finger to create a pause into which she could insert a caveat for Ardin. "It's time you come with me." Ardin had no idea where Tetta could be leading her.

"Is it a surprise?" Ardin asked.

"Yes!" The guru's tone grew more excited as she noticed Ardin's attention wandering into the ethers. The grey eyed Tetta felt her cover fading as the girl locked in on the distraction.

Pause, pause, pause...

Nick looked into the swirling ball at the center of the table in the conference room. Using his intention he was able to pilot the ball between the address he had given for the location of the body in Over-the-Rhine, and the location under the Banyan tree where Decius had told him Ardin's jiva consciousness was hidden.

Nick had watched as Pluto effortlessly shred Decius' plan into confetti sized pieces. The ball filled with fog and when it cleared, Nick could see Amelia and Miguel's heads nodding as their awareness flickered off and they seemed to be as lifeless as Ardin's body.

As if he was consulting a crystal ball, Nick asked the foggy orb what he should do. Through the fog, Jojo's face emerged. Looking much like Auntie Em in the Wizard of Oz movie, Jojo was calling, "Ardin! Ardin, where are you?"

"Jojo, wait!" Nick found himself transported through the ball landing closely behind the boy to start chasing after him. Jojo looked over his shoulder when he heard his name called only to see that it wasn't Galahad, Archie, or Karen following him, but the man he had seen waiting in the cab for the waitress on the dark side of the Wait Zone. Suddenly Jojo stopped and wished with all his might that Ardin could hear him.

"Ardin, I need you! Please help me!" Jojo begged.

"Did you hear that?" Ardin asked Tetta.

"No," Tetta dismissed the question and reached for Ardin's hand. Ardin heard Jojo calling her again, and stepped back from Tetta.

"Why not?"

"Because there's nothing to hear." Tetta's voice sounded distorted and filled with static as Ardin withdrew her attention from her again. Decius felt his disguise fading without the energy of Ardin's faith invested in it.

"You must come with me if you are to receive your boon!" Decius scratched to remain apparent as he started to fade from view.

We interrupt this scene to bring you a note from the Narrator as there really isn't time to have a webinar!

The funny thing about bodhisattvas is that no matter how many times they are repeatedly warned to put on their own oxygen masks first, they will likely forget. Just let them hear a shout out from a person in need no matter how distant, and they will do whatever it takes to get to wherever they're needed even if it means crossing over two or more dimensions, and leaving a primo viewing spot for the fireworks.

In a flash, Ardin was at Jojo's side dreaming in her dream that she was dreaming him in his, which might sound a bit surrealistic, but it's actually closer to everyday life than most of the dreams that were taking place all around them.

Back to our story...

This is weird. Ardin felt as if she was in a bubble. She was relieved to see recognition in Jojo's eyes when he looked at her.

"You see me?" She mouthed the words, but Jojo only heard the thought.

207

"Arrrdinnnn! Jojo ran to her as the sound of her name tripped over his every step. Jojo tried to give Ardin one of his crushing full throttle hugs but found himself bounced backward by a translucent bubble of air that came between them.

"Jojo!" Nick Green waved his hands trying to get Jojo's attention as he watched him bounce off what looked like completely empty space. "Stop! I want to help!"

Jojo, who is that? Ardin wondered.

"He's a bad guy!" Jojo yelled to make sure his words went through the squishy barrier.

Think, Jojo, Ardin urged the boy.

"I can't remember his name!" Jojo yelled again.

No, Jojo. Think. Then you won't have to yell, Ardin explained.

Ohhh. Jojo tried a thought. *This is cool!*

Yeah, Ardin agreed. *How can I help you?*

"Jojo!" Nick shouted. "If you can see Ardin, tell her she's in danger!"

"Don't you try to hurt her!" Jojo shouted back at Nick. "I'll squish you!"

Jojo, that's not nice. Ardin bent down and smiled at Jojo. *Maybe he does want to help. Ask him why he thinks I'm in danger.*

Oh I know that Ardin! You are kidnapped. Jojo nodded his head as he saw the words reach Ardin's awareness.

No Jojo, I am just being tested. Ardin laughed at the idea that Jojo thought she was in danger. *Really, I'll be home soon.*

Nick Green had slowly made his way closer to Jojo and could see that Jojo was telecommunicating with someone. Nick was not as well practiced as Trisha who had taught him most of what he knew, but he had to give it a try.

208

Ardin?

Yes, Nick.

I'm an old friend of Miguel's.

That's not true, Jojo insisted. *He's a bad guy!*

It is true, Jojo. We were beat cops together. Nick's eyes pleaded with the boy's. *I made some mistakes, but I never meant to hurt anyone.* He looked back to the air above Ardin, imagining she was taller, as she knelt down next to Jojo.

Look, this is not about me. Nick was finding it difficult to think slowly enough to keep track of his thoughts.

You can speak to Jojo and I can listen to his thoughts, Ardin suggested.

"Okay," Nick hoped Jojo would think nice thoughts. "The woman you think is Tetta, the one who brought you – Ardin – here... she is not a good person. She's not even a lady, she's a man, a... uh... bad guy." Nick checked in with Jojo who was patiently listening for Ardin and then tried to imagine the height that Ardin's eyes might be relative to his own. He looked into the empty space and continued, "Well, he took your mind and some other guy got your body."

Nick worried what he was saying wasn't making any sense. "I can't explain it all right now, but if we don't get the two of you back together as one, something bad is going to happen. I can take you where you need to go, but you have to trust me.

Ardin looked at Nick and felt into his heart space the way Tetta had taught her. It was filled with sadness, regret, and the slightest hope. *I think he's telling the truth Jojo. What about you?*

Jojo sized-up Nick and looked at Ardin. *So far I don't think he's lying. Wait, I'll let you know if we should trust him.* "Where are you taking us?" Jojo asked.

"We have to get up to Twelfth Street," Nick informed him.

If you want to go, Jojo thought to Ardin, *I think it would be okay.* Ardin started walking up the bank. Nick ran ahead and started leading them toward Eggleston Avenue.

"If we go this way, we will get around a lot of the crowds" Nick explained his choice to use a street less central than Vine Street. Jojo wasn't sure he liked the idea, but he felt better because he knew Nick couldn't really see Ardin.

"Jojo, we need to hurry!" Nick urged. "If we don't get her back in time...." Jojo started trotting alongside Nick and Ardin followed.

As they crossed Central Parkway and started weaving through the mixed use buildings on Main Street, Nick sensed a drop in Jojo's trust level. He reached out his hand and Jojo barely noticed as he clasped his hand into one that was the same size and almost as comforting as Miguel's. Nick remembered his connection with Jojo in a scene like this, then turned his thoughts to chili cheese coneys and root beer to keep from sending the wrong message to Jojo.

"I'm hungry." Jojo expressed as they ran around the corner onto Twelfth Street. The sidewalks became littered with dreamtime drunks and panhandlers, people shooting up in alleys, and couples arguing through open windows. The dreaming state in Over-the-Rhine could be scary to a boy. More than one child felt the hope that passed as Jojo and Nick ran by and they started to follow behind.

"Jojo, I don't think they can come too," Nick shouted. "This isn't a game." Ardin heard Jojo briefly consider Nick's concern.

Tell him they're helping, Jojo, Ardin requested, sounding a little breathless. *I can't explain it but they seem to be helping me.*

"Ardin says the kids are helping her." Jojo looked at Ardin, the light he always saw around her seemed to be dull. "She's fading" Jojo informed him. Nick looked at his watch. It was 9:00pm and the streetlights were on. He felt confident they would make Vine Street in a matter of minutes, but he wasn't sure if there might be something in the air, some block, that could be holding Ardin back or draining her.

Jojo listened to Nick's thoughts, finally confident Nick truly intended to help. Ardin felt reassured as they made their way across Sycamore.

Pause, pause, pause...

Karen watched Archie as he zoned in on Galahad who was zoning in on Jojo and alarmed to find him running, in Over-the-Rhine with his hand clenched in the palm of Nick Green's fist. Silently Galahad sent a message to Archie.

You've got to be kidding me. Archie replied to Galahad's order that he surf to the coordinates Hrim had given Miguel and Amelia. *How do you think I'm going to get this woman to come with?*

Leave her behind then. Galahad thought back. *Jojo's in trouble.*

Archie looked at Karen. It had been a long time since he had met such a feisty dame and he wasn't ready to let go of the red head.

Hang on, Sweet, Archie thought to Karen who looked surprised to hear his voice in her mind. *We're going to take a small trip.* Archie held out his hand and Karen instinctually grabbed on. She was having trouble comprehending her experience as it was happening just as she couldn't believe possible when Jojo told her about his adventures with Amelia and Miguel in the Wait Zone a year ago.

What she knew for sure was Archie appeared to be one of the guides Jojo insisted lived where he went when he dreamed. She thought her best chance of finding Jojo and Ardin was to go along with the guide and hope for the best. Even if she was only dreaming, she thought she should make the most of her time. As she looked into his eyes, Karen felt Archie begin to shake and then she felt herself dissolve into a whirlwind of energy. If she wanted to change her mind it was obviously too late. Her life was in the hands of the Englishman.

Ardin was excited to see Karen slide out of thin air and wondered who her companion was. She wanted to hug her, but there was even less of a connection with her than with Nick.

"Mrs. Bradford!" Jojo delivered his thud of a hug as he ran across the street and wrapped his arms around her hips. Karen stepped backward as she absorbed the impact of the boy's body against hers.

"Jojo, honey." Karen was careful not to seem critical, "How many times do I have to ask you to ask before you hug?" Jojo looked up.

"Sorry. But we found Ardin!" Jojo proclaimed. Karen looked around at the buildings.

"Where is she?" Karen frantically pulled Jojo off her hips and tried to take his hand so he could lead her to Ardin.

"She's right here. Can't you see her?" Jojo pointed to what looked like empty air to Karen.

"Jojo, are you imagining this?" Karen prepared to explain that not everyone could see the things he made up in his mind.

"No ma'am," Nick stopped her. "Ardin is here and Jojo really can see her."

"No! She can't be!" Karen believed Nick was telling her Ardin had become a ghost.

"Shut up, you fiend!" Archie pushed Nick hard against a wall.

"Have I taught you nothing in the year you've been here?" Galahad yelled as Archie held Nick in place. "Going after the little boy! You whack job!"

"No!" Nick insisted, "Ardin is alive and we can rescue her, dammit!" Nick tugged at Archie's hands, "Just let me go and I'll tell you what you need to know."

"You can tell us while I hold ye," Archie insisted, and Nick delivered the short version of what he had seen in the swirling ball on the conference table.

"If we're quick, I think we can get Ardin back in her body, if Decius doesn't pick up on us." Nick finished and looked around. Archie and Galahad were clearly locked in thought processing the particulars, Karen stared at Nick in complete disbelief, while the mere mention of Decius caught his attention and the thread went through him like a needle pulling Decius into the scene.

A mix of smoke and sparks preceded Decius as he appeared before the group on the corner of Twelfth and Vine. "Hello my dear." He nodded to Ardin who recognized the grey eyes she had been seeing in Tetta's face. "And you!" He turned to Nick. "You thought you could get around me did you?"

Decius shot a ball of fire at Nick, which struck him in the chest and threw him back against the building. Galahad and Archie cowered momentarily which Decius took as a sign that he didn't need to bother with them.

Twirling on his heel, Decius focused his attention on Jojo. "Come away from there boy." Decius produced a fudgesicle in his had to lure Jojo.

"Get away!" Jojo squared off against Decius who didn't see Archie coming as the Englishman dove for Decius at the knees and took him down hard against the pavement. Galahad jumped on top and tried to steer Decius' hand away from Jojo as it randomly shot great balls of fire across the street and into the air.

"Jojo!" Nick shouted just before he added himself to the fracas. "She's in the basement!"

Come on Ardin! Jojo darted for the front door of the corner building and ran through the foyer to the basement door and down the stairs to the hallway below. The door to the Maintenance room was open, and Jojo slipped inside with Ardin.

Ardin looked at her body laying on the bed and wondered what she was supposed to do.

Get in, Ardin! Jojo urged, afraid the others would descend upon them at any moment.

I don't know how, Ardin tried to explain. *I never had to try before.*

Karen Bradford stood in the doorway taking in the scene. Amelia and Miguel were asleep in chairs. Karen resisted the urge to slug both of them with her purse. Jojo was talking to Ardin who remained invisible to Karen. Ardin's body was lying under a blue blanket on a bed. Karen was paralyzed with fear that Ardin might be dead. She breathlessly watched as the blanket over Ardin's chest rose and fell with her breath.

"Lie down, get in!" Jojo shouted at thin air as far as Karen could see.

Ardin wore an expression Jojo had never seen in Ardin before. He looked up and saw Karen. "She's afraid! Please!" Jojo wrung his hands with worry. "Please, help her get in her body!"

Ardin watched as Karen reached out and pulled Jojo close to her, wrapping her arms over his shoulders, and laid her hands on his heaving chest. "It's okay, Jojo, it's okay." Karen tried to seem reassuring even as the while scene was shaking her to the core. Acting in the same way she would to appease any child in her classroom who was afraid to try something new, Karen sought to comfort Jojo if no one else.

"Ardin," Karen looked into the empty air at the height she was accustomed to seeing Ardin's eyes. Ardin felt as if Karen was looking deep inside her. "I know you're afraid honey, but you need to... get back in your body."

Ardin smiled as she heard Karen think how stupid that sounded. "Try laying down honey, like Jojo said. We're here for you." Karen lied, not knowing how she could possibly help the invisible girl if something did go wrong.

Ardin moved over to the side of the bed and sat down. Lying back, her spirit was slowly enveloped by the body. Jojo panicked as he was losing sight of the only part of Ardin that seemed to have any life. For a moment longer than Jojo could bear, Ardin's body remained on the bed unmoving. Jojo slid out from under Karen's hands and ran to the bedside. Karen watched as he tried to shake Ardin by the shoulders but his hands went through the 3-D body.

"Ardin, please!" Jojo shouted.

Karen moved across the floor and put her hands on Jojo's back trying to comfort him. Jojo listened as the balls of fire ceased making the noise as if they were being shot from guns. "They're coming to get her!" Jojo shouted.

Amelia awakened to Jojo's cries for help. She opened her eyes and stepped out of her body. It was the weirdest thing she had ever felt in the dream experience. She shook Miguel and pulled him into the space between planes.

"I know what to do," Amelia told him. Tetta taught me. You have to help. We need to build a bridge from here to Tetta. Are you ready?" Miguel nodded.

As Jojo continued to try to awaken Ardin, Karen held him tighter. Amelia placed Miguel's hands on Karen's shoulders as she smiled at her mother. Stepping next to Jojo, Amelia put one hand over Ardin's heart and one hand over Jojo's as she tuned in the energy she knew as Tetta.

The door banged open and slammed against the wall as Decius saw his whole plan was unraveling. He grabbed Miguel by the shoulders and tried to wrestle him away from Amelia as the room began to fill with light. Suddenly Decius felt himself being pummeled by Galahad as Archie and Nick joined in the melee. The moment the threesome connected with Decius they simultaneously balanced the resistant energy that had been slowing things down and provided the boost needed to mend Ardin's severed thread. In an instant the whole crowd was plowing through the illusion of space and time like a train without a brake.

"Arrrr-diiiiiiiinnn!" Jojo landed with a thud. He flinched as he heard one thud after another pound the ground around him seven more times. Jojo was afraid to look. He was crying so hard his eyes were squeezed tightly closed and wouldn't open.

"Jojo." He heard Karen's voice through otherwise absolute silence except for the sound of his own sobs. "Open your eyes. Look up."

Jojo opened his eyes and saw Ardin standing with Tetta under the Banyan tree. Tetta was cupping her hands around a glowing orb about twenty inches above Ardin's head as Ardin knelt on the ground. As Tetta engaged a sequence of hand gestures, the orb brightened and grew in size. Then, as if it had been magically opened by the combination of movements, a brilliant light shot upward as it began to pour golden light over Ardin. Tetta continued to make movements as if she was ladling the light over Ardin's head and shoulders into her heart. Jojo watched as the light shimmered over the top of Ardin's beautiful blonde curls to surround her body in a field of white light that was so brilliant Jojo thought he could hear

216

it.   When Tetta's hands were empty, Jojo heard Tetta advising Ardin.

"On this, the sixteenth anniversary of your manifestation in this lifetime, your full potential has been unlocked.   It is up to you to fulfill the plans you have set in motion.   In a short while the light you have received will take its proper place in your heart and patiently witness every choice, every commitment, every thought you make."   Ardin opened her eyes and gazed at Tetta bathed in the light that was shining from her.   Tetta embraced Ardin.

"Is Ardin okay?" Jojo whispered to Karen who knelt next to him and supported him with her shoulder.

"I think so, Jojo."   Karen smiled weakly as she wondered who Tetta was and what exactly was going on.

"She's fine," Tetta assured Karen.   "Nice work getting them here."   Tetta complimented Amelia's ability to awaken from Pluto's spell and move things between planes, under his radar.

Tetta turned to the group and made a pronouncement. "Please join me in recognizing the Green Tara, the bringer of mirth and liberation to tens and hundreds of thousands, alive and well with us today!"

"It *is* she!" Narada was deeply affected by her presence and bowed graciously toward Ardin.   "Namaste!"

"But I thought her name was Yeshe Dawa?"   Max, was kneeling on the ground holding a somewhat improved yet very frail looking, very weak, Malchus in his arms.   "Malchus has caused himself great harm to protect her and now you're telling me she's somebody else, not the princess?"

"They are one in the same!" Narada explained to Max. Call her what you will: Princess Yeshe Dawa, Green Tara, Kuan Yin, The Virgin.   She is a blessing to all cultures in the world appearance.   She is joy, she brings levity yes, but she also dispels fear and worry. Balance has been restored this day!"

"Yes, Max," Tetta added, "and look at you. She is the reason that even you are on your knees, demonstrating compassion for someone other than yourself. It took a long time, but you have finally learned the meaning of selfless service."

Max hugged his friend and felt his form give way as Malchus' inner organs were failing. "But what about Malchus? He should not suffer for my stubborn ways! Help him!" Max pleaded with Ardin.

Ardin walked over to Malchus who was shivering in Max's arms. "My friend."

"Don't look at me," Malchus begged Ardin, disgusted by his appearance. "I failed you." Malchus' body seemed to be imploding.

"Perhaps, but not in the way you may think." Ardin waited for Malchus to look at her before she continued. Slowly he raised his head to find out why she stopped speaking.

"Malchus, you disappoint me because you fail to fulfill the one reason I keep going around on this crazy wheel of life."

"But princess, I have been here for you in every lifetime."

"And why did I keep coming back?" Ardin knelt beside Malchus and took his hand. A strange peace came over him.

"So that all sentient beings could know Nirvana," Malchus quietly answered.

"And what are you?" Ardin asked as she dabbed his forehead with an easily materialized cloth.

"A sentient being?" Malchus wished Ardin would stop caring for him. "I don't deserve your kindness, princess."

"Yes you do! For all the effort you have expended grasping at this world appearance to protect me, you must

218

spend at least an equal amount of time enjoying the effortlessness of the truth, that we are all One in the Same."

The color began to return to his cheeks as the light that was in Ardin poured into Malchus. Max watched his friend seem to be growing younger.

"So you have been delaying my work Malchus, and you need to move on!" Ardin turned to Max. "Do you think you could connect him with his Moksha Meter and teach him how to use that thing?"

Max nodded and smiled weakly as he began to feel embarrassed for the way he felt toward her when he was younger.

"You two!" Ardin giggled. "Your presence was once the only relief I got from the hard time the monks were always dishing out."

"You knew we were there?" Max was surprised and then horrified as the full load of inappropriate things he said crashed through his mind as if he had just said it yesterday. "Son of a — "

"...*better not pout, better not cry...*" an expletive eraser on vacation from the gates of Heaven, flew in to the tune of the Christmas song. Max swatted at the miniature angel, "Go away, you're two holidays ahead of yourself." Max quickly recovered from the slip into his usual self and helped Malchus to his feet.

"*Comic* relief, of course." Ardin smiled. "I don't think you knew what you were getting yourself into Max when you and Malchus established the only way anyone would know how I was faring on my journey. Had your Moksha Meter not gone down, the disaster that had been set in motion might not have been traced back to my spirit." Ardin took Max's hand and his heart melted as he dropped to his knees. "Thanks to you I may continue on with my work."

219

Burch popped into the scene and was finally able to recognize the energy he had been watching as it posted to Max's Moksha Meter. "Namaste, Bodhisattva!"

Tetta stepped forward to deliver the news. "Burch, Ardin has determined that Max here has demonstrated the kindness and selflessness that through the Law of Similars would work to reset his Moksha Meter. Furthermore, his levels will surpass previous levels given the added assistance of his alter egos." Ardin smiled at Burch who worked to stifle his resentment.

"I see." Burch cast a not so loving sideways glance at Max who was beaming along with Galahad, Narada, and Archie over the fact that they had managed to do something self-less. Burch acknowledged her wishes. "I will make the reparations Bodhisattva."

"Be careful not to get a swelled head about it." Tetta reminded the four egos. "That would just be making more work for your selves. You're not finished yet." Max did what he could to look humble. It wasn't much of an improvement to his grandiose demeanor.

Tetta turned to face the group with her arms outstretched as Ardin's eyes travelled from face to face. "Ardin, while you have fresh awareness of your true nature, I invite you to address those gathered here now, and impart any wisdom or instruction you have to offer."

As Ardin walked toward Decius, Pluto and Trisha, Karen gasped with concern for her. Decius shuddered with fear at the thought of the retribution he would pay for having deceived her for so long.

"Emperor, I wish to thank you for your service." Decius quaked as he was immersed in Ardin's forgiveness. "You have risked innumerable turns on the wheel of life in order to provide me with this opportunity to stand here now, enlightened, and ready to serve humanity."

Karen was dumbstruck by the appreciation Ardin was demonstrating as she included Pluto and Trisha in her expression of gratitude. "Because the people will benefit, you need not suffer one more moment of fear for your actions regarding me, unless it is your preference to do so."

Decius knelt down and bowed his head as he faded from view.

"This is not fair!" Pluto groaned as he chose to suffer the dissatisfaction of unfulfilled desire. "We have worked so hard. We almost had it all," Pluto snarled.

"Pluto," Hrim stepped up beside Ardin, "you are free to return to the underworld. The damage that you have done to the world economy will now serve as fodder for correcting injustice and improving opportunities for humanity."

Pluto let out an agonizing shriek. "You're fooling yourself Hrim! Humans will never understand the folly of greed. They will never see how their desires only guarantee their suffering." Pluto seethed at Ardin who smiled peacefully nonetheless.

"You are wasting your time, Princess." Pluto's head and shoulders steamed with rage.

"I'm sorry you feel that way, Pluto." Ardin was completely unaffected by his anger. Without another word, Pluto was absorbed into the ground beneath the Banyan tree.

Trisha remained alone in the place where her two departed companions had once stood. She looked past Hrim to Nick and attempted to see if there was any hope.

"We've been here before Nick, haven't we?" Nick remained silent.

"You have made your choice, Trisha," Hrim said as he continued to take care of the details while Ardin began to walk toward Nick. "Trisha, you will be taking the express elevator from the penthouse to the basement as the muse to the Roman god you chose over your best interests. We will check on you from time to time via your Moksha Meter which Burch is presently resetting for sub-zero readings."

Trisha quaked a little as her comprehension of Hrim's words caught up to images of the future he implied. Her head made several short jerks as she looked from Hrim to Nick to Amelia, Miguel, and Jojo. Then, without a sound except for an ever so slight pop that was almost like a sloppy kiss, Trisha dropped out of sight, through the dust at her feet.

Ardin led Nick toward Miguel who was barely withstanding the heat of Amelia's angry stare.

"Why didn't you tell me you knew Trisha *and* Nick were here?"

"I was worried." Miguel doubted Amelia would accept his reasons for holding back the truth.

"Next thing you know I'm going to find out Shima is here too!" Amelia's body, mind and heart stopped as truth about her missing step-sister filled her mind. Amelia's lip trembled but she couldn't utter a sound.

"What's wrong?" Karen joined the group with Jojo trailing quickly behind her.

"They're all gone." Amelia looked at Karen.

Karen looked at Amelia not understanding that Amelia wasn't talking about what she already knew, but the permanence she now understood it to have.

"Yes, honey, but you're here and Jojo and Ardin are safe." Karen searched Miguel's face trying to comprehend what truth he had withheld from Amelia, and tried to find words that would improve her daughter's suddenly pale complexion.

"Amelia," Tetta made an effort to intercede, "try accepting that no matter how things come to us, they do so only when we are able to handle them." Amelia tried not to include Tetta in the anger she was feeling for not being told the truth.

"Ardin has been on this journey through the wheel of life for thousands of years," Tetta continued. "However if she was conscious of her destiny before she could exercise discretion, she probably would have been medicated to the point that she could not actualize the intention with which she was born."

Amelia considered how close Ardin had been to residential treatment at various times in her record. "But that still doesn't explain why you didn't tell me."

"Because it was out of bounds for us to do so," Hrim defended Miguel's choices. "You needed to remember on your own."

"Remember what?" Karen asked sounding frustrated that she felt left out.

"Out of bounds!" Tetta, Hrim, Amelia, Miguel, Ardin and Jojo stated in unison. Karen stepped backward overwhelmed by the intensity of their combined focused attention.

"Miss Tetta?" Jojo quietly approached the Guru.

"You have been very brave and well behaved tonight, my dear," Tetta complimented the boy. "What can I do for you?"

"Could you please tell me, who is Ardin?" Jojo feared losing his friend now that she knew she was someone else.

"Oh, Jojo." Tetta softly chuckled hearing his thoughts. "Ardin is a special soul, much as you are."

Ardin placed her arm around Jojo's shoulder and pulled him close as she poked him playfully.

"Ardin is joyful." Tetta explained. "She embodies and imparts joy." Tetta smiled as Jojo thoughtfully attempted to decipher the meaning of her words. "She likes to be happy and she helps others be happy, especially when they are taking things too seriously." Tetta simplified, "She appreciates the importance of play." The guru glanced around at the circle as it gathered closer.

"Some people believe something has to happen to make them happy. They connect their joy to conditions on the job, at home, in relationships, and their possessions. When someone doesn't have something he or she believes will make them happy, they only have desire, and don't feel happy until they can trade it in for that which they want."

Tetta locked eyes with Amelia. "Ardin helps everyone see that these conditions are not a recipe for happiness but suffering. When we let go of the belief that the source of our happiness, joy, and contentment lies outside ourselves in something, someone, or some circumstance, we can all be as free and joyful as a child, and, as another fine teacher put it, enter into the kingdom of Heaven. That is what masters like Yeshua and Yeshe Dawa teach. Tetta gazed into Jojo's wondering eyes. That is who Ardin is, or at least who she can be. And for that matter, you too can be little one."

Tetta and the others watched as Jojo contemplated her words for a moment. "Is Ardin allowed to come home with us?" he asked. The group broke out in laughter.

"Silly!" Ardin wrestled Jojo playfully in her arms. "You can't get rid of me that easily. Besides," she smiled at Karen. "I get to learn how to drive now!" As the enlightened awareness of the Princess Yeshe Dawa that had been dispensed by Tetta was finding its way to the core of Ardin's being, her sense of humor was revitalized and flushed to the surface.

"I still feel like I'm missing something!" Karen asserted.

"The fireworks!" Jojo, shouted in alarm. "We missed the fireworks!"

"Ah Jojo!" Hrim scooped the boy into his arms and loaded him on to a branch of the Banyan tree. "That's the beauty of time, sometimes it moves too slowly, like when you're taking one of those math tests in school." Jojo stood up on the level limb and looked out. "Sometimes it moves too fast when you're having fun." Hrim levitated to land next to Jojo on the branch and invited the rest to join the sentient creatures that lived full-time among the leaves of the original Banyan tree.

"It just so happens your patience completely stopped time, in time for you to remember that it's time to watch one of the most impressive expressions of light in the 3-D world from the optimal viewing point known in all the planes."

"Mr. Hrim, sir," Jojo addressed his friend using the most respectful vernacular he could apply.

"Yes, Jojo?"

"Could you please say that again?" Jojo requested.

"Why, yes, my dear friend." Hrim took a deep breath and shouted, "Its show time!" The sound of fireworks launched into the awareness of everyone on the Banyan tree which was suddenly submerged in darkness while the sky lit up right over them.

"Wait!" Karen shouted, but the fireworks were covering the sound of her voice. "I don't understand!" Tetta could hear Karen perfectly in her mind, and sat down on the branch next to her keeping her eyes on the fireworks. In the background the heavenly choir and two of the four Beatles alternated with other dearly departed rock and rollers, plus Michael Jackson, to provide a musical interlude that mixed with the sounds of launches and explosions.

"Tetta!" Karen shouted. "Is that your name?" Tetta nodded. "What happens next?" Karen was shouting as Tetta put a damper on the noise of the fireworks. Karen blushed at the volume of her voice.

"In a little while it will be time to awaken." Tetta calmly explained. "It will be Monday morning, Labor Day. A total of 24 hours has elapsed since Ardin disappeared. Amelia and Miguel will physically be with Ardin when she awakens in Over-the-Rhine. They will bring her to the condo where you and Jojo are currently asleep on the couch. You will likely forget everything you have seen here and feel very confused about what happened and what to do about it."

Karen couldn't imagine that she would forget the bizarre events that had transpired. "What can I do to remember? Apparently she is much more special than I could have known. What do I need to do differently?"

"Not one thing, Mrs. Bradford." Tetta kept the discussion professional as if she was the principal in a school talking with a teacher about a gifted student.

"Just treat her normally and let things unfold as they will. She may be the first female Buddha, but for now, she's still a teenage girl. And you are the best thing she has going." Tetta smiled as she watched Karen take the compliment to heart and soothed all of the doubts she had entertained about her motherly abilities.

"Do you do this often?" Karen asked. "You know, time travel and all this strange stuff. Do you like it? Can I learn to do it?" Tetta smiled at the brimming curiosity of the science teacher.

"In dreams you may visit anyone, anywhere, anytime. Days may transpire in the last second before you reawaken to the dream you think of as reality with all its associated limitations. Mastery begins with developing the ability to be awake in one's dreams and then ceasing to be identified with any dreams. However, even the masters and gods have their little place of ascension which continues to be a dreamy part of the fabric of time and space." Karen held her breath trying to imagine an appropriate response as she failed to process most of what Tetta had just said.

"I'll send you a brochure, okay?" Tetta turned to watch the fireworks and Karen decided she would wait to ask more questions until after she read the brochure.

"Oh! One more thing!" The damper dissolved and Karen's words were overrun by the fireworks as they hit their peak with a volley of low explosions followed by a series of high boomers while sparkling light spilled like waterfalls off the bridges to the river below.

So, Hrim. Amelia thought spoke through the sound of the fireworks, eager to get his input.

Hrim turned down the volume of the fireworks in the area surrounding him and Amelia.

"I'm not quite sure I understand what went on between the princess and Max." Amelia began.

"What's not to understand?" Hrim transitioned into teaching mode.

"Well I thought the deal was for Max's moksha to go down as Yeshe Dawa did well, but it plummeted when Ardin was abducted. What kind of good was she doing by being kidnapped?"

"Ah well, yes," Hrim searched for a way to explain. "Max and Malchus really didn't know what they were talking about. It couldn't work out as they had planned."

"But clearly, there was an effect." Amelia waited for Hrim to deliver a better answer.

"Amelia, you watched two men dreaming in a time and place millions of years and countless universes away from where they started. They were unfamiliar with the customs. The link was established but how it would play out wasn't really up to those two." Hrim checked to see that Amelia was understanding him. "No one can suffer from a bodhisattva doing her work. It was impossible for Max to lose points if the princess did well."

"But his meter…" Amelia started but stopped at Hrim' shushing motion.

"While the bet was impossible," Hrim clarified, "it was nevertheless floated into the ethers and was used by the jivas involved to send out a distress signal when it became necessary. This is why Max's moksha meter suddenly manifested all the good the bodhisattva accomplished throughout history in a way that seemed to be without a cause that Burch could catalogue." Hrim shook his head. "As long as I've been around, I'm still learning new things."

"So did Max really need to do good things to win his moksha back?" Amelia understood the appearance of debits on the meter to be merely illusion.

"It couldn't hurt." Hrim chortled as he and Amelia watched Max and Malchus taking in the fireworks from the ground below the Banyan.

Amelia was relieved to have access to her guide again. She wanted to know about everything she had seen in her many webinar peep shows in-between her waking moments over the last twenty-four hours. But the issues associated with her own forgotten past felt heavy in her heart.

"Do I remember everything now?"

"For the most part." Hrim smiled at her. He could tell Amelia didn't want any more surprises. She was trying to understand why Miguel and the guides had withheld information about Trisha, Nick and Shima.

"We didn't withhold information Amelia." Hrim answered her thoughts. "The information was always available to you. It was your beliefs that held you back. There were things you learned but could not accept, so you clung to beliefs that seemed to make it manageable." Hrim smiled at Amelia and she let go of her rising resistance to the idea that she would cling to anything. Hrim continued as Amelia began to consider how she could possibly not believe in anything.

"As long as one has beliefs, one is limited to the extent of one's story. So it may seem that one who doesn't believe anything may have the upper hand, but what makes a "belief" is one's *attachment* to a thought. The dedicated atheist and agnostic are just as limited as anyone devoted to attaining eternal peace."

Hrim paused to let his teaching sink in. She could see how not believing could actually be a belief, but she was unsure where Hrim was heading.

"This is actually the point all of these systems of thought set out to prove and then were mistaken as the proof. It's the belief in and attachment to time and life and all separate experiences that creates these appearances. In truth there are no separate things which may be brought together, and thus not even oneness as this is only comprehendible via comparison to separateness. There is no illusion separate from the reality, Amelia, but the beliefs even at this level must be reconciled in order to advance, even as there is no advancement necessary. When this is accomplished you will remember everything."

Amelia's dazed expression of dwindling comprehension cleared as the lilting tone of Hrim's voice went quiet. She tried to recover her concentration and returned to the webinar material.

"I seem to be getting better at surfing." Amelia blurted out and blushed as Hrim broke into laughter.

"Seriously Hrim." She didn't want to lose her opportunity to catch up and make sense out of the things she's seen. "Another thing I'm still wondering about is all the lessons on time. If I saw Max's past with Malchus and Yeshe Dawa, why didn't he remember?"

"Max couldn't remember his dream, as you often can't remember your own dream experiences," Hrim began. "You were attracted to Max through your studies of time and karma, which introduced you to the story of the Seven Sleepers." Hrim paused to scan Amelia's thoughts.

"I still don't get it," Amelia admitted.

"That's the beauty of it." Hrim continued, "When Decius cut off the connection between Ardin and Malchus the night of the kidnapping, he sloppily missed the link made to Max during those 208 years." Amelia nodded.

"The block was established only to prevent intentional connections by those Decius knew to be connected to Ardin. You circumvented the block without intent as you came in through the back door of your webinar studies and connected with Max. That's what gave you the inside scoop we needed to break the case."

"You mean it was an accident?" Amelia summarized her understanding of Hrim's explanation.

"Basically, yes." Hrim nodded and smiled as Amelia's thoughts indicated she was disappointed that she had only stumbled upon the truth.

"Your thoughts are all over the place most of the time anyway." Hrim addressed Amelia's frustration growing. "It's not just you Amelia. Even though you think you should be able, you really can't keep your mind fixed in that linear illusion for very long before it goes wandering off in all directions. That's why meditation is so important. to consciously getting behind the workings of the mind." The one thing Amelia did worse than remembering her dreams was meditate. She glanced at Miguel wishing he was not privy to the poor evaluation Hrim seemed to be assessing.

"But you did remember Amelia." Hrim reminded her, "And just in the nick of time!" Hrim reminded her.

"Did you say Nick?" Miguel moved into the quieting bubble that surrounded Amelia and Hrim. "What about Him?"

"Nick is doing better." Hrim turned to field Miguel's worries as they popped out of him like a baseball pitching machine. "He made great strides to overcome his fearful ways."

Miguel couldn't imagine Nick ever being fearful.

"Greed and judgmental tendencies are born on fear Miguel, the fear of not having or being enough. Fear is born on the idea that we are all separate." Hrim took the opportunity to pierce Miguel's attachment to his own beliefs. "When one sees through all things, not as a separate being observing another but through the eyes of the beholden, then one has taken his or her true place in all that seems to be and has transcended the limits of time and space which never existed in the first place, and returns to that from which one was never lost to a place where time and life were never measurable as they never could be as this is eternal and, I might add, priceless. Then one no longer abides with fear."

Amelia smiled at the poetic rhythm of Hrim's words, and the reflection of her previously dazed state now washing over Miguel's face. Hrim waited until Miguel snapped out of it.

"But Nick got some points, right?" Miguel searched Hrim's smiling wrinkles of wisdom for hope that Nick's good behavior had been recorded in his Book of Life the same way Max's moksha had been restored.

"I don't think he'll be returning to the dark side of the Wait Zone." Hrim nodded toward Nick as he cheered the fireworks with Jojo. "The two of you will have more time to catch up with each other."

The silencing bubble dissolved and the volume of the fireworks was restored as they reached the climax. For the next few minutes there was no way anything anyone said mentally or out loud, other than *Ooohhh* and *Ahhhh* could be distinguished from the cacophony of powerful blasts in the air, and then it all suddenly stopped, leaving behind just the smoke and ashes, reminding everyone of the journey they had made over thousands of years to get through the last twenty-four hours, give or take a divine moment.

"Ta-daaa!" Jojo shouted.

"TAA! DAA!" all the sentient beings on the limbs of the great Banyan tree repeated.

Cincinnati native, C. Pic Michel, is a teaching artist working with creatively talented and challenged youth and adults. Bouncing between a wide range of venues from her studio hermitage to corporate workshops, residential programs, and prison projects, has given her an eclectic mix of motivations to write, the certainty that it's best to give up all hope of understanding the meaning of life, and the determination to effortlessly live, laughing as much as possible, in the moment.